# Wolves
## on the
# West Side

Novels by Michelle L. Levigne
*Published by Mundania Press*

*Bitter Sweet*

*Wolves on the West Side*

*Shatter, Scatter*

# Wolves
## on the
# West Side

## Book I of The Emerald Necklace Series

# Michelle L. Levigne

Mundania Press

A Mundania Press Production

Mundania Press LLC
6470A Glenway Avenue, #109
Cincinnati, Ohio 45211-5222

To order additional copies of this book, contact:
books@mundania.com
www.mundania.com

Cover Art © 2007 by Trace Edward Zaber
Book Design, Production, and Layout by Daniel J. Reitz, Sr.
Marketing and Promotion by Bob Sanders
Edited by Heather Bollinger

Trade Paperback ISBN: 978-1-59426-254-8
eBook ISBN: 978-1-59426-255-5

First Edition • April 2007

Library of Congress Catalog Number: 2006927883

Production by Mundania Press LLC
Printed in the United States of America

10  9  8  7  6  5  4  3  2  1

# Chapter One

The storm came from nowhere that July evening, pounding the Cleveland Metroparks with hail and driving rain from all points of the compass. First the storm churned and spun everything outward like an invisible centrifuge. Then it pulled everything inward, as if the riverbed had become an enormous drain and the Bonnie Park picnic area would vanish, sucked down through the fabric of space and time.

The people who dashed for shelter didn't think about such things. They gasped and shivered, coated with ice and debris, blinded by rain, stunned. Moments ago, there hadn't been a cloud in the sky. Rain blew horizontally. Swings clanged and wrapped around the support poles. The wading pool filled with sand and pebbles from the Rocky River, dozens of yards away. Trees toppled. On Pearl Road, horns blared, brakes screamed and traffic snarled when the traffic lights died in a momentary power surge.

Lightning flashed purple, green and blue, and a heartbeat later the lights came back on. Traffic lights flashed once, then settled into their usual pattern, but the cars sat still at the intersection where Pearl Road and Valley Parkway met a few seconds longer. The rain slowed to mist. People who hadn't made it to the pavilion shelters or to their cars came to a stumbling halt, picking their way through piles of melting hail. The Rocky River, which had been only a foot deep now raged along the banks, brown and foaming like in spring flood.

Marty Hosgrove, an off-duty EMT for Middleburg Heights, had gone to Bonnie Park after his shift ended to relax before going home. When the storm hit, he and his partner, Lori Wilkins, abandoned his neon green Frisbee to dash for shelter. The two friends stepped out from under cover of the picnic pavilion and grimaced at the churning, brown expanse of the west branch of the Rocky River.

"I got this awful feeling we should be looking there," Mike said, hooking a thumb toward the river.

"Then why look at all?" Lori shook her head, but she grinned and followed him down the muddy slope. "What's that?" She pointed at a lump of what looked like rags, tangled in the branches of several fallen trees stretched across the river.

He looked and snarled a few curses.

"Marty?" She hurried to the edge of the water.

"Somebody's dog, probably. Poor thing is bleeding. Look at that." He shook his head and gestured at the streaks of watery red streaming through the water as it rushed downstream.

A man shouted and stumbled out along the tree trunk that touched the bank. He gestured at the same spot in the river that Marty and Lori stared at.

Grace and Jack Harsey stopped on the way to their car, drawn by the shouts. They were both soaking wet, but the evening had warmed already and something strange in the air made them both feel slightly giddy about their drenched condition. Grace linked her arm through her husband's and they hurried across the parking lot and toward the embankment built of raw stone.

A moan and a splashing sound caught their attention when they were still a few dozen yards away from the scene of all the shouting. Grace glanced down over the low stone wall into the water and gave a little scream.

A girl sat in the high water, her leg wedged between stones and a fallen tree. She shivered, white-faced and dark-haired and stared up at Grace with wide, blank eyes. One arm was bruised and swollen and visibly crooked.

Grace didn't stop to think, but put both hands on the top of the wall and swung her legs over. She went in past her knees in the rushing water. A moment later, Jack joined her. It was a matter of moments to get the child's leg free and pick her up to carry her out of the water. That was when they discovered she wore nothing but rags smeared with blood and black with char. Jack supported Grace as they stumbled along the edge of the river to the shallows, where the two uniformed EMTs and the blond man worked together. Grace sat on a fallen tree and cradled the girl on her lap to share her body heat. Jack raced back to their car, to get the blanket they kept in the trunk for emergencies.

Marty and Lori were too busy with their own emergency to notice. Grace watched, feeling sickened as she realized what she saw. Marty and Lori climbed out along the tree limb to join the stranger. The red hair in the water belonged to another girl. Half her clothes were burned away, the remains scorched and blackened and shredded.

Lori took a few seconds to assess the situation. It was a mercy the girl lay in the cold water of the river, and a greater mercy she was unconscious. The child's face was swollen and bruised, and when Lori lifted her eyelids her pupils dilated unevenly. Both arms were broken. From the bruises and raw strips of skin over the child's body, Lori guessed most of her ribs were broken as well.

It was an even risk all around in moving her. The child could bleed to death before a rescue team arrived with proper equipment.

The rising floodwaters could drown her. She could succumb to hypothermia. Or moving her could damage her internally, leaving her paralyzed, or puncture vital organs. The stranger chose before the two EMTs could even start the debate. He reached in and broke branches, forcing them to lift the child before she went under the churning water.

Jack and Grace followed Marty's truck to Southwest General, both of them silent, no need to confer. The child clung to Grace, not even moaning when the motion of the car jarred her.

The emergency room at Southwest was in an uproar when the Harseys arrived with their shivering, bruised bundle. The little girl's face had swollen and darkened with massive bruises and Grace feared she might choke or even suffocate if something wasn't done. Her leg was discolored and the returning warmth in her flesh promoted bleeding. She shivered and clung to Grace with long-fingered hands and sharp nails, eyes half-closed. Grace held her close and sat down to wait while Jack harangued the overworked front desk nurse.

Grace looked around for the two EMTs who had beaten them inside. She was surprised to see the man, his wet clothes smeared with blood, come racing out to meet Jack and grab hold of his arm. For some reason, she thought no one had noticed them in the greater concern for the girl in the water.

"Where's the kid?" he demanded, and gestured for a doctor, who had just emerged from a room, to join them.

Jack pointed to Grace. The two men hurried over to her.

"This can't be a coincidence." The doctor frowned and went to one knee to get a closer look at the child huddled against Grace. "What are the chances of two brutalized children—"

Grace braced to have the child taken from her arms. The girl roused from her daze and lifted her head from the woman's shoulder. The doctor gasped when he saw her face, swollen and shiny red from the pressure.

"That's a broken jaw, at the very least. Come on, sweetheart, let me help you feel better." He smiled and reached both hands to slide the girl from Grace's embrace.

A low, rasping sound emerged from the child's throat. She shifted closer against Grace and yelped as she put pressure on her oozing, discolored arm. When the doctor persisted, she tried to bite him. The reckless movement earned another yelp of pain.

"Maybe I should carry her?" Grace offered. The doctor ignored her and rapped out a series of incomprehensible medical orders. Two nurses jumped to respond.

In moments a needle appeared, which the doctor stabbed into the child's arm—answered by another attempt at biting. Then suddenly the struggle stopped. The child's dark, green-ringed eyes glazed over, her lids drooped and she let out a growling moan. She gave Grace such a pitiful, pleading look the woman nearly burst into tears. Then the child collapsed, like a marionette with cut strings. A nurse dragged a gurney over, and she and the doctor transferred the child from Grace's arms to the gurney and whisked her away.

"Wait," Grace said, reaching out to the EMT before he could follow them. "What about the other girl?"

"We have no idea yet. What kind of sicko would beat up on two helpless kids and then dump them in the river?"

*≈ ≈*

The redhead child stayed unconscious, lost in a nest of monitor wires and IV tubes. The hospital staff and Social Services labeled her Jane Doe. They doubted she would survive.

The other girl had a high resistance to the tranquilizers. She struggled so much after they set her broken arm and leg and wired her jaw, the nurses had to strap her into her hospital bed. They named her Jenny Doe.

No one had reported any children missing who matched their descriptions. The machinery of inquiry began to move, looking for children taken from other states, patterns of abuse and body dumping. The girls didn't look anything alike, certainly not enough to be distant cousins, let alone sisters.

*≈ ≈*

That night, a shower of silver sparks paralyzed the security monitors and blinded the nurses on duty on the floor where Jenny Doe whimpered and fought her medication and the restraints on her arms and legs. She grew still when the swirl of silver sparks hovered over the bed.

A man stepped into the room, invisible until he walked through the thin streak of moonlight sliding between the shade and the windowsill. His clothes were too large, borrowed from the discards in hospital stores. He was barefoot, his golden beard patchy from burned spots. His face bore bruises to match hers. His blue eyes glistened with tears as he looked at the child, her swollen face and wired jaw, the cast on her arm and leg and the caterpillar tracks of stitches for her deeper cuts.

"She's here, Princess," he whispered, and rested a scratched, long-fingered hand on her dark head. "She'll be all right. You'll be all right. I don't know where we are, but I swear on the Bendici and on the Greening Lands, I'll find a way home for all of us."

"Kh—na—" she managed to say through her swollen, immobilized mouth.

"I don't know where he is. Nowhere near us. I'm sorry. I promise I'll find him." He shook his head. "Sleep. Heal. You are a hunter born, but even the fiercest need to rest. Understand?"

The girl glared at him for a moment, then tears filled her eyes before she nodded and closed them.

"I will be here," he whispered. "You won't know me, but you'll know I'm a friend. Until I can send us all home, ignorance is bliss." He stroked his fingertips down the side of her face, leaving another trail of sparks. "When you need to know, you will know. Stay true to her, and someday you will find your way home. But only together. The door will only open when you are together," he finished on a sigh, and a catch in his voice. A faint shower of silver, healing sparks bore witness to his words and sealed them.

In another moment, the pain lines faded and the child relaxed visibly, finally sleeping.

He walked past the nurses, unseen, cloaked in a shower of silver sparks as soft as moonlight. Up two flights of stairs, to the room where the other girl lay encased in so much machinery, she nearly vanished among the technology.

"What evil did you do?" he said, bracing his arms against the doorframe.

In the few minutes it had taken to find the child's room, years had landed heavily on his shoulders. New wrinkles in his face outlined his nose and mouth and eyes. He no longer looked like a lithe young man in his early twenties, but a man nearing his forties, scarred by time. He caught a glimpse of himself in the stainless steel surface of the monitor and a mirthless, silent chuckle shook his shoulders.

"Who would be so cruel, so afraid, they would attack innocence? Sleep, little one. Your parents are gone and an entire world of wizards live in fear of you and the Wereling bound to you in blood. You can't go back." He held out a calloused hand as if she could see it. "This is a mirror world. Find the power sources. Grow in wisdom. Grow in strength. Grow in allies. But remember nothing of what and who you were until there is need. It is the only way to survive."

A shower of sparks spun out from his outstretched hands and wrapped around the still, pale form in the bed. Even in the moonlight and shadows, a hint of color appeared in the child's pale skin and her chest moved visibly as her breathing improved. She moaned in her sleep, eyelids fluttering.

"It's all I can give you. My magic is bound to no land, so I have no ready source to replenish it. Your champion waits and will find you and know you," he murmured, and slumped back against the doorframe, his knees nearly folding. White streaks appeared among the gold of his hair. "I am a healer of minds and bodies, with some gift of illusion. Useful to you for now, but nothing to help any of us go home. You will have to find the door and open it. Someday. When you are grown and strong and ready to battle her enemies. Hear your mother's last words. They are your key and your map.

"Shatter ties that bind to land

"Bind to time, shifting sand.

"Shatter ties to all you love,

"Earth below and sky above.

"Scatter, all companions blown.

"All is new and heart is gone.

"Scatter to the mirror world,

"Destiny and need unfurled."

As the last words rasped out of his throat, he sagged forward, going to his knees. More streaks of white touched his hair and his entire frame shook with weakness.

A footstep in the hallway startled him. Shuddering, he flicked his fingers through the air, drawing up another shield of silver sparks.

When the night nurse walked in to check on Jane Doe, she noticed nothing wrong. She checked the monitors and made notations on the chart she carried. A pleased smile curved her lips as she checked the child's pupils and brushed gentle fingertips over little fingers emerging from the casts.

"You're a strong little gal, aren't you?" the nurse whispered. "Just keep fighting, honey. Just keep fighting."

⁓⁓

In the morning, the duty nurse was startled to find a man sitting in the corner of the waiting room on the pediatrics floor. She reached for the call button for Security, then paused, distracted by a few silver sparks that danced across her eyes. When she blinked them away, she smiled at the poor man who had spent the night waiting for news. It took a moment, but she snagged a cup of coffee for him from the dispenser on the end of the floor, and a Danish from the big box some grateful parents had sent up.

"She's going to be just fine," she said, approaching the man. "You really should go home and get some rest, Mr. Dorayn."

Dorayn nodded, mumbling thanks for the coffee and Danish. He glanced down the hallway where Jenny Doe lay sleeping. When he left, he had a list of names, phone numbers and schedules, so he could call at all hours of day or night and find out how the girls he had helped rescue were doing. Bo Timmons, the social worker in charge of the girls, noted his name in his files, and didn't notice the silver sparks that kept him from wondering why there was nothing but a name, Anton Dorayn; no phone number or address. The sparks kept him from instigating a police investigation into the stranger's background.

# Chapter Two

Grace Harsey came back in the morning to check on the girl she and Jack had found. She brought a teddy bear, fuzzy green slippers and a coloring book and crayons. The girl stopped struggling against her restraints when Grace walked into the room. Bo Timmons hovered in the doorway and watched as the woman settled down with the child. There was an attraction between the two, and Bo was delighted to see the girl quiet under Grace's influence. The hospital staff worried she wouldn't heal properly if she couldn't sit still.

Then he noticed something strange. The girl, maybe eight years old, laughed at the slippers—what little laughing she could do through her swollen, wired mouth. She hesitated when Grace handed her the teddy bear, ran her hands over it and actually smelled it before she accepted it. But stranger than that was the child's reaction to the coloring book and crayons. From her puzzled little frown and the way she examined the book and then the crayons, Bo would have sworn she had never seen anything like them before.

He put that consideration aside. What mattered more was that the child behaved for Grace Harsey, and the woman obviously cared for her. Until they could identify both girls and find their families, they needed places to put them. Preferably, families that could give both girls one-on-one attention. Bo knew it wasn't any too soon to start talking about fostering Jenny Doe with the Harseys.

Grace was astonished when he made the suggestion in the little waiting room just down the hall from Jenny's room. She sat down slowly, her eyes wide, gaze turned inward. Bo held his breath, afraid he had listened to his gut instinct once too often and he was finally wrong. Then the woman smiled.

"You have no idea how long I've wanted...she really does like me, doesn't she?" Grace murmured.

"Ma'am, you're the only person she's taken a shine to. I could swear the kid tries to claw and bite everyone who comes near her. Of course, everyone else has a needle or they do something that hurts her." The two shared a smile at that. "You, though, I think she'd do anything for you." Bo relaxed now and settled down on the couch opposite her. He opened up the folder he carried under his arm. "All the medical expenses are paid for by the county, of course, and you'll get a monthly stipend for clothes and other expenses—"

"I'm not worried about that," she hurried to say. "You haven't had time to check out my family. Isn't there a long process to go through?"

"This isn't like adopting, and yes, we have to do a thorough background check. Especially after what that little gal has gone through. But you know something? I trust a kid's instincts a whole lot more than I trust investigations into bank accounts and criminal records and family histories. Jenny there likes you, she trusts you, and that's going to make a world of difference in her recovery, mental and physical. You like her a lot too, don't you?"

"It's like she grabbed hold of my heart the first moment I saw her." Tears touched the woman's eyes for a moment. "Jack and I can't have children. We've talked about adopting, but it always seemed like such a big hurdle to cross."

"Fostering is kind of like test-driving a car. If it doesn't work out, well …" Bo shrugged.

"Children are not cars," she retorted hotly, but that spark of anger faded under his friendly smile. She nodded. "I understand what you mean, though. Well, I'll talk to Jack and we'll get back to you. How soon do you need to know?"

"Jenny isn't going to leave the hospital any time soon. The more she fights, the longer it'll take her to heal. On the other hand, the sooner she's able to leave, the faster she'll heal. She really doesn't like this place."

"She thinks it smells bad here," Grace said with a chuckle. Bo gave her a confused look. "She held her nose several times while I was in there. She's a smart little thing, trying to communicate with her mouth all wired shut. She's a fighter, not scared at all."

"Good for her."

Two nights later, Jenny Doe escaped her hospital bed restraints with the skill of Houdini. She hobbled down the dimly lit hallway, leaning into the wall to stay upright, her cast clicking softly against the linoleum, shivering in her thin cotton gown. She growled when the first nurse spotted her and approached. Then she shifted into overdrive, clicking like castanets, ducking and evading the grasping arms of two more nurses and three orderlies. She found the stairwell and scrambled upward. The hubbub followed her.

She made it to the door of Jane Doe's room. The little scream of anguish that escaped her tight-wired mouth caught the attention of the nurse on duty. The girl leaned against the doorframe, shivering, tears filling her eyes. She tried to lunge into the room when the nurse approached her, but the woman had grown up playing football with five older brothers and didn't hesitate to tackle the child. Gently. Muffled words spilled from Jenny's mouth, and her pursuers realized something important.

She didn't speak English.

It wasn't that she was stubborn or unable to speak, or too dazed to understand the staff tending her, but that she didn't understand their questions. The nurse held onto the struggling girl as the hunters from the floor below caught up with them. They all were astonished to hear the child babble through the wires holding the broken bones of her jaw together.

"Lari—Lar—a," she managed to say, and pointed at the girl in the bed.

Jane Doe woke. Her green eyes fluttered open and her head turned toward the commotion as the other girl battled to get to her. A soft, weary smile lit her face.

"Aggie," she whispered, startling everyone. Then her eyes fluttered closed.

"That settles that," the head nurse said, and gasped as she got an elbow in her gut. She passed the struggling child over to an orderly, who pinned the child's arms to her sides. "They know each other, they belong together." She grinned her thanks and nodded as a nurse came into the room with a sedative.

Jenny Doe—now Aggie—gave a little shriek that turned into a howl when she saw the needle. She held out her one good arm to point at the sleeping girl.

"Lara," she mumbled through swollen lips, and growled as the needle sank into her arm.

Jane Doe's name was changed in the hospital records to Lara. Jenny Doe's name was changed to Aggie. Their last names were still mysteries. It was enough, though, to help refine the search for the girls' identities and backgrounds and families just a little bit more.

༽ ༼

When Grace arrived the next morning, Bo immediately went to meet her before she reached Aggie's room. He laughed at the woman's astonishment, and was relieved when she was pleased with the incident. Some prospective foster parents cancelled the fostering arrangements when the child did something contrary to first impressions. Grace just smiled and shook her head.

"She's a fighter, isn't she? That's good. Jack needs someone who will resist him, not just sit there and let him pick on her."

"Jack?" Bo felt his stomach drop. "Your husband—"

"Isn't exactly thrilled at the idea of fostering a girl. Especially one so badly injured. He agrees with me that Jenny—no, her name is Aggie, isn't it? Aggie needs me, and he won't deny that I've...quite fallen in love with the little rascal," Grace added with a chuckle. "I think maybe he feels like a failure, that we never had a child of our own. If Aggie had only been a boy, he might not resist so much. He needs a son."

"Well, if Aggie keeps this up, she'll be more than a match for him."

"Good." She gestured down the hall to the girl's room. "Is there anything else? I'd like to spend as much time with her as I can today."

Bo bowed and gestured for Grace to lead the way.

✂ ✂

After that midnight awakening, Lara improved so quickly, the hospital staff put her and Aggie in the same room. They estimated Lara was ten to Aggie's eight, and the older girl took the lead in learning. Nurses and doctors and other members of the hospital staff soon took to standing outside the door, listening to Lara babble to Aggie in whatever language it was they spoke, interspersed with English words. Aggie picked up the words, managing to be understood despite her wired jaw.

No one noticed the blue sparks that often jumped between the girls during those times. Everyone who came into contact with the girls was too busy trying to unravel the mystery of who they were, how they had come to be in the river and what language they spoke.

Grace came to love both girls and spent as much time as she could with them each day. She became the intermediary between them and Bo, the social workers, examiners for the school district and anyone else who dealt with them. Her husband, Jack, came to visit from time to time. He took a shine to Aggie immediately, laughing at the tough little girl who wouldn't let her injuries slow her down.

Lara, however, with her disconcerting way of looking right through people, he could only tolerate. Grace knew better than to suggest they foster both girls. Lara's shattered leg would never support her without a brace and years of therapy. The Hendersons, living in Olmsted Falls, were foster parents who specialized in physically handicapped children, and they agreed to take Lara and ensure the girls kept in contact.

✂ ✂

In a Pittsburgh hospital, a battered, sullen boy with black hair and hazel eyes recuperated from a broken leg and three broken ribs. He refused to say a word and only tolerated the nurses and doctors. He had been found in the Allegheny forest after a horrific storm that same July evening that deposited two battered girls in Cleveland.

Nine days after that storm, just before the boy was about to be released to Child Services for fostering, Anton Dorayn followed the fading trail of silver sparks that led him to Pittsburgh, by way of the Allegheny forest. He wandered through the hospital, talking to nurses, orderlies, candy-stripers, anyone who would talk to him. A cloud of silver sparks made sure everyone thought he was a wonderful man, and were eager to help him. No one noticed most of his questions were about the boy.

No one saw him walk into the boy's hospital room near midnight. Sparks danced around his fingertips and the ends of his white-streaked blond hair and settled in the deep grooves in the weathered skin of his face. He leaned on the rail of the hospital bed for many long moments and studied the boy.

Hazel eyes snapped open. The boy woke growling, teeth bared. The sound caught and died in his throat when he saw the man standing over him.

"Dorayn?" he rasped.

"You're in a mess, aren't you, young prince?" Dorayn shook his head. "No less of a mess than I'm in. I only have enough to glamour people, understand me, Kaenarr? I can't get us home. We'll need the others before we can find the doorway."

"Aguirra? Alaria?" Kaenarr sat up and reached for the man. Padded restraints hobbled him. He bared his teeth and bent his head to try to bite the thick canvass.

"They're safe. Let's concentrate on getting you safe, shall we?" Dorayn pushed down the rails of the bed. He sighed and muttered a curse when the restraints holding the boy in his bed stopped the movement of the rails. "You've been causing trouble like always, haven't you?" he scolded as he unbuckled the restraints and set the boy free.

Kaenarr grinned and slid over the side of the bed, landing on the floor on all fours. He winced a few times, and rubbed at his bound ribs. His outline started to blur.

"Not here. I don't have enough magic to hide what you are, if we're caught." He caught the boy by the collar of his hospital robe and forced him back to his feet.

They clicked and thudded down the hall, the boy lopsided in his cast, stiff from all the bandages wrapped around his lacerated arms and legs—and too proud to lean on the man who guided him. A faint dusting of silver sparks kept them from being seen when they had to pass through well-lit areas, but those sparks grew fewer and fainter as they made their way past nurses' stations and doctors and maintenance people working the midnight shift. Finally they found the stairs and slid and stumbled down to the ground floor.

The alarm went off when Dorayn pushed open the door leading outside. Kaenarr howled and went to his knees, hands pressed to his ears. Dorayn reached for him, but the boy snapped at him. His outline blurred. His cast crackled as if about to shatter.

Abruptly, a yearling wolf huddled on the floor where the boy had been. Black fur sparkled with silvery residue of magic. The wolf leaped up and darted out the open door, limping on one twisted hind leg. Dorayn cursed under his breath and raced after the young wolf.

Bright lights startled a yelp from the wolf. He turned so sharply he somersaulted. Someone saw and shouted. A truck squealed to a stop in the parking lot. A security guard shouted for backup and fired. The young black wolf howled and dove at the man.

"No, you idiot," Dorayn moaned, and flung his hand in the direction of the boy-turned-wolf. Silver sparks flared at his fingertips...and then died.

The truck gave chase as the sleek black form darted across the parking lot, fleeing into darkness again.

In the morning, police found a shivering, bruised, feverish boy in a cast, bandages and hospital gown huddled in the middle of a garden on the university campus. They couldn't get any answers out of him because he couldn't speak English. He still wore his hospital identification band, and that sped up his return trip to the hospital.

The boy growled and tried to bite anyone who touched him. That, combined with the mystery of his disappearance from the hospital and tales of a wolf racing through the southern half of town prompted a local gossip rag to dub him 'Wolf Boy.'

Dorayn returned to the hospital as soon as he heard the boy had been found, but no clouds of silver sparks charmed the staff into giving him answers this time. He aged another decade as he battled bureaucracy and tried to track down the people who had answers. Because of the furor caused by the gossip rag, the staff of dedicated social workers made the boy's trail vanish. All Dorayn could learn was that a family had agreed to foster him and the system was doing everything it could to help them stay anonymous, for the boy's sake.

Dorayn returned to Cleveland with a heavy heart. He knew it would take years before the three children would be strong enough to return to their home and take up the battle that had nearly killed them. He only hoped he could find the boy and reunite him with the two girls before that time came. He was only a healer, after all, not a wizard, an enchanter born to the kind of magical power that had ripped through the fabric of space and time that separated worlds.

# Chapter Three

Two weeks after that freak storm in the Metroparks, the Harseys brought Aggie home.

Aggie sat in the back seat, her leg stiff and streaked with red caterpillar marks from stitches. Her newly released arm hung in a sling to take pressure off it. She stared, wide-eyed and silent, as her new foster-parents drove down Eastland, past the Baldwin-Wallace College administration building and the Children's Home, and turned right onto Bridge Street. Their Century home was only a few doors down from the Berea Area Historical Society's museum, and Aggie startled when her gaze landed on the two sandstone lions sitting on the front step. She reached forward to touch Grace's shoulder. The woman turned in the front seat.

"What is it, Aggie?"

"What?" She pointed as they passed the lions.

"How do you explain a museum to a poor kid who's just learning English?" Jack muttered. He gave his wife a crooked smile as he said it.

A smile was an improvement, Grace knew. Jack still wasn't too sure about fostering Aggie, but he *had* insisted on repainting the room she would stay in. He had even argued with Grace that a kid who could survive the battering she took didn't want flowers or fairies on her bedspread. He argued for a nice bright plaid but settled for ponies. The fact that he took an interest in the girl's presence in their home told Grace he was weakening. He admired the toughness of the child.

"I'll certainly try to get her to understand," Grace responded as they pulled into the driveway. "Come on, Aggie. Let's go see." She opened her door and climbed out, then pushed the seat forward and reached back for the girl to help her climb from the back seat.

Aggie hopped out, barely any awkwardness in her movements. The doctors had been amazed at her progress, after the battering she took. Holding hands, the two went down the sidewalk to the museum. Grace knew she probably looked ridiculous, grinning so widely, but she felt wonderful. She felt as if she had never been complete until she had found this child to call her own, for however long or short a time she stayed with them.

Aggie led the way up the sidewalk to the museum's front door, eyes wide, gripping Grace's hand tight in her eagerness. She dropped to one knee on the front step and pressed both hands against the left-hand lion.

"What?" she repeated.

"These are Fred and Rosie," Grace began, tapping the lions on their heads in turn.

For the life of her, she couldn't remember which was which. She doubted it really mattered. She went through a very brief history of how the lions were carved decades ago and their part in Berea's history. She didn't feel foolish, as Jack said he did when he talked to Aggie. How could she learn English if she didn't hear it being used, Grace reasoned.

"Fred lion," Aggie said, nodding and stroking the stone mane. "Rosie lion," she said, after scooting over to the other side of the steps without actually getting up. She grinned and looked up to Grace expectantly.

"Yes. Very good." She hugged the girl. "Fred lion and Rosie lion. Is Aggie hungry?" She patted her own stomach. "Lunch?"

"Hungry." Aggie pressed both hands over her own stomach and made a growling noise, then burst out laughing. She muttered something in her own language, patted both lions, then gave her hand back to Grace and let the woman lead her away.

*~*~*

Aggie's room on the second floor looked out over a backyard full of Grace's flowers and Jack's patio and barbecue pit, which angled down to a drop-off to Coe Lake. Aggie sat a long time on the wide window seat, her nose pressed to the cool glass, watching bats flying in the moonlight. Her new mother had put her to bed hours ago and Aggie had obediently closed her eyes and lay still when Grace pulled the sheet up to her chin. She stayed in her bed, trying to hold still, knowing Grace would check on her a few times, like the people at the hospital did.

Now, past midnight, she couldn't stay still any longer. Her new parents were asleep, so Aggie knew it was safe to move around. She went to the window seat and pushed the curtains aside and drank her fill of the night.

A tiny tear escaped her left eye. Aggie closed her eyes tight, willing the tear away. There was an aching feeling deep inside that had nothing to do with her still-healing scars and bones.

Lara was still in the hospital. Aggie knew they were supposed to stay together, but she hated the smells of the hospital and was glad to leave it behind. Lara understood far more than she did, and had explained that she would be going home to new parents soon, too, but that they would see each other almost every day.

So she would wait until Lara had a new home too, and they could be together again.

Right now, though, there was something she didn't have to wait for. She grinned as she thought about it. Aggie liked mysteries and exploring and seeing new things. She could do that now. Lara had explained to her that this was a different place from home, and people here didn't understand the things that made them different. Aggie didn't like having to hide and lie, especially not to Grace, but Lara was older than her and smarter, and she knew it was her duty to obey and protect Lara. If she made a mistake and made people angry or afraid of them, how could she do her duty?

Questions such as where their home was and where were their parents and why did the people here speak a different language—those were questions Lara couldn't answer. Aggie didn't understand why Lara couldn't heal them both, or where her twin brother, Kaenarr, was, or what had happened to them to make them so badly hurt. She sensed these were questions that would have to wait, too. She sensed there were many things she should remember, things she should do—but something stopped her from remembering.

She could wait. She was very good at waiting. It was a game she often had played with her father and uncles, deep in the cool green forests of the Greening Lands. But waiting didn't mean sitting still when she was in a foreign land. Waiting meant exploring and getting all the answers she could, and preparing for the right moment to act. All good hunters knew that, and her father had told her she would someday grow up to be the greatest huntress of them all.

Aggie opened her bedroom window and looked out. The sill was wide. It was a drop of maybe seven feet to the top rail of the deck, and from the deck another five feet to the ground. Easy to do. Aggie climbed up onto the sill and crouched there a moment. Her let hurt a little. She knew how to make the pain go away. The thought of what she wanted and needed to do brought a little whimper from deep inside.

She leaped from the sill, aiming for the upper railing of the deck with her hands. Halfway down, her hands morphed into paws with tiny, sharp claws and hair coated her arms and legs. Her bones ached where they had been broken, just for a moment, but when she landed on all fours in wolf shape her entire body tingled with a sense of well-being that made her want to lift her voice and scream exultation to the moon.

Aggie swallowed down that feeling. She knew in this foreign place, no matter how much she liked her new parents, she had to walk quietly and stay in the shadows. Nothing here was familiar, and she had to move carefully until she understood her new path.

The little black wolf jumped down from the railing to the thin strip of grass around the deck, where Grace's flowers didn't grow. She glanced back over her shoulder once, making sure she could indeed leap back up to her window and get back into her room. She thought it would be funny, but she knew Grace and Jack would not be amused if she showed up on the front step in her pajamas and rang the door-bell to get back in.

That worry taken care of, Aggie darted around the side of the house and across the front lawn and down the street. She stayed in the shadows between the streetlights and her fur stood on end as she approached the center of downtown Berea. Her eyes and ears told her she headed into a maze of concrete and lights and buildings—but her nose told her the park, filled with moonlight, grass and trees lay on the other side of all that light.

Aggie twitched her tail as she darted past the grindstone set up at the entrance to the park road. She stretched out her legs and ran along the asphalt curve of road so her claws clicked. She shivered under her fur as the scents of water, mud, grass, trees and dozens of wild animals filled her head and finally drove away the stink of the hospital.

Then, when she started across the arched stone bridge, she felt a tingle of energy, an itching-tickle that was so familiar she nearly lifted her head to the falling moon to howl a question half-filled with exhila-ration. Her half-grown legs stretched out far, fast and furious as she raced along the edge of the curving Valley Parkway road. She was a dim blur, low to the ground, there and gone so quickly the people illegally in the park only saw a flicker of movement. The lucky ones saw a few sparks from her claws scraping against the asphalt and gravel along the berm.

She loped down the slope of the road into the ford and up the opposite side. She followed the curving road, listening to the sense of knowing in her mind. It was like a quiet voice in the middle of a whirl-ing maelstrom of confusion that offered her a shelter and a stable place to stand and anchor herself.

Aggie was only eight years old. She didn't understand half what went on in her head, or why she couldn't remember much of anything from before the storm—but she knew enough to listen and trust the sense of knowing that seemed to be her only guide.

She crossed Pearl Road, and prickling energy called to her. She turned off the sure guide of the road and crossed dewy meadows and cut through stands of trees until she came to a place where clouds of blue and purple and green sparkles buzzed in swirls like playful hor-nets.

Blue, she knew, was very good. And green was even better. Green meant good smells and sweet things, plants growing in her hands and laughter. There was purple that was friendly, protective, full of fun and treats. And then there was purple that made her bones ache and her blood scorch. She couldn't understand that.

The energy swirling through the air crackled and spun around her. Blue and green sparks tried to cling to her fur. That tickled. She opened her mouth in a doggy grin and panted.

Streaks of blue clung to the fallen tree stretching over the quietly bubbling waters of the river. Aggie lowered her nose to the water and sniffed and knew this was the river where she and Lara had landed. Faint through the smells of car exhaust and dozens of people and animals playing in the river, plastics and food and charcoal smoke, grit dumped into the river and wild animals coming to drink, she smelled the lingering scent of her own body, and Lara's, caught on wood and stone. She smelled their blood and pain, and the scent of a man and his magic.

Her lips pulled back from her teeth in a silent snarl. Aggie knew something had been taken from her memory and hidden, and she didn't like it.

Aggie could still smell the blood where it had washed up against rocks as the level of the water began to descend. Blue sparkles clung to the tree where shreds of cloth and red hairs still clung. Purple hovered in the air, trying to attack, trying to destroy the few remnants of the child who had been there. The energy buzzed, but Aggie could sense it fading. In a few more days, it would be gone.

She didn't know how she knew that. She only knew that she could trust the sense of knowing.

Nodding, Aggie turned and trotted back up the road, through the park, into Berea, into the backyard of the Harseys' house. It was easy to jump up onto the deck railing and through her open window and to shift back to human form as she leaped back into her bed.

She was sound asleep, curled up with her knees to her chin and smiling faintly when Grace came to check on her at seven the next morning.

❦❧

The authorities gave Lara the last name of Monroe, mostly because they thought both girls said 'Lara Mon' or something like it. The Hendersons took Lara home still wearing a cast on her shattered leg. She had enjoyed a miraculous recovery, but no one had much hope she would ever use that leg without a brace and crutches. The Hendersons' most recent foster child had been gone for nearly a month by that time, so they could devote all their attention on Lara. Their son, Mike, was nine and bored at the thought of another physically handicapped girl living in their house.

The Hendersons' next-door neighbors were the Terrels. Their son and daughter were Greg, thirteen, and Allison, seven. Allison had two goals in life: to become a nurse and to marry Mike. As soon as the little girl saw Mike settle in the back yard with Lara her first day in the house, she came tearing over to visit, carrying an injured kitten she had brought home from the park the day before, against her parents' wishes.

Greg hurried to bring his sister back and keep her from intruding. He stopped with his apology half-spoken and stared when his gaze met Lara's.

"Hey, Greg." Mike finally looked up from his book, after trying unsuccessfully to ignore Allison's chatter. "This is Lara. You know that killer storm we had a couple weeks ago? She was beat up in it." He shrugged and rolled his eyes.

"Hi." Greg put down the plant book he had tucked under his arm and held out his hand to shake Lara's. He flinched, feeling a stinging, tickling sensation that raced up his arm when their fingers touched.

"Hello." Lara smiled and held out her hands for the kitten. Allison finally fell silent and settled down at Lara's feet.

Only Lara saw the blue sparks that danced at the ends of Allison's straight, pale gold hair and around her fingertips. Only Lara saw the green sparks that spun around Greg's lean, blond figure like orbiting moons. She couldn't understand why or how the green sparks collided with the blue that leaped from her own fingertips to meet his magic. She only knew she had found good friends.

Mr. and Mrs. Terrel came over that evening for dinner. They had to, because both their children spent the day visiting with Lara, telling her about the neighborhood, running errands, bringing her books, making plans to get her into Allison's wagon to ride down to the park. They were pleasant, but Lara didn't like the way they stared at her, the way they forced themselves to smile.

She didn't like the faint purple sparks that flared up from Mr. Terrel for just a moment when he walked in the door. She didn't like purple magic, but she couldn't remember why.

Lara sensed the Terrels didn't want their children spending time with her, but they didn't do or say anything about it. Why?

# Chapter Four

At the end of the week, when they were sure Lara had settled in, Grace Harsey brought Aggie over to study and spend the day. Aggie didn't wait for Mrs. Henderson to guide her, but followed her nose around the side of the house to the back patio, where Lara had been enthroned for the day.

"Lara!" She laughed and broke into a quick skipping run and crossed the yard. "I like my new house—do you like yours?"

"In English, Aggie." Lara smiled and held her arms out and the two girls hugged, careful of her remaining bruises and the cast that made everything awkward.

Aggie sighed and rolled her eyes, and then noticed the boy and girl with shaggy, pale golden hair coming into the yard.

"She has blue sparks just like you," she whispered, ignoring the injunction to speak in English. "He has green. Green magic is very good."

"I know." Lara wrinkled up her nose at her younger friend. "They can't see it, though. Don't say anything. I think this world doesn't have any magic."

"In English, Lara," Aggie retorted and giggled.

She obeyed, though, and soon after being introduced to Greg and Allison, decided they would both be very good friends.

❧

As August slid into September, Bo Timmons grew discouraged. No matter what he tried, he found no clue to the identities of the two girls. Not a single sign that either girl belonged to someone who missed them. It was as if they had fallen from the sky when the storm split it open.

Aggie and Lara picked up English quickly and soon chattered as easily as the children in their neighborhoods. They studied together, and all the educational counselors and tutors agreed they had a long way to go, but caught up rapidly. Lara had genius potential, and she made it possible for Aggie to learn more rapidly than anyone had thought possible. At the rate they were going, both girls could start into public school the next fall. Lara would go to school in Olmsted Falls and Aggie would go to Roehm Middle School. By that time, both sets of foster parents agreed with Bo, the girls would be sufficiently acclimated they wouldn't mind being separated all day long.

Jack Harsey acclimated to Aggie's addition to their lives faster than either Grace or Bo had hoped. He blustered and seemed almost ashamed to enjoy teaching Aggie to make paper airplanes or throw a baseball or shoot baskets with him in the driveway. Grace watched the two and smiled, reassured that no matter how Jack might complain, he had fallen in love with the scrappy little girl just as thoroughly as she had.

Aggie gained enough vocabulary quickly enough to entertain even Jack with her questions and how she put concepts together. She threw herself into learning everything, exploring everything, experiencing everything to the fullest. It was Jack who suggested they take her to Cedar Point amusement park on the last weekend it was open in September. Grace didn't particularly care for the park herself, but any initiative her husband showed when it came to Aggie, she encouraged.

Aggie didn't care for the crowds. The multitudes of shifting smells and sounds kept her in a state of quivering overload for hours until she was almost numb with it. She stared, open-mouthed at the first ride—Cedar Downs, a carousel that simulated a horse race. Grace had to coax her through the turnstile and up onto the plastic-coated horse, legs extended as if caught in mid-flight, mouth open and eyes wide with the effort of racing. Aggie sat stiff and straight on the horse, gripping the metal bar coming up from the saddle, but only until the carousel started to move.

Then a wide grin took over. She mimicked the other children, kicking the plastic horse to get it to move faster, leaning down low over the animal's neck as if to cut wind resistance. She let out little yipping sounds, enough like the other children's excitement the Harseys didn't notice she sounded more like an excited puppy than a child.

When the ride ended, Aggie leaped off and looked for the next one. She picked up immediately on Grace's reluctance, so she latched onto Jack as her partner. Jack Harsey bloomed that day, telling Aggie everything anyone would ever want to know about the history of the park, of amusement parks in general, of each roller coaster and spinning ride. He talked, using words far beyond her expanding vocabulary and Aggie drank up every word, eyes wide and shining, an eager audience that only made the words come faster.

If the fascination with spinning, falling, racing rides drew the two together, the games section of the park sealed the growing bond between man and child. Aggie didn't have the strength, but she had the hand-eye coordination and innate balance and accuracy to win at nearly every game of skill they tried. Jack spent nearly forty dollars at the games booths, and the two came away with so many stuffed animals and gaudy trophies they had to take four trips to the car to put them away during the course of the day.

Grace didn't complain about the money or the silliness of the toys. She bit her lip against tears every time Jack said, 'That's my girl!' when Aggie triumphed in a game.

"We have to get her into Little League next summer, Grace," he said, when they finally tore themselves away from the games area to find supper. "The kid's a natural. How about gymnastics? I bet she'd tear apart the Olympics if she had a chance."

"That sounds good. If she's still with us," Grace couldn't resist adding. She nearly laughed at Jack's scowl, but she smothered the sound, choking on emotion when he rested a hand on Aggie's shoulder and a proud smile lit his face.

Maybe Jack finally had a son, after all.

꘏ꕤ

Aggie understood enough to feel left out when she saw other children walking past their house to attend Loomis Elementary school only a few blocks away. She stayed at Grace's side, helping her shop, learning chores and how to ride a bike, playing basketball with Jack and studying every day with Lara.

Grace took hope as the days passed and no one showed up to claim Aggie. She dreamed of the day she could talk Jack into adopting. Aggie was everything she had ever wanted. Sometimes Aggie's energy and inquisitiveness exhausted her, and she was glad when Jack came home and took over. They went to basketball and football games together, and played basketball in the driveway every night until winter weather kept them housebound.

There were moments, however, when Grace feared they would lose the girl without anyone taking her. Times when Aggie wasn't anywhere to be found and Grace walked around the house or yard with her heart in her throat, calling, half expecting to be told Aggie had been a figment of her imagination. She had to fight terrified anger when the girl reappeared from seemingly out of the ground and gazed at her foster-mother with her big, muddy-green eyes and the oddest look on her face. Part tears, part longing, part exhilaration.

Sometimes at night, Grace would go into Aggie's room and just stand there, watching the girl sleep. She always did that when Aggie said a foreign word or stumbled over a concept that Grace expected her to understand.

By Christmas, Aggie stopped using foreign words altogether. Grace didn't know if that was good or not; healthy or a sign of deeper problems. She only knew she was relieved and felt a little more secure. She honestly couldn't imagine life without the inquisitive, energetic child.

On Christmas Eve, Jack came home with the preliminary paperwork for adopting Aggie. Grace cried, and Aggie cried when she couldn't get her to stop crying. When the Harseys explained what the papers meant, Aggie grew very quiet and her eyes went wide and she turned so pale they were both afraid she would fall sick right there in front of them.

Then Aggie laughed and spread her arms wide. She leaped on them and hugged them and drowned them with questions. Grace never heard ninety percent of the questions after Aggie's first question: "Can I call you Mommy and Daddy now?"

Jack nearly cried when he heard that.

He gave Aggie a baseball, mitt and bat for Christmas, and a plastic pitching machine to set up in the backyard when spring came. Grace laughed and told herself to be grateful her husband hadn't bought the girl a football and helmet, cleats and shoulder pads.

⚜

Aggie slipped out of the house at least once a week to run in the moonlight and explore the Metroparks. She learned her way around Berea and then through the park system, stretching into Middleburg Heights, Strongsville and Olmsted Falls. When she went to Olmsted Falls and called with her mind, Lara would slip out of the house and meet her, but she was hampered by her crippled leg and brace. No matter how hard she concentrated, Aggie could never get Greg or Allison to hear her mind-call, though sometimes blue and green sparks of magic would drift out of the house, as if they answered her in their dreams.

That summer, Jack announced he wanted to take Aggie with him to work, so she could understand what he did for a living. Grace teased that he wanted to train Aggie to take over the business, and asked when he would start calling it Harsey & Daughter Construction. Jack laughed with her, but he got a thoughtful light in his eyes.

Aggie was quiet all during the ride to the construction site, an office building at the edge of the industrial park in Strongsville. She stayed by Jack's side and smiled and shook hands when he introduced her to the people working in the office trailer, and then took her around the site.

A lean, tanned, white-haired man sitting astride a girder three stories up caught her attention, without calling her or waving. She stole glances at him as she followed her father around the construction site, until she had met everyone on the ground. Jack stopped to answer a few questions from a man holding a big roll of blueprints. Aggie watched until the two men started talking about dimensions and stress factors and liveload. She turned around to look at the man again.

He took his hard hat off, nodded to Aggie and smiled. She smiled back. She saw the natural ladder of girders and temporary scaffolding around a section of wall being bricked in. It only made sense to use it to climb. Jack didn't notice Aggie had left his side until she was nearly to the top. The white-haired man came hurrying across the girder to meet her and lead her onto a platform of plywood sheets.

"That's not quite safe now, Princess," he said, but he grinned at her, and plopped his hardhat on her head.

"I know you," she said in her own language.

"Ah, Princess," he said in the same language, and his smile faded to sadness. "Don't you know it's safer to forget?" A single silver spark shot off each fingertip and filled her eyes for a heartbeat. Aggie blinked and her knees tried to fold.

"Aggie!" Jack hurtled off the pulley lift, nearly losing his own hardhat. "What do you think you're doing?"

"It's okay, Mr. Harsey," the white-haired man said with a chuckle. He went down on one knee next to Aggie and slid an arm around her shoulders. "At this age, they're all just monkeys, anyway."

"Sorry, Daddy," she murmured. "I thought—I thought I knew him." She hated the feeling of tears trying to erupt.

"Well that makes sense, I guess." Jack nodded. "Thanks, Dorayn. I guess I owe you again."

"No you don't, sir." Dorayn shook his head. "You hired me without any records or references. That's a lot."

"You saved my little girl's life." Jack's hearty laugh told Aggie, as clearly as the fading bitterness in his scent, he wasn't angry. "That's a debt I'll never finish repaying." He nodded and smiled down at Aggie now. "Of course you remember Mr. Dorayn, Honey. He helped save you and Lara when you were in the river, remember?"

"Mommy pulled me out."

"We wouldn't have known you were in the river if he hadn't shouted and jumped in after the two of you." He held out his hand for hers. "Let's get back down on the ground again, all right? Mr. Dorayn works for Daddy now, and we should let him do his job."

"Nice seeing you again, Aggie. You go home with your Daddy and be a good girl, all right?" Dorayn said. He winked at her.

Aggie nodded, grinning. She liked Mr. Dorayn. She wasn't sure why, but that knowing sense deep in her gut told her he could be trusted, no matter what.

※ ※

Aggie did well when her parents sent her for gymnastics lessons, but she simply didn't care enough to continue. They let her quit after only a year of lessons. Grace was amused to notice Jack wasn't disappointed. She speculated that perhaps gymnastics was too much a 'girl' thing for his taste. Aggie loved baseball and basketball, and she was nearly a fish when the family went to Wallace Lake or the Berea pool to cool off and relax. That, her love of basketball and her grace and speed in running were more than enough to satisfy Jack that 'his little girl' was going to be a star athlete.

The day Aggie started at Roehm Middle School, he boasted to Grace that Aggie could get into any college she wanted; twenty top colleges would offer her athletic scholarships and she could write her own ticket for the rest of her life.

"But Jack, don't you want Aggie to go into construction with you? Wouldn't it be wonderful to hand Harsey Construction over to her someday?" Grace teased. "We should get her more interested in math, teach her drafting, teach her about concrete and welding and—"

Jack gave her a disgusted look, then burst out laughing a moment later. They laughed together, holding each other.

Aggie heard but really didn't listen or even consider what her parents' words meant. There was too much life out there to experience, too much to explore and learn. Now that she was attending school, she didn't see Lara—and Greg and Allison—as much as she wanted. They could only get together on the weekends. Aggie left the studying and planning to Lara, who always helped her with her homework. She never appointed herself Lara's guardian and assistant, but that was what she was, what she did. Both girls sensed their roles had been chosen for them since they were born.

# Chapter Five

Dorayn didn't need much. He rented an efficiency apartment, rode the bus in the winter and a bike in the summer, bought only enough clothes for work and saved his money to search for the boy, Kaenarr. During the winter, when Harsey Construction slowed down, he took his vacations, always going to Pennsylvania to pick up the trail that had gone cold long ago. His only indulgences were books, because knowledge was power, and the supermarket gossip magazines. He followed up every story that even hinted of wolves in the city.

He wondered, sometimes, how the people of Northeastern Ohio would react to know they had a Wereling, a werewolf, living on the West Side. He wondered if Aggie remembered what she was, her potential and her heritage.

~ ~

The summer between seventh and eighth grade for Aggie, she and Lara planned a picnic at Wallace Lake with Greg and Allison. Greg drove and Mike Henderson tagged along at the last minute, which delighted Allison. When they arrived at the picnic grounds, they drove from one spot to another, and found every table and outdoor grill occupied. It seemed every family in Berea had the same idea. They ended up going down Valley Parkway and across Pearl Road, to Bonnie Park.

Aggie said nothing, but she watched Lara. They went through the park several times a month, by car, taking shortcuts from one place to another. They had never stopped here. Her parents never came to Bonnie Park and Aggie never asked why. It was just one of those things they never talked about. Lara didn't seem troubled, and Aggie wondered if she even remembered this place and how they had come to be here.

*It's all right.* Lara looked sideways at Aggie and smiled as they got out of Greg's car. *It doesn't hurt, if that's what you're worried about.*

*Do you remember a lot?*

*No. Enough, though. Flashes of images. I think it's good for our healing to come back here.*

*The magic doesn't come here.*

*Then what do you call that?* Lara laughed softly and pointed at a swirl of blue and green and purple sparks above the water and the rotted remains of a fallen tree.

"What are you looking at?" Allison asked, and turned to look where Lara pointed. She frowned and took a few steps closer to the bank of the river.

*She can see them!* Aggie held her breath, waiting for something momentous to happen. Then Allison frowned and shrugged and turned back to helping unload the car.

*They have some magic.* Lara picked up a plastic grocery bag and limped toward the nearest table. *Maybe their presence is enough to bring out whatever magic still remains from our...crossing over.*

*Crossing over?* Aggie helped tote charcoal and cooler and picnic basket to the table. *That's right—we crossed over. How come I couldn't remember that until now?*

*Probably for the same reason I can't remember where we crossed over from.* Lara shrugged. "Let's worry about it later, all right? We're here to have fun."

Greg ran into difficulty lighting the charcoal for their hamburgers. Mike put down his computer theory book and stepped up to the grill to help him. Allison had to stay near Mike, even though the older boy ignored her. That left Aggie and Lara with nothing to do, so they took a walk down along the raw stone wall that bordered the curving bank of the river.

"This is so weird," Lara whispered, as she and Aggie strolled through the shadows. "I've been here a few times with Allison and Greg. When their parents don't know—I don't know why, but they don't like it when we go to the park together. Anyway, we just drop things at the recycling bins, or watch a baseball game or something. All the times I've been here, I've never seen the sparks like you told me about."

"Maybe we have to be together to see it?" Aggie offered. Except for that first night in the Harseys' home, when she had run down here, she had never seen any colors, as if the magic throbbing through the stone and soil at this place had truly faded to nothing, just like she had sensed.

"I don't like purple," her friend whispered, coming to a stop twenty yards from the fallen tree.

Sparks danced across the water. Blue and green sparks stayed together, almost like dancing partners. Aggie grinned at the observation and wondered if it was her imagination or it really did happen that way. Purple sparks, however, stayed away from the other two, spinning around in clumps.

"It's not a bad color," Aggie offered. "Not by itself."

"No...but he...the one who was using it...The one who hurt us. He was purple."

"But the one who helped us was purple, too."

"That's right." Lara tried to smile. "I bet you didn't remember that until just now."

"You're right." Aggie shrugged and arched her back. "I wish I could shift to wolf for a few seconds, to see the other way."

"If you want to end up as a news item, fine." Lara glanced back at the picnic table. Faint glimmers of light meant Greg had finally succeeded in lighting the charcoal.

"Do you think the magic is trying to find us?" Aggie looked at the sparks of magic. How fast could they move? Faster than her? Aggie could pick up small items like stones, money and other things she could hold in her hand, shift into her wolf shape, run somewhere, and have the item still in her hand when she shifted back. She didn't want to find out if she could carry Lara away, if they had to run for their lives.

"No," Lara finally said, after frowning at the water in silence for several long moments. "It's just leftovers, with nowhere to go."

"How do you know?" she whispered.

"I don't know. I just do."

"I'm so sick of that. It's not fair. It's like someone has put all our memories in a big, dark box, and we're only allowed to reach in once in a while and pull out something."

"There's probably a psychological term for it, after all the trauma we went through."

"Yuck. Is that what you have to study in high school?" The two girls grinned at each other.

"Knowledge is power," Lara whispered. "The more you know, the more power, the more weapons and defenses you have." She blinked and shook her head, as if waking up. "I started studying psychology, just to figure out what's going on in my head. There's a block in our memories. Either the trauma of what happened to us caused it, or someone put it there."

"Why?" Aggie shivered, feeling that she ought to know the answer. It frightened and angered her.

"To hurt us more, or to protect us, I guess. We have to try to get around that block, or tear it apart, if we want to remember and have answers."

They rejoined the other three by the picnic table while Aggie digested this bit of news. She didn't like the distant light in Lara's eyes. It spoke of pain and loneliness, and that made Aggie feel guilty, because she was supposed to shield Lara. Someone had promised long ago that they would be friends and support each other always. Who had made that promise? When? Where? Why? Aggie didn't have those answers. They hid behind that block Lara mentioned.

Dan Moon became a partner in Harsey Construction in the fall of Aggie's sophomore year of high school. Dan had been recommended by a college friend of Jack's, and moved up from Columbus where he had been second-in-command at a similar company. The plan was to use Dan's contacts to begin Jack's long-awaited expansion of the company.

Lara had a part-time job at the Berea Library, so Jack decided it was time Aggie learned to help Grace with the company bookkeeping. Aggie spent two afternoons a week at the site after school, helping out in the office. That meant Dan spent most of that time with Grace and Aggie, learning the business.

Aggie liked Dan. He smelled good—clean, not half-washed and covering up his bad hygiene with cologne and perfumed deodorant. He walked softly instead of clumping around as if he wanted to stomp the foundations to pieces. He always had a smile for her and Grace and always had a funny story to tell them.

The only employee of Harsey Construction whom Aggie liked more was Dorayn. She always made sure she spent at least half an hour with him whenever she visited a construction site, talking about anything. He always had interesting stories and he always listened. He didn't think she was strange when smells bothered her or she reacted to sounds other people couldn't hear. Whenever they talked, she remembered little bits and pieces of the time before the storm.

Lara liked him, too, and Dorayn always had a joke for Lara or a treat when she drove Aggie to the site in the Hendersons' car. They told him what they never told anyone; memories, seeing sparks of blue and green magic, and the feeling that if they could just turn the right way, they would step through a slit in the air and find their way home. Wherever home was. Dorayn listened and offered advice, and he never gave them that confused, worried, uneasy frown that other people gave them.

Aggie wished she could tell Dorayn she could turn into a wolf, but she feared that would hurt their friendship.

Dan didn't like Dorayn. He claimed it was because the man encouraged Aggie to take stupid risks on the site. The first time Dan saw her climb up to the top of the building where Dorayn took measurements, he panicked half the workers. Jack was used to Aggie breaking safety rules, and knew she would never lose her balance. He slapped a hard hat into Dan's hand and told him to make sure Aggie wore it, and went back to work. Aggie tried to made sure Dan wasn't watching when she went in search of Dorayn, but the longer Dan worked with her father, the harder that became. Almost as if he watched for her to come to work.

Aggie didn't like Dan enough to like that much attention.

Lara speculated that Dan didn't like Dorayn because Aggie preferred to spend her free time on the site with him, rather than Dan.

Aggie couldn't believe that. She didn't want to believe that, because she didn't like Dan that way. She decided that Dan disliked Dorayn because he wanted power among the construction crew, and Dorayn had power without even trying.

The white-haired, leathery man didn't say much and he didn't play the power games that Aggie sensed among the construction crew. The best analogy she could find was that Dorayn didn't belong to any particular pack and Dan believed everyone had to belong to a pack, whether it was his or another. Dorayn didn't try to fit in. There were those in Harsey Construction who left him alone, and others who admired him, but other than Aggie, he had no real friends.

"Maybe that's part of why he doesn't like Mr. Dorayn, either," Lara said, when Aggie refined her theory. "He wants you to be only his friend, and nobody else's."

"That's stupid!" Aggie felt her face heat up. "I'm fifteen and Dan is thirty! He's not interested in me that way." And yet, Dan Moon was more than good-looking. He was strong and graceful, a hard worker, smart and spoke respectfully to her father.

"Want to bet?" Lara wrinkled up her nose at her and switched to another topic, much to Aggie's relief.

Four days later, the girls went on a hayride with the youth group from the church Lara attended with the Hendersons. Aggie went to avoid Dan, who was coming to the house that evening to discuss business with Jack and Grace.

The air was damp and chilly and she smelled an ice storm hovering in the distance. The youth group had invited the fifth and sixth-graders, along with the middle school level, so girls screamed and raced across the parking lot with boys chasing them and other children whined and complained. The piles of manure out back of the barns smelled better than some of the children they would have to ride with in the wagons.

"Why did we agree to this?" Aggie grumbled as she climbed to the top of the wobbly bales of hay inside the tractor-drawn wagon.

"You're sworn to protect me, and if I have to spend another Saturday night at home listening to that little slut crowing about all her boyfriends..." Lara shuddered and forced a bright smile onto her face.

The 'slut' in question was twelve years old and had only been with the Hendersons two weeks. She came from an abusive home and according to the psychological and medical reports Lara had 'borrowed' from the county's computer system, she learned to earn love by giving sex to every adult who showed any interest. Her way of making friends at her new school was to sneak into every shadowy corner with boys and give a show. Knowing that didn't make it any easier for Lara to put up with the unfairly gorgeous, foul-mouthed girl. Aggie and Lara felt decades older in their sense of restraint, decorum and basic hygiene.

"Besides." Lara heaved herself up onto the last bale and stretched her bad leg out along the side of the wagon so it wouldn't get in anyone's way. "This should be fun. Exercise, fresh air, time with our peers—all that good stuff."

"Well, fresh air at least," Aggie muttered. She much preferred tractor exhaust, mud, hay and animal smells, to her closed-up house; aromas of her father's bronchitis, menthol inhalers and tea brewed so long and hot it was gagging bitter. If Lara hadn't called, Aggie would have made some excuse to escape and then spent the evening as a wolf, running through the Metroparks. The lowering clouds would reduce the revealing moonlight and the crowds of weekend walkers and hikers would be next to nil because of the threatening rain. No one would see her. Even if they did, how many people knew a wolf on sight?

The last of the group crowded into the wagons, chattering and giggling, some groaning about how hokey it was to go on a hayride, others digging for handfuls of hay to throw.

Mike Henderson had come on the hayride to get away from his new foster sister, too. He climbed up on the top level with Lara and Aggie and held onto the support pole closest to him. He nodded to them and turned to look out over the slightly muddy field just as the tractor started forward with a jerk and went into an immediate sharp turn.

Several girls shrieked, mostly laughter, as the wagon tilted left. Aggie and Lara held onto poles next to them. Aggie privately admitted Mike was smart to foresee what would happen, even if he was a computer geek and too good-looking. If he would just pay attention to Allison, she thought she could like him.

More shrieks followed and two big bruisers stumbled sideways, knocking into Cleo, a chubby Oriental girl sitting on the railing. Aggie nudged Lara and gestured down as Cleo started to fall. Hands reached out to catch her.

The hands missed. She landed on her back in the muddy, hay-strewn grass. Shouts rose up for the driver to stop. The tractor kept turning, dragging the wagon after it.

"No!" Lara shrieked, and lunged forward, as if she could catch the fallen girl.

The left front tire headed straight for Cleo, who rolled onto her side and got to her knees. More shrieks erupted, more people shouting for the tractor driver to stop. He didn't hear above the grinding noise of the engine. Aggie guessed he thought they were just goofing around.

Blue sparks streaked from Lara's hands, straight at the tractor. The engine died with a squeal-groan-scraping sound, like something had seized up in the block. Cleo curled up, hands over her head and screamed.

Aggie had no sympathy for her. What good did screaming and

hiding her head do? But the tractor had stopped, and that was the important thing.

"I saw what you did," she whispered to Lara, who had landed on her knees on the lower level. Aggie reached down to help her friend up. "You didn't tell me you could do that."

"I didn't know I could." Lara tried to smile, but she looked pale. Blue sparks lingered in her eyes. "I think I pulled something...sort of."

# Chapter Six

The tractor was dead. Few people realized that, with all attention on Cleo. She continued shrieking even after Mr. and Mrs. Willis, the youth leaders came to check on her. Aggie and Mike helped Lara down from the jackknifed wagon and across the muddy yard to the picnic tables around the bonfire pit.

*Well, that was an interesting experience,* Lara commented.

Aggie decided not to comment. She felt a little woozy in the stomach and barely heard when Mike asked if Lara was all right. Aggie needed to move, not sit. Mike stayed with Lara while she got hot chocolate and hot dogs from the people tending the bonfire. Then to both girls' relief, Mike left them alone.

Everyone around them kept busy in the chill, playing football or sitting around the fire, talking and roasting marshmallows under the watchful eye of the Willises. Those who managed to escape did so as soon as they could, sliding into the encroaching tide of the evening dark to explore the farm.

*Am I supposed to be able to zap tractors?* Lara asked as she bit into her hot dog.

*I...don't think we have tractors back where we come from.*

Lara thought for a moment. The sparkle of humor in her eyes faded. She shook her head. *No. You're right, we don't. I think we should be able to do this, but maybe not so young.*

*I don't know.* Aggie gave her a wide grin, mouth open and teeth bared like a wolf just daring another beast to be stupid. *I feel pretty old right now.*

*Me, too.*

"Hey, what's with you two?" Crash Murtock roared, coming up behind them. Both girls jumped and he laughed. "Come on and join the fun. Duck!" He belched laughter as a football sailed over their heads, so close it stirred Aggie's hair.

*Why is a guy like that hanging around with a church group?* she demanded.

*He either has to go to youth group events, or his parents will send him to military school.* Lara sighed and crumpled the paper from her hot dog. *They should have sent him to the Foreign Legion.*

"Well, who's going to be the lucky girl tonight, huh?" Murtock said and thumped down on the bench between the girls. He laughed when they gave him blank looks. "It's dark out, y'know? Plenty of hay to roll in, if you know what I mean." He waggled his eyebrows at them and grinned.

*Yuck.*

*You're so right,* Lara thought back. They traded grins and burst out laughing.

"Can't believe your good luck, huh? I'm completely unattached and eager to please."

*His brain is what's unattached.* Aggie leaped to her feet to evade his groping hand.

Lara wasn't so lucky. Murtock pulled her close against his side and laughed. That got Aggie angry. She wasn't supposed to let things like that happen to Lara.

"That's not how the game is played, Murtock," she snapped, and slapped his hand just before it slid across the front of Lara's sweatshirt. The stereotyped dumb jock just gaped at her, but his grip on Lara loosened. "Like Uhura said to Sulu, I push you away and you come back."

"Huh?"

"He never saw that episode of *Star Trek,*" Lara said. She managed to slide down the seat as Murtock's arm dropped off her shoulders. *What are you doing?*

*Giving the jerk a taste of his own medicine.*

Murtock grinned and leaped off the picnic bench, reaching for Aggie. She turned and ran back behind the barn where the wagons and tractor were stored. There were two couples already giggling and whispering, huddled together among the extra bales of hay stored there.

*Aggie, he's too big for you to fight.*

*Who said I was going to fight? I bet he gets so scared he pees his pants.*

Lara pressed both hands over her mouth to keep from laughing. Aggie darted into the barn. She paused three steps into the utter darkness, just out of the line of moonlight and firelight that seeped through the three-foot gap in the doorway.

"Hey, Aggie?" Murtock chuckled. "I remember that episode now. The evil empire one." He stepped through the doorway and stumbled into darkness.

Aggie went backwards, moving on her toes, wishing she could have slipped out of her boots before she ran. It didn't really matter what she was wearing when she shifted to wolf, though, but she wanted to be light on her feet before that.

"Uhura had that hot uniform. Bet you'd look really great in one of those, huh?"

Aggie growled, letting the wolf come up to the surface.

"Ooh, baby, are you hot for a good time or what?" Murtock turned toward the sound.

Aggie shifted to wolf and darted forward, knocking Murtock backwards with one swipe of her paw. She landed in the shaft of weak light and turned to face him, teeth bared, saliva dripping from her fangs, lips rolled back to expose all the sharp white and dripping red.

"Ah...nice...doggy?" he whispered. The aroma of incontinence filled the barn.

Aggie snapped her teeth and lunged at him, stopping just short of Murtock's folded knees. She growled, shifting the sound to a howl that was unmistakable.

Murtock shrieked even louder and shriller than Cleo had when she fell off the wagon. He scrambled to his feet and ran, falling over himself to get out the door. Aggie shifted to Human and went further into the dark barn. She thought she heard and smelled something that would double her revenge on Murtock.

*Well?* Lara asked, as an uproar of voices followed Murtock's screams and the sound of his pounding feet grew fainter. *Did he pee his pants?*

*And then some.* Aggie found what she was looking for and knelt. "Hello, pretties. Want to help me play a trick?"

When a band of rescuers spilled into the barn, they found Aggie sitting on the floor in the shaft of moonlight, playing with five week-old spaniel puppies and their aged mother. When she suggested that Murtock's wolf was actually the mother dog defending her pups, everyone laughed.

✍ ✎

Dorayn hit paydirt. A gossip rag on the west coast had managed to access sealed records and published the legal name of the 'wolf boy' found in the Allegheny National Forest. Brody Cooper hadn't been adopted, but the reporter insinuated that he had stayed with his foster parents since being smuggled from the Pittsburgh hospital. There were even a few photos, but they were smudged, likely taken from a long distance, in the rain, and computer-enhanced. Dorayn studied the grainy black-and-white photos until his eyes ached. Brody looked enough like Kralnar to be his son, enough like Aggie to be her brother.

Dorayn knew he had found the third child. His inner guide, the bit of magic that had never faded no matter how long he stayed in this magic-lacking world, told him Brody was still in Pennsylvania. That narrowed the search considerably. He would find Kaenarr, now called Brody Cooper.

Now, how to get Brody to Cleveland and reunite the twins, once he found the boy?

✍ ✎

Two weeks after the hayride, Aggie came home from basketball practice to find both Lara and Dan had been invited for dinner. She had heard rumblings from her father that Dan would be coming over to work on company business and plans for expansion, but why had Lara been invited?

"Your Mom thinks we should hit 'American Werewolf' tonight," Lara said, when the two had retreated to Aggie's room. They had ten minutes for Aggie to wash and change.

"You're kidding. Dad thinks the only reason it's stayed in town this long is because I keep going to see it." Aggie stepped into her connecting bathroom, shut the door and peeled out of her workout clothes. *Dan didn't seem too happy. Do you know what's up?* She had time for a basin bath, nothing more.

*I think your Mom invited me over as a shield. She never lets you go to work alone anymore, so I think she thinks Dan is after you. Big time.*

Aggie couldn't laugh, like the last time Lara had suggested it, because she knew it was true. The last few times she had worked at the construction site, she had felt Dan watching her a little too intently. She couldn't figure out if his look, his scent were hungry or possessive, or both. A girl could be highly flattered by his attention. After all, Dan was good-looking, successful, had his own place—and he smelled good.

*Dorayn says I should be careful of Dan and his buddies, all the new guys he's brought to work for Dad. He won't say why, but I trust Dorayn more than anybody.*

*Mr. Dorayn is...* Lara grinned when Aggie opened the door and stepped back into the bedroom and picked up her fresh sweatshirt and jeans. "Long day on the computer, at school and the library. My head hurts. I think if Mr. Dorayn doesn't trust Dan, neither should you."

"Did you ever wonder where Dan got all his money? He's awful young to have so much to throw around. Daddy asked him a couple times, and he just laughs and says it's his, free and clear and he doesn't have to answer to anybody how it's spent, so why should Daddy worry?"

"I'd worry," Lara said. She rested a hand on Aggie's shoulder. A blue spark leaped from her fingertip to tickle Aggie's nose. "I don't like how he looks at you. Like he's going to eat you."

"Do you ever see purple sparks in his eyes?" Aggie whispered.

Neither girl said anything more on that subject, but it stayed in Aggie's mind all through dinner. She noticed Dan wasn't too happy to have Lara with them. His scent turned bitter-hot, negating his spicy cologne, when Grace announced the girls were going to a movie immediately after dinner.

"Yeah, your Dad says you really like that werewolf movie. Kind of a long time for a Halloween revival to be out, huh?" Dan said with a grin. He never looked at Lara or spoke to her, all through dinner. Aggie wanted to shift to wolf just long enough to slap him with her claws for his rudeness.

"The Berea Cinema has been trying a lot of things to stay alive," Jack mumbled through his double serving of death-by-chocolate cake.

"Wish I could go with you, but I have work to do."

Something in Dan's tone, the way his gaze raked over her, made Aggie think he wanted to go with her, specifically, just to sit next to her in the dark. Lara concurred.

*Some guys think they can get away with a lot in the dark,* she offered as she took a mouthful of cake.

Aggie waited until Lara picked up her glass of milk to wash the cake down. *Then he'd find out werewolves are real.*

Lara barely kept from laughing and shooting chocolate cake and milk out her nose.

"American Werewolf in London" had come to Berea for Halloween week, but had proven to be such a hit it stayed on. Aggie had seen the movie five times and didn't really care if she saw it again. Dan had promised, or threatened, to take her to the movie the last time Jack had mentioned it at work. She didn't want him following through, now. Lately, something about Dan made her fur stand up on end, even when she wasn't in her wolf body. Lara was right: Dan was just a little nicer to his partner's daughter than he should have been.

"I thought you didn't like horror movies," Lara grumbled as Aggie paid for their tickets to see the movie.

"But this is so wrong, it's a comedy," Aggie insisted. She shivered, feeling the fur on her insubstantial wolf body raise. She sensed watching eyes.

A scruffy pair of young men with three-day growths of beard and matted hair filled her view. They wore a kind of uniform of camouflage pants and ragged sweatshirts, neon colored hightops and stocking caps. They watched her and Lara to the exclusion of the other girls paying for tickets. The other girls were in larger groups, or were with boyfriends.

She kept her assessment short and kept surveying the sidewalk in front of the Berea Cinema, but the pair saw her notice them. From the corner of her eye, Aggie saw the blond nudge his darker partner and they headed toward her and Lara.

*Let's get in now.* Aggie took a grip on her friend's elbow to support her and her bad leg in a fast walk through the front doors. They bypassed the concession stand, though the chocolate covered raisins and peanuts seemed to shriek her name.

*You're not getting anything?*

*In a minute. I just want to get us lost in the dark.* Aggie showed Lara a mental image of the filthy duo.

*Chocolate boosts us both, but you're going to need more than chocolate if they become a problem.* Lara moved into an empty row of seats ahead of her.

*Worse—it's that time of the month, and a full moon.*

*Lucky you.* Lara tried to smile. They had learned years ago that chocolate was like a drug for them. They had only eaten half their servings of chocolate cake at dinner, and that had been enough to make them slightly giddy.

A breath of air thick with stale sweat and unbrushed teeth warned Aggie. From the corner of her eye, pretending not to notice, she saw the scruffy pair settle into the seat behind her and Lara. This would not do. It wasn't like there weren't any other seats in the house. At fifteen minutes until the show started, only a quarter of the seats were filled.

"I need some popcorn big time," she said and stood. "Want anything?" *Don't look now, but the boys from 'Deliverance' are sitting right behind us.*

"Yes, but I don't know what." Lara made a face and levered herself to her feet. Her leg brace creaked extra loud. "I'll have to come with you."

"I hope nobody takes these seats while we're gone. They're the best seats in the house."

Aggie prayed the pair wouldn't follow them. Were they stupid enough to believe the girls hadn't seen them and would actually return to those specific seats?

None of that mattered when they reached the concession stand. She bought her usual lemonade and two boxes of chocolate-covered mints. Lara kept it simple with a box of Dots and a bag of chocolate snowflakes.

*Expecting trouble?* Lara asked, as they linked arms and took their time returning to the theater.

They took seats halfway down on the left, where she could keep an eye on the unwashed pair. Aggie settled down and looked around as she took her first sip of lemonade. She almost choked when she realized she couldn't find their smelly shadows.

*Don't look now,* Lara thought to her as the seats behind them creaked and groaned.

Banjos?

*Where's Burt Reynolds when you really need him?* Lara glanced at Aggie and rolled her eyes.

They burst out laughing even though Aggie knew this was not a funny situation. If they got up and moved, would the two follow them? Probably. As long as the ventilation system pushed the aroma away from Aggie and not toward her, and the unwanted pair kept their mouths shut during the movie, she and Lara were better off not moving.

Aggie usually enjoyed "American Werewolf" because it was so silly and unrealistic. She giggled through most of it this time, laughing aloud in anticipation of the shocker scenes that were so outrageous they weren't frightening. A few people turned to glare, but Aggie noticed the looks were directed at the two sitting behind her and Lara. Maybe people couldn't believe a girl would laugh at a horror movie? The smelly pair made comments under their breaths but Aggie couldn't smell or hear them, so she didn't care. She threw herself into enjoying the movie, laughing at the insult to shape-changers everywhere—*were* there other shape-changers anywhere?—and escaping into a world where she wouldn't have felt quite so odd and unprepared.

She actually forgot about the filthy pair until the movie ended and the lights came up. She and Lara stood and giggled as they quoted outrageous lines from the movie while they waited for the rest of the audience to leave.

"You really like gore, huh?" a gravelly voice asked, accompanied by breath that smelled like a dirty fish tank a week after the fish had died of polluted water.

Aggie turned slowly, all her bubbly feelings dying. *I really hate it when jerks steal my chocolate buzz, y'know?*

"It's not real," she said slowly, and gave the speaker, the dark-haired one, a half-lidded stare that had made football players and punkers at school leave her alone.

It didn't faze the greasy young man. He grinned and leaned forward, gusting more rotting breath at her. Aggie imagined if he was cut open, half his organs would be gone to black slime.

"Ever do it on a tombstone? Wanna hit the Flats?"

This was worse than pimply-faced boys trying to hold her hand or put their arms too far around her during square dancing in gym class.

"We don't date," Lara said, and gave Aggie a shove, hard enough to make her stumble out into the aisle.

"Don't have to call it a date," the blond one said, grinning wide enough to show three rotten teeth and two gaps. "You as hot as your hair looks?"

*I wish...* Lara turned her head and refused to look at either one as she and Aggie stalked out of the theater. *I wish I could start fires, instead of just zapping engines.*

# Chapter Seven

*They aren't following*. Aggie couldn't quite believe their luck. She hooked her arm through Lara's to support her as they hurried across the lobby, aiming for the door. She wished there was a larger crowd that night, to help them vanish. But a larger crowd would slow them down, too.

The filthy pair came out onto the sidewalk just seconds after Aggie and Lara emerged. The last thing she wanted was to lead them home. She could just imagine Jack Harsey bringing out his rifle and threatening them. Usually Aggie appreciated her father's protectiveness. Other kids knew about it at school and if she didn't want to go somewhere or do something or be with someone, she only had to use her father's strictness as reason. That earned her sympathy from her age-mates and she didn't get the harassment they could hand out.

This time, however, Aggie suspected her father wouldn't leave it at just a threat, because these two aggravating boys wouldn't know when to stop. They already proved they didn't have the brains to take a hint, and they were probably numb-wits who believed that when a girl said no she meant yes. What if Jack actually loaded his rifle this time, instead of just waving it as a talisman against unwanted visitors?

*Down the alley*, she said after only a few seconds considering their options.

An apartment building shared a large, badly lit parking lot with the theater, accessed by two badly lit alleys littered with storm-driven debris, rubble and puddles. Aggie thought if she and Lara could get down the alley quickly enough, they could cut through the apartment building and out the other side, hopefully leaving the filthy pair in the dark, looking for them, maybe creating a nuisance so the police would be called. Meanwhile, she and Lara would already be down Front Street and heading toward Bridge and safety.

There were no other people in the alley ahead of them. Aggie guessed everyone had either parked on the street in front of the theater or went down the other alley. What was wrong with her, to make so many wrong choices? Why wasn't she paying attention lately?

"Hey, girls, what's your hurry?" the dark-haired one shouted. "You scared of the dark?" He and his friend guffawed.

"I wish I could make them afraid of the dark," Lara muttered.

Aggie muffled a giggle as a plan sprang into her mind. She pointed at the single light bulb high overhead that created a weak yellow puddle of light ten yards wide.

*Think you can zap that like you did the tractor?*

Lara opened her mouth to answer, then grinned. She stopped and leaned against the wall and closed her eyes, concentrating. The two jerks behind them let out excited yelps. Did they think the girls had decided to wait for them?

The light died with a loud *snap*. Aggie pressed both hands over her mouth to stifle a giggle as the two boys immediately crashed into each other. They cursed and hit the walls.

*All right. Step back and hide, and turn it back on.*

*What?* Lara reached out and grabbed Aggie's shoulder. *You didn't tell me you wanted it to come back on.*

*How are they going to see me? You can do it—I know you can.*

*Okay. If you say so.*

Something pulsed through the darkness, a feeling that was almost a sound, vibrating in her bones. She and Lara could simply flee out the other end, but the pestering had gone too far. They didn't have to put up with the harassment. They had the means and the knowledge—albeit spotty—to protect themselves from anything and anyone.

*Here it comes!*

Aggie leaped almost before her claws and fangs appeared. The light came on and the two filthy boys twenty feet away let out yells of delight—which turned to shrieks as a black wolf raced down at them. She snarled and opened her mouth wide, teeth gleaming. She raced past them, going between them. They dove aside, one slamming his face against the brick wall of the outside of the theater, the other falling against the brick and sandstone facing of the building next door. Aggie ran another five steps, then turned with a backflip. She came back at them and the two let out shrieks and went to their knees. Aggie leaped over them and raced back down the alley, past the niche where Lara hid. She vanished into the half-lit darkness of the parking lot at the same moment the two boys scrambled on hands and knees out the street end of the alley.

When a policeman appeared, Aggie had changed shape and returned to Lara. They crouched in the alley, leaning against the side of the building, giggling themselves breathless. It took nearly five minutes to get their breath back and enough control of themselves to answer his questions.

Grace came to the front door when the police car dropped the girls off. Aggie wondered what her mother would think if the lights had been flashing. That started her giggling, but she managed to squash the sound behind her hand. Lara looked close to breaking out in fresh giggles, though. They held hands, tightly enough to hurt.

"They're okay, ma'am. Some boys were harassing them, probably on drugs or drunk or something. The girls are just fine. They weren't in any danger. I think someone saw the boys bothering them and decided to step in and help." The officer turned to look at the girls as they came up the flagstone walkway to the front door. "You sure you're going to be all right?"

"Sure. We're fine. Those guys were seeing things. I mean, we just came out of a horror movie, right?" Aggie said. "Mom, you should have seen these jerks, trying to hit on us. They must have been high. But they tried to follow us down the alley and the light went out for a few seconds and they must have run into each other and...well, there were just me and Lara in the alley. No monster. No wild animal." She giggled. "Unless you think I'm a wild animal?"

"I think the girls need something to calm them down, ma'am, and a good night's sleep," the officer said.

"What the girls need is better police protection in this town," Dan muttered. He stood by the open front door and watched the police cruiser drive away.

Aggie and Lara burst out in more giggles. Dan turned, and for a moment there was a fierce, ugly look in his eyes that made Aggie want to scream and shift to wolf and run at him, claws extended. The moment passed, shattered when Dan swore under his breath, voice harsh.

"Dan—in front of the girls," Jack scolded.

"Sorry." Dan offered them his charming smile. "I just don't like thinking that I was less than a mile away when Aggie was being harassed by some spaced-out freak on drugs."

"Puh—lease," Aggie muttered, which earned a few sputtered giggles from Lara.

"Are you two sure you're all right?" Grace stepped toward them, gesturing as if to herd them into the kitchen. "What did you have to eat at the theater?"

"This is more than just too much sugar, Grace," Jack said. "They're hysterical."

"We had enough chocolate to feed an army!" Aggie called over her shoulder.

"That explains a lot." Grace sighed and rolled her eyes, but she smiled. She knew how both girls reacted to chocolate.

Dan didn't believe the explanation, judging from the whispered argument that came hissing down the hall into the kitchen. Aggie felt the tension in the house drop by two-thirds when she heard the front door close and the rumble of Dan's truck as it started up out at the curb.

An hour later, Lara and Aggie had settled into the twin beds in Aggie's room to giggle and make plans for the weekend. The phone rang. Jack's startled exclamations piqued Aggie's interest. She shifted to wolf, leaped off the windowsill and crept up to listen in at the kitchen window.

"I don't know whether he's an idiot or just too good to be true," Jack said, after hanging up the phone.

"Now what happened?" Grace asked. China clicked and silver rattled. Aggie guessed her parents were having their evening ritual hot herbal tea before going to bed.

"Dan went down to the jail to talk to those two criminals who were harassing the girls. Read them the riot act. Officer Crayne called to let me know. Turns out one of those slimebags has important relatives and his lawyer is threatening to sue *us* for emotional abuse!" He snarled something under his breath. Aggie heard the creak-bang of Jack dropping into his chair at the kitchen table.

"Well, Dan really had no business—"

"Dan cares about our family, Grace. Not just my business. I'm glad there's someone else looking out for you and Aggie. If anything happened to me...well, these last few months have shown me how alone I've been, business-wise, and how important it is to have a partner who can take care of things. I'm glad Dan cares enough about Aggie to get involved."

"A little too involved, if you ask me."

"Honey?"

"She's fifteen, Jack. Dan is twice her age. I don't like the way he looks at her sometimes."

"As long as he doesn't try something he shouldn't, is it really so bad when a man admires your little girl?"

"That's just it." Grace stood up and came over to the sink. Aggie could see the top of her head in the window. "She's still our little girl. Wait until she's at least out of high school before you marry her off to your business partner."

"Marry her off?" Jack chuckled, but it was an uneasy sound. "Sweetheart, do you really think I'd do that?"

"You need Dan's money and connections. He has a good reputation, and I was fully behind you when you formed the partnership. But if he won't abide by the contract unless he gets Aggie, too...what are you going to do, Jack?"

Aggie turned tail and ran, back to the porch railing and the long leap up to her windowsill. She leaped onto her bed and then shifted back to Human. Lara had heard it all, through Aggie's ears and their mental bond. The two just looked at each other, with nothing to say.

⚭ ⚭

Jack must have said something to Dan about his visible interest in Aggie, because he didn't come to their house as often as he used to. That relieved her, and yet she admitted she liked having someone as mature, strong and handsome as Dan Moon interested in her.

Aggie knew boys in school were interested in her, but she didn't like any of them. She sometimes wondered if she had any right to want a mate, when she was so very different from all other girls in the world. She was sure she came from a place where everyone was like her. And if that was so, why should she settle for a man like Dan Moon, who couldn't run with her on four feet, read the world through his nose, howl on moonlit nights and feel the rhythm of life everywhere?

Aggie's sophomore year flew by, caught up in helping Lara find her own apartment and shop for furniture and dishes and all the exciting little details that made her so jealous of her best friend. Lara found an apartment in a converted three-story house practically across the street from the library, so she could walk to work even in the worst weather. Then came the flurry and fuss of graduation. Lara was valedictorian and no one was surprised. She had earned several scholarships, and chose to invest them at Cuyahoga Community College, taking evening, weekend and Internet courses, so she could keep working at the library.

Lara confessed she wasn't sure what to major in, when she and Aggie went for a walk in Bonnie Park a few days after graduation. She was good in so many subjects, and nothing really appealed to her as a specialty.

Then something glimmered at the edge of Aggie's vision, yanking her attention away and stealing the teasing comment from her lips. She shook her head, squinted, then opened her eyes wide. She realized Lara had stopped and looked at her, waiting.

"Do you see..." Aggie stopped, feeling rather foolish with the question poised on her lips.

"See what?" Lara looked out over the river as it curled around the picnic area at Bonnie Park.

"Sometimes, it seems like just before I close my eyes..." Aggie shook her head, a tiny growl rising in her throat. She looked around, made sure they were alone, then shifted to wolf to see more clearly and from a different perspective.

"That drives me crazy sometimes."

*Huh? You're used to it.*

"I know, but it still bugs me. How come I can't change shape?"

*Maybe you don't know your other shape yet. And there are dozens of things you can do that I can't. Like you get those visions. Don't tell me it's just remembering something you read or saw or heard before. It's like you can link your brain into the computers. Just wait until you get your own computer and you can link into the Internet all the time.*

"Once all the bills for my apartment are paid up, that's the next thing on my list," Lara said with a sigh and a smile.

*And you can zap things, cut off the flow of energy or reconnect the flow. You know what people are going to say before they say it. You can read half the teachers' minds at school.*

"Only if there's something to read," Lara said with a snort.

*I think you can teleport. Just short distances. Like to make up for your bad leg. I know there are times I've seen you at the back of the room, and I don't feel or smell or hear you move, and then suddenly you're at the front. Or in another room. I think you teleport when you're not aware.*

"That's not a very useful talent."

*Thinking sometimes makes something impossible.*

"Talk about impossible—where do your clothes go when you shift shapes?"

*'Tweening spaces.* Aggie-wolf stopped short, her mouth dropping open. She shifted back to Human and scrambled back up onto the picnic table where they had been perched to watch the flow of the river. "I never remembered that word until now. The 'tweening spaces. It's like a fold in reality. A holding space. A place that's two places at the same time. Maybe that's how you do your teleporting. Your body knows how to find the folds, but your conscious mind still needs to remember how. When you're thinking about it, your brain gets in the way of what your body wants to do."

"Yeah. Really useful. You get the craziest theories sometimes."

"Maybe, but they seem to work, don't they?" She smirked.

"Lots of impossible things work for us, and nobody else. I wish we could find others like us. Just so we don't feel so odd," Lara whispered. She shook her head and a faint, bitter aroma that Aggie linked with angry fear and hurt wafted around her for a moment. "So what's so impossible right now that you can't tell me?"

"It's..." Aggie took a deep breath and forced the words out. "Sometimes when we're here, I half-close my eyes and I could swear I can see another...place. Same general landscape, but with more trees and no parking lot, no fire circle, no signs warning kids to stay out of the river. You know? Maybe what this place would look like if people hadn't come through and bulldozed things."

"Hmm." Her friend nodded. "I've noticed that too."

"Why didn't you tell me?" She grabbed Lara's shoulder and shook her, pretending anger. "We're a team, remember?"

"I remember, but I always see these things when I'm alone, when I'm tired, and...on mornings when I've had bad dreams about the storm. You never dream about the storm, do you?"

Aggie didn't have to ask which storm Lara referred to. There was only one storm in their vocabulary and memory.

"No. Not really. Or at least if I do, I don't remember when I wake up."

"I dream about it all the time, seems like." Lara held up her hand, blue sparks weaving around her fingers for a moment. "There's something special about the Metroparks. I only get the double vision in the Emerald Necklace. Maybe I should spend the summer researching the history of the park system."

That summer was hard on Aggie. She took on more office work so Grace could concentrate on public relations for Harsey Construction. Her mother became involved in local charities and artistic groups, meeting the movers and shakers in Cuyahoga County and in the Cleveland development and renovation market. Dan didn't push his attention on her when they were alone in the office, as Aggie had half-feared, however. That, and being able to talk to Dorayn every day helped, but didn't counteract the restlessness that gnawed at her. She felt uneasy all summer.

What could she blame? Her rapidly approaching junior year? The fact that Lara had graduated and they weren't able to spend most of their summer together as they had hoped? Or the way Dan was so very protective of her in a very gentlemanly, flattering way, so she really couldn't complain to her father? Or maybe the fact that Aggie had no idea what she wanted to do with her life? High school juniors were supposed to start figuring that out, weren't they? She hadn't a clue.

Her dreams of running through a misty forest with someone who felt like her other half, who vanished when she stopped to look, didn't help matters any.

Sometimes she woke from dreams where a voice called to her to run, to explore, to call to others like her and be their heart and mind and voice. Sometimes she ran in wolf shape and knew, deep in the hot depths of her wolf heart, sensed with her wolf mind, that she was born to lead, to rule, to run at the head of a—of a what? What was she? Wolf or Human?

She had to find others like her, to get that answer. She had to go Home.

Wherever Home really was.

That meant leaving the Harseys and Berea and the only home she could remember. Why did that thought hurt so much, even at the times when she knew Berea wasn't her true home?

Dorayn took two weeks off at the end of October and followed his newest lead to Mercer, Pennsylvania. He hoarded his magic, refusing to waste it in futile attempts to follow the streaks of blue, green and purple magic that still sometimes writhed and teased in the air around the Metroparks and pointed him east. East to Pennsylvania. He waited, wishing he could use the computers for research like Lara did. His magic recoiled from technical things, while Lara's magic seemed to grow exponentially when he watched her working on the computers. He wondered if she would laugh when he told her about her parents and her heritage. Should he tell her before the gap between worlds opened again? Why torment her with knowing and no proof? He wanted to ask her to help in his search for Kaenarr, the boy named Brody Cooper, but he wasn't even sure Aggie and Lara remembered that

Kaenarr existed.

They were still far safer and happier not knowing.

His months of searching and phone calls and making friends with the right people led him to a custom woodworking shop outside of Mercer. His magic flared, silver sparks dancing around his fingertips when he approached Cooper's Fine Cabinetry and the door opened and a young man walked out, carrying a rocking chair for a customer.

From his coarse, blue-black hair and wide shoulders to his liquid grace to his long, sharp nose and deep-set eyes with green and brown rings, he was Kralnar's son. Dorayn half-closed his eyes and roused his magic, and he saw the shadow of the wolf following the high school boy. He stood in the gravel parking lot, watching Brody Cooper wrap the chair in blankets and load it in the customer's trunk. Dorayn laughed quietly when the woman tipped Brody with a tightly folded bill and the boy grinned and shoved the money in his pocket. High school boys were always short on cash. He wondered if Brody had a girlfriend, what he liked in school and how well he fit in.

"I know you," slipped from Brody's lips almost the moment he turned and saw Dorayn watching him.

Dorayn nearly flung the forgetting magic at the boy, a knee-jerk reaction. He caught himself in time, prompted by curiosity and weariness. It was hard being the only one who remembered. Brody might only be Kralnar's physical image; he might have inherited his mother's watchful, cunning, deep-thinking nature. Guerrleen could be cold-blooded, but she had been the wisest choice of all the Werelings as Kralnar's mate, to counter his hot-blooded nature. For the first time in years, Dorayn let himself wonder how the Wereling rulers had reacted to the loss of their twins. Or if they were even alive.

"Do you, now?" His fingertips itched from the pressure of unused magic.

"From...the storm." Brody frowned and rubbed his temples.

"Is that all you remember?" Dorayn knew he hadn't been close enough to affect the boy's memory on that disastrous escape attempt from the hospital, but he had tried anyway.

Or Brody could have blocked his memory all on his own. The gossip rags and years of snooping, rude reporters, plus his own knowledge that he didn't belong in this world, could have done more to block the young Wereling's memories than any magic.

"You're...a friend. I think." Some of the wrinkles smoothed around Brody's eyes and mouth.

"That I am, young prince." Dorayn held out a hand, tingling with silver sparkles of magic. Brody didn't even flinch when they shook hands. "Do you like woodworking?" He gestured at the shop.

An hour later, Dorayn had a detailed tour of the shop and the business, and had much to think about. Brody and his two foster-brothers all worked in the shop. Stan Cooper was an artist and unashamed to admit he preferred the fancy work, leaving the actual building, designing and contracting to his boys. He spoke with pride of Brody's skill with his hands, his uncanny ability to eyeball a project and know just how much wood and nails, varnish and stain they would need.

"Sometimes he doesn't even measure. Just jumps right in and cuts and gets it right. And his sense for wood..." Stan grinned and clapped his foster-son's shoulder. "Don't know how many times he's saved one of us from trouble, running into knots and hidden nails or other trouble in the middle of a piece of wood. And the money he's saved us, when someone tries to sell us lumber that's rotten in the middle."

Dorayn nodded. Guerrleen had given that gift to her son, a touch of green woodland magic mixed into her Wereling blood.

"So," he said, looking around the shop, "you see yourself staying here for the rest of your life, making furniture? I envy you, that kind of security."

"Eh, who knows with these boys? Eddie, my designer, he should be an engineer. An architect. All my boys are going to college and making something of themselves." Stan gestured toward the other end of the shop, where the two younger boys sat in front of a drafting board, scribbling on a design for a kitchen island unit. "Brody..." He winked at his foster-son. "He might just be happier in construction. Outdoors. Lots of heavy work, not the fancy details. Know what I mean?"

"I do indeed." Dorayn nodded slowly as inspiration struck. "Have you approached the union, to check out an apprenticeship?"

Mercer wasn't that far from Cleveland, after all.

He had known from the night he lost Brody at the hospital, he couldn't bring the twins together in any way that might attract attention. The same magic that had flung the three children to this world hadn't found Aggie and Lara, though Dorayn knew it lingered in the Metroparks. He avoided the Metroparks, despite the leakage of magic that strengthened and revitalized him. If magic could seep through to replenish his stores, then tracking magic could find him. The children were safe, until they discovered what and who they were. Dorayn knew he was the weakest point in the protection he had woven around them.

Then again, perhaps the magic that threatened the children had weakened, just as he had weakened and aged during this long exile from the Greening Lands. Or, it could simply be sleeping, hoarding its strength, waiting for any uproar that would reveal where the Wanderer's child had come to rest. The reunion of the Wereling twins had to be quietly done, slowly, in a way that wouldn't attract attention.

By the time Dorayn headed back to Cleveland three days later, he had introduced Brody to the Carpenter's Union and had planted in his mind the notion of applying for a summer internship in Cleveland.

# Chapter Eight

"I'm not going to the Snowflake Dance."

Aggie tried not to hold her breath as the silence congealed in the car. It felt colder inside, despite the heater, than outside in the slushy darkness of the park road in early November.

Maybe she should have held her breath. Grace fought a rotten cold. The bitter tang of her medicine in her sweat mixed oddly with her menthol cough drops and the vinyl fumes of the brand-new Saturn.

"That old rule about girls needing a chaperon to attend dances died when *I* was attending Berea High," Grace finally said. "Besides, you still have two weeks. Quite a few boys might get the sense to ask you out. Or you could ask them. Nothing wrong with a girl asking a boy to go out."

Aggie bit her lip to keep from saying her father certainly didn't agree with that viewpoint. How could she explain to her mother that even if some young fool was desperate enough to ask her to go with him, she didn't want to go? They had gone to SouthPark Mall to look for a present for Jack's birthday next week, but her mother had wandered over to look at the formal gowns. Aggie had felt sick then, like she did when she had a rare nightmare about the storm, falling and the fire and nearly drowning. She hated feeling helpless, and the rituals of high school always did that to her. Every step toward the great unknown of graduation made her feel more trapped and helpless.

It made her want to scream until the roof shook. It made her want to run forever, until she ran the flesh of her paws.

"Mom." Aggie tried to laugh to fight the tendency to hyperventilate. "I'm a better athlete than three-quarters of the guys in my class. Heck, the whole school. They won't ask out a girl who makes them look like wimps. Besides, I don't have the looks." She grinned, baring her teeth and leaned back into the corner between the seat and the door.

"You're a nice-looking girl, Aggie. I know I sound old-fashioned, but if you wore a dress once in a while and did something with your hair—"

"If I actually looked like a girl, the guys might treat me like one.

Come on, Mom, do you know how guys treat girls nowadays?"

"Aggie..." Grace sighed. Her sideways glance melted into a smile. "Is Dan giving you a hard time?"

Aggie looked out at the frozen surface of the fishing lake made from the old sandstone quarries, glowing a soft, almost eerie white in the sparse moonlight through storm-heavy clouds. Maybe it was this late night drive through the deserted park that depressed her, combined with two fruitless, exhausting hours searching for a sports video or jersey Jack didn't have.

"Dan knows I don't approve of a man his age trying to monopolize your time. Especially since you're still in school," Grace said, slowing for a patch of ice across the road.

"You talked to him? Why?" Aggie grinned at the strip of icy, snowy road lit by the headlights.

"Oh? I wasn't supposed to see him breathing down your neck during that last business social? Why do you think I kept sending you into the kitchen for more appetizers?"

"You're my Mommy and you were protecting me from big bad Dan." Aggie laughed. "You impressed all those bigwigs among the developers Dad's trying to cozy up to, that's for sure."

"A man's home life reflects how his business is run." Grace gasped as the car made a loud popping sound and lurched to the left across the road. It headed straight for the rocky barrier around the fishing area.

Aggie bared her teeth as the car went airborne for a moment. She hated falling. Jumping was one thing. Falling with no idea where or when she would land brought on nightmares of fire and being pulled in ten different directions, landing so fast and hard water was like concrete.

All four wheels slammed down hard and the car skidded on slushy asphalt, abruptly slamming to rest against the sign that informed passersby the trees along that section of park road had been donated by the Berea Kiwanis.

Both women let out little shrieks—then silence. A hard, icy rain slammed into the windows from all directions.

"Aggie?" Grace sniffed and reached across the seat.

"I'm okay, Mom. How about you?"

"Fine. I think. I should have let that nice salesman talk me into the car phone. That felt like a flat tire."

Two minutes later, with the flashlight on her mother's key ring, Aggie determined they had *two* flat tires. She knew how to change a tire, but they only had one spare. She brushed the sleet off her hair and face as she climbed back into the car with the bad news.

"We aren't too far from home. Maybe ten minutes to walk out of the park. I could go to the police station and call Dad. Or even walk home."

"I'm glad you know your way around. I've never been in the park after dark. It all looks like an alien world." Grace gave her a considering look. "Have you been in the park after dark?"

"If I have, it's always been alone—or with Lara." Aggie grinned, earning a raspy chuckle from her mother that turned into a cough. "You're not going anywhere with that cold and the rain coming down like it is. You stay here where it's nice and warm and listen to the radio. I'll be back in no time." Aggie handed the keys back to her mother. She hit the latch on the door. It didn't open. "Mom?"

"Oh, all right. But be careful. I feel bad enough as it is, letting you go alone. I'd never forgive myself if you got hurt." Grace unlocked the door.

"I'd never forgive myself if your cold turned into pneumonia." Aggie tugged her pea coat tighter and stepped out into the slush and mud piled around the car where the sliding wheels had dug furrows. "Now lock up and don't open until a policeman shows up, hear me?"

"This is Berea, not New York or Chicago or Los Angeles—"

"Or the rough side of Cleveland, Mom?" Aggie crossed her eyes and slammed the door before her mother could laugh.

Aggie trotted around the first bend in the winding park road, putting trees between her and the car, just enough distance before she shifted to wolf and ran. A flicker of light up ahead caught her attention. Aggie skidded and strained her eyes to see through the icy rain. Was that a car?

The white-blue glimmer of light vanished, replaced a moment later by a flicker of red. Tail lights. The car had turned off the bridge she needed to cross to get into downtown Berea, and turned right instead of left. Maybe if she ran—

Sleet slapped her face and added to the layer of slush on the asphalt and hibernating grass and the waterfowl habitat off to her right. Voices penetrated the hissing. Aggie faced into the wind, taking deep, slow breaths to taste the air. Nothing came to her nose and tongue but the damp and cold, and the wind was from the wrong direction.

Glass shattered.

Grace Harsey screamed.

A man laughed.

Aggie bared her teeth and ran. Gloves and jeans and pea coat vanished before her hands touched the ground. Claws and horn-tough pads dug through the slush, clacking against the frozen asphalt. The half-hidden moon saw a black wolf tear through the trees, leaping the bike path, arrowing across the road in one long, dark leap.

They were four, all dressed in dark clothes that smelled of beer and cigarettes, dirty sweat and the acid tang of metal; guns held close to the skin. The tall one held Grace by her throat, bending her backwards over the hood of her car. The one with no hat and a shaved head rifled through the contents of the car. The one with a cigarette in the corner of his mouth pulled out his gun and aimed it at Grace, snorting laughter when the woman whimpered.

The short, fat, pimply one saw the wolf leap across the road straight at him.

He shouted and raised his gun. Fired. Another gun went off. His bullet missed, coming close enough to scorch Aggie's ear. The tall thug swore and leaped backwards. Grace yelped and slumped, sliding down the side of the car. Aggie caught the pimply one's shoulder with her jaws, raking open his jeans jacket with her right front paw, catching his patched jeans with her rear claws. He screamed and went down. The other three ran.

Grace shrieked—the sound broken off by sudden coughing. Aggie smelled her mother's blood and flung herself off the man. She stumbled, transforming back to Human before she took two steps. The man never saw, scrambling to turn over and stumbled away, whimpering, leaving a trail of blood.

"Mom?" Aggie couldn't breathe. She was afraid to even touch the woman who stared at her with such wide eyes, her face pale, blood seeping around her fingers, through her coat, pressed so tight and hard against the gunshot hole low in her ribs.

"Oh...Aggie."

"I'm sorry."

Incredibly, Grace smiled. She shook her head a little and reached out a hand to her daughter. Aggie took it. She felt the chill in her mother's flesh, felt the blood trickling out of her body, smelled death creeping close, waiting to take his prey.

Until this moment, she thought the battering she had taken and survived in her childhood was the epitome of helplessness.

"So that's what you are," Grace whispered.

"I'm sorry." Aggie went to her knees in the slush and tried to put her arms around her mother without moving her. The woman was in a blessed state of shock and felt no pain for now. Aggie would have smelled her mother's pain, bitter and sharp and sour, mixed with her blood and the stink of medicine in her breath. It just wasn't there.

"Sweetheart...I wish you had told me." She tried to smile, but a shudder racked her body and she gasped. The trickle of blood through her fingers steamed in the icy air.

"I wanted to. Mom, I can carry you to the police station—no, I can drive on the stupid flat tires!" She slid her arms around her mother.

"It's all right," Grace whispered, her eyes closing. "I understand. So marvelous...magic. I knew you were...magic from the...day we...found you." She smiled, never reacting as Aggie lifted her and slid her into the front seat of the ransacked car. Glass from the shattered window was all over the inside of the car. It cut Aggie's hands through her gloves, cut through the knees of her jeans, but she paid it no attention.

"Yeah, just like Superman," she said, resurrecting the old family joke.

No, it had only been a joke between her and Grace. Jack didn't like being reminded that 'his little girl' hadn't been born to them. He didn't want to remember Aggie had been found, and not brought home as a newborn.

Aggie pushed that thought to the back of her mind and finished gingerly sliding her mother across the seat. Turning, she wriggled into the driver's seat and reached for the keys in the ignition.

They weren't there.

A growl escaped her. Aggie glanced at Grace, who seemed even paler in the dome light of the car. Biting her lip against crying in rage, she slid out and searched the floor of the car. Then the slushy ground where the muggers had stood around her mother. She found broken glass scattered all along the road, right in the path the car had taken. Nothing else.

If Lara were here, she could find the keys. Lara was good at finding things.

"Lara—" Aggie swallowed hard, refusing to give in to the helplessness that threatened to send her running, racing, tearing through the trees and snow, across the rotting ice, screaming her anger and fear and hurt to the uncaring sky.

Lights blinded her, magnified and distorted by the tears she couldn't hold back. Rubbing her eyes with her torn, wet gloves, Aggie saw a police car slide up behind the Saturn. She ran to the officer as he got out.

⸙

Lara got to the emergency room at Southwest General Health Center before Jack Harsey. She stumbled in through the sliding doors, no coat over the extra-large Berea Braves football jersey she slept in, her leg brace outside her green sweatpants, in ratty blue tennis shoes without socks, her red curls tangled and wet from the shower and her fern-green eyes wide with worry. She never gave the police officer questioning Aggie a chance to shoo her away, but slid into the next chair and wrapped arms tight around her. She said nothing. They never needed to say anything to understand each other.

"Excuse me, miss, but—" the officer began.

"I really need my friend here," Aggie said, her voice rough with repressed tears. She showed her blood-streaked hands to Lara, Grace's blood mingled with her own cuts, and her friend let out a little gasp of sympathy, tears gleaming in her eyes.

"Aggie!" Jack roared, coming through the doors. He stumbled across the pale linoleum. "Officer, what happened? Where's my wife? Aggie, are you all right?" He shoved the officer aside and slammed into the chair on Aggie's other side. He reached for her hands, stopped short by the sight of the blood.

"Mr. Harsey?" The officer jerked his head toward the admitting desk, asking him to follow. Jack nodded and gave one more glance to Aggie before getting up. His eyes flicked to Lara then and his concern faded into something that Aggie had long ago decided was a mixture of resignation and humor. "The short of it is, your wife and daughter had a flat tire out by Wallace Lake. Someone decided to play stagecoach robber and spread broken glass on the road, waiting for the next car.

"Your daughter made her mother stay in the car and started walking to the station for help. Four men forced your wife out of the car, shot her and ran. Your daughter says a big dog attacked—maybe a passerby tried to help, siccing their dog on the men. Several people living on the edge of the park heard the gunshots and called us. We got there as fast as we could."

"My wife?" Jack's voice broke.

Aggie smelled his agony, bitter and salty-weak, mixed with his late-night beers coming out in the sudden sweat pouring from his body. Her father always sweated when he was afraid or nervous or shocked.

"I don't know, sir. I've been busy getting the story from your daughter. She's had quite a shock." Mild reproof touched his voice.

Aggie couldn't understand that. Grace was the focal point; Grace was the one they had to worry about.

"Lara, could you—" The rest of the words caught in her throat as she looked into her best friend's eyes and Lara could only shake her head.

"I know a lot of things, but I have no idea how to help her," Lara whispered.

"But you can. I know you can."

"I know I can, too, but I don't remember *how*."

"Why does this always happen to us? It's there, in the back of my head, like how you—" She stopped short. "Dorayn."

"He's a healer," Lara whispered. "Silver magic. How come we never remembered until now?"

"Where is he? He can—" She looked up as her father returned to her side. "Dad?"

Jack shook his head, tears filling his eyes, making his chunky face redder than usual. He sat down next to Aggie and put an arm around her shoulder and turned her just enough to rest her head on his shoulder. He was the one who needed the comfort, not the one offering comfort. Aggie slid out of Lara's steadying support and leaned against her father, letting him pretend to be the strong one.

He didn't cry when the doctor finally came to tell them Grace was in serious condition, but she would recover. He held Aggie close and his dignity even closer, thanking the doctor and nurses and the police

officers who had helped. He arranged for the car to be towed to the
dealership for repairs. He kept his arm around Aggie all the way home,
into their house and up the stairs and hugged her—wordless—before
she went into her room.

Aggie picked up the phone as she listened to him go back downstairs to his den, close the folding doors and go to his liquor cabinet.
She left a message for Dorayn and whiskey fumes floated through the
house as her father numbed his grief. She was the one who called Dan
and the crew at the construction site in the morning and told them the
news about her mother; who answered the phone call from the polite,
sympathetic reporter from the *News Sun*; who called Berea High School
and told them she wouldn't be in.

Jack was still asleep after she finished those chores, reeking of
his liquid comfort even through the closed doors of his den. Aggie
didn't write him a note, knowing she would be back long before he
woke up. She stepped out the back door without shoes or jacket,
dressed only in jeans and black T-shirt. It was an unspoken rule never
to shift to wolf in daylight or where people could see, but today she
didn't care.

She had to run, or scream. She lunged off the deck and landed
on all fours, running, her tail high and her fur bristling. As if they
sensed the storm brewing inside her, none of the neighbor dogs made
a sound as she tore through backyards on her way to the park. Aggie
ran, paying no attention to where she went, instinctively seeking the
thickness of the trees and the shadows. She ran until the snow seemed
to steam where her paws touched and the chill air burned in her over-
heated lungs.

It did no good. It never did. But she still had to try and outrace
the pain.

Her mother's words rang through her mind. *Aggie rode in the
ambulance, holding her mother's hand and staying out of the way
of the EMT as he worked frantically to stabilize her blood pressure
and stop the bleeding.*

*"You're old enough,"* Grace whispered. *"You should find out where
you come from."* *She smiled, struggling for breath. Her pulse turned
into a butterfly under Aggie's hypersensitive fingers. "That's been
the problem all along, I think. You need to know. You need to go
home."*

*"I know,"* Aggie said through a throat locked tight by tears. *She
refused to cry them, knowing it would turn into a howl and she would
tear the inside of the ambulance to shreds in her helpless rage.*

*"You've never really been happy here, I think."*

*"I've been very happy. You're my Mother. You wanted me."*

*"You stayed for me?"* Grace's face brightened for a moment.

*"Mom, where would I go? I don't remember anyone but you."*

*"You have to remember,"* Grace whispered, just before the am-

*bulance pulled up to the emergency room doors and the flurry of technicians and doctors and nurses separated them.*

≈≈

"She knows," Aggie said, when she appeared at Lara's door three hours later. "Mom saw me turn wolf and she smiled and she knows and it doesn't freak her." Then she burst into tears.

She and Lara ended up on the floor in the tiny living room, huddled together under a mound of blankets, eating chocolate and vegetarian pizza and wine coolers and just being there for each other. Aggie didn't have to say anything. Her grief had torn her mind wide open and Lara saw every second of last night through her eyes.

"She knew," Aggie finally said, when the movie Lara put into the VCR for background was nearly done. "She knew what I was but she wasn't scared. She wasn't angry I kept secrets from her. She called it magic. When I think of all the time I wasted, all the secrets and things I hid from her—"

"How were you supposed to know? We're too different," Lara said. She caught a handful of Aggie's long, curly hair and tugged. That bit of teasing earned a smile from her. "We knew from the day they found us we were different and we didn't fit in, and we had to be careful."

"*How* did we know?" she challenged. "Where do we come from? How did we get here? Are there other people like us? Why are we the way we are? How come we can't do the same things? Why do we always *know* things, but we don't know *how* we know or why we couldn't remember them before?" Aggie's head throbbed. Her hands itched from running. She could still feel the land under them as she raced over mud, stones and matted grass, through slush and melting snow.

"I don't know. Maybe it's time we started looking," Lara admitted, looking away.

"That's what Mom said. She said I was old enough to know." Her voice cracked. "I think she told me that because she thought she was dying."

"Your mother isn't going to push you away when she recovers. I know I'm the smart one, but I didn't think you were that stupid," Lara drawled.

Aggie stared at her for a few seconds, then a jerky, broken stream of laughter spilled out of her. They hugged. She felt the aching inside her melt and release and flow away, like ice jammed into places that had been dark for too long.

"It's time we faced our past, or we might never have a future," Lara continued, her voice softening. A thoughtful expression touched her eyes.

"Do you ever try to remember, or do you just get nightmares?"

"Both." She shrugged. "When weird things happen and I remember tiny bits... Yes, someone hurt us—"

"Tried to kill us," she corrected softly.

"Kill. Yes. But there is someone else who loved us very much. I remember laughing and running through a forest and...apples ripening in my hands, and someone holding me very close and tickling me." A spark of laughter briefly gleamed in her eyes. Lara sighed. "Mostly, all I remember is the storm."

"Isn't it funny how we always say *the* storm, not *a* storm?"

"Sometimes it seems like we were born in that storm."

# Chapter Nine

Aggie's days took up a new pattern. She went to school, then basketball practice, then spent the evening in her mother's hospital room, studying and keeping her company until visiting hours closed. Several times, she found Dorayn standing by her mother's side, holding her hand, watching her sleep. Aggie knew she had seen...something, but she could never remember what she saw or what she and Dorayn spoke about. She only knew she felt less fear and worry for her mother when Dorayn visited.

When the nurses grew insistent, then Aggie went home. Jack wasn't much company, wrapped up in his worry for Grace and his liquor cabinet. He never checked on Aggie once she went up to her room. She always waited until she heard her father stumble into his room and the trail of whiskey fumes had dissipated from the air, then she went downstairs, stepped outside in her bare feet and shifted to wolf.

The police could follow their paltry leads, trying to find the men who had set the trap in the park and shot her mother. Aggie would hunt her own way. She knew what the men smelled like. She knew what one of them tasted like, the blood that filled the air, the stink of their fear and anger, the drugs and alcohol that filled their bodies and seared their souls. She knew, even if she couldn't tell the police.

She knew she had seen those men before, just glimpses, but she couldn't remember where. Maybe they simply came to the park often, for their own warped kind of hunting. She dared to hope they would come back. Aggie vowed to look for them, seek their scent and faces and watch them. She would learn their patterns and habits and get enough information to trap them, hand them over to the police. They would be caught and punished.

After she exacted a little revenge of her own.

She wondered sometimes what those four brutes told their friends about that night, what they thought they saw, and what they told each other and themselves. Was she nothing more than a vicious dog, or did they know what a wolf was? Did they realize that her attack wasn't the ordinary actions of a wild animal? Did they have only nightmare glimpses of her to remember? What about the man she had clawed?

What had he told the doctors when he went to the hospital? Or had his friends been afraid to go, and doctored him themselves?

What if he was dead?

Aggie didn't want him dead. She wanted him to suffer. More than that, she wanted to capture the man who had shot Grace.

She went to the park every night, until Jack began checking on her before he stumbled into his room. Aggie pretended to be asleep, waiting until he looked in her room and the bitter aroma of his nightly whiskey filtered through the air. Once he checked on her and left, she got up and slipped out of the house. Her father always drank himself to sleep by midnight. After that, she was free to vanish, but she didn't go every night.

She was still a high school student, after all, and had a responsibility to her team and her classes. Aggie was determined to get perfect grades to please her mother. Basketball didn't mean anything to her, but the physical stress helped relieve the pressure and helplessness pounding inside her.

When Grace came home from the hospital, just two days before Thanksgiving, Aggie changed her pattern. Someone had to be awake if Grace needed something. Jack cut back on his drinking, but Aggie refused to leave all the work to him. She changed her hunting pattern to twice a week on weeknights and then every Friday and Saturday night.

She had found three lost children, by that time, who reported a big black dog led them back to the main road and their frantic parents. She had stopped so many attempted car break-ins, Aggie no longer bothered to count.

⁂

"Aggie, are you spending all your nights in the park?" Lara asked when she and Aggie were alone in the kitchen, Thanksgiving Day. The girls had decided to make dinner by themselves and refused to let Jack or Grace in the kitchen.

Her relief over Grace's recovery had softened the driving need for revenge and justice. It surprised her to have Lara bring up the subject. She thought Lara couldn't read her mind without her knowing. At least, she hoped so.

"Nights in the park?" Aggie echoed.

"There have been a couple dozen reports of a black dog scaring off burglars and helping people in the park lately. Five people identified it as a wolf, but they've been laughed down because there haven't been wolves in this part of the country in over a century."

"What about the wolf hunt in Strongsville back—"

"That was a wild dog, a coyote hybrid, not a real wolf," Lara snapped, interrupting, which was rare for her. "What are you doing? What if someone decides the stories are true and tries to capture you?"

"It's not like I'll be naked when the sun rises," she said with a shrug.

"Aggie!" They both glanced at the kitchen door. In the momentary silence, they could hear the movie Jack and Grace were watching. "I'm worried about you," Lara continued in a softer voice. "What are you doing in the park so much?"

"Looking for the creeps who shot Mom," she admitted with a sigh.

"They have guns."

"Look, they didn't shoot me when I attacked them—what makes you think they'll shoot if they see me watching for them? And that's all I'm doing. Just watching. I want enough to tell the police so they get caught. That's all I want."

"All? You want revenge."

"It's not your mother who got shot while your back was turned."

"I know." Lara rested a hand over Aggie's. "What good can you do?"

"I've done a lot of good, helped a lot of people. The park rangers do a good job, but they can't be everywhere."

"You're getting a reputation. There's a story going around about the Wolf of Wallace Lake."

"Really?" For a moment, Aggie felt a light-headed sense of pride and delight in what she was doing.

Then the sensation fled. Maybe Lara was right. If people knew she was there, if they started to believe, others would believe and re-actionaries would come. People who wanted to capture the freak, or people who wanted to kill it for sport, or just plain wanted to destroy anything special.

'Different is dangerous' was the rule she and Lara lived by, to stay safe, to hide what they could do and what they were.

"Okay," she said with a sigh. "I'll slow down, and I'll be careful." Aggie searched for some other topic to distract Lara and avoid more lecture. "So, how are things going with you and Greg?"

"They're not, though I get the feeling he wishes they were. Between his classes at Cleveland State and our conflicting work schedules...what's the use of having my own place and all the privacy I could want if we can't get together to use it? Besides, it could just be my imagination that he's interested, you know?" Lara shrugged and managed a lopsided grin. "I just don't know how to handle it when a guy's interested in me. I mean, he's so active and I'm so slow!

"He's into trees and all that wildlife stuff and conservation and botany and I'm into my computers and learning everything about anything, just for the fun of learning. Greg isn't a book-hater by any means. He's so smart and he knows so much about things that matter to him, but..." She sighed and rested her head in her hands, the heels of her hands pressing into her eyes. "Am I wrong? Maybe he isn't interested in me after all?"

"Greg's shy, I guess. Allison says he's interested. She says Greg really doesn't pay much attention to girls. Except for you. She says you've been the center of his interest, girl-wise, since the day you moved in with the Hendersons. Allison says he comes out of that Nature Boy trance of his whenever someone mentions you. Only you. It might take him a while to realize he has to do something about it, but I think he's interested."

Lara turned bright pink, from the tips of her ears to deep into the collar of her shirt. A wide grin brought wrinkles to her face.

"Well, it's not like anybody talks about me at their house. It's not that his parents dislike me, but..." She shrugged.

"It's like the way they avoid going anywhere near the park and won't even talk about it?" Aggie guessed.

"Exactly." Lara sighed. "They're nice people, but there is something definitely weird going on."

"Maybe they know what we are, and they're trying to forget?"

The two stared at each other for several long moments, until the smell of scorching butter for the sweet potatoes intruded. Neither one spoke about it, but Aggie let the thought stay at the back of her mind. She would mention it to Dorayn, if no one else. Instinct told her Dorayn understood things nobody else in the entire world would understand.

Later, when Jack slipped into his after-gorge doze, Grace came out to the kitchen to join the girls. She made a face when they wouldn't let her help clean up, but didn't protest when Aggie guided her to the kitchen table to sit down. The girls worked in silence and Grace said nothing for a while, merely watched them, pleasantly exhausted instead of drained by her pain and the struggle to heal. Aggie sensed the difference in her mother and welcomed it. She wondered, though, what had brought Grace out to watch them work.

"Lara." Grace had sat still for so long they almost forgot she was there. "Can you...change like Aggie?"

"If I can, I still can't remember how," Lara responded with a grin and a shrug, after only a moment's hesitation. The humor shattered a crackling, tight feeling in the air that had grown gradually on them.

"Do you remember anything of how you ended up in the river?" she continued, her voice softer.

"Somebody tried to kill us."

"Somebody tried to kill you," Aggie corrected her. She felt an uneasy chuckle catch in her throat. "I really hate it when I get these little bits and pieces of memory, and no idea where it all fits!" She nodded, tasting in her mind the truth of what she had just remembered. "Somebody tried to kill you, Lara. You and your parents. I was just there on the sidelines."

"No." Lara put down the plastic tub of leftover stuffing. Her eyes were wide and her hands shook. "There were two of you."

"Kaenarr," she whispered.

They stared at each other, tears in their eyes. The memory hurt, but they welcomed it. An image flickered between their minds, of a black-haired, hazel-eyed boy with bruised knuckles and dirty feet and full of tricks. They each contributed pieces, until Aggie thought she could hear his voice and even smell that particular sweet-stink odor of little boy sweat.

"Who?" Grace asked, breaking the silence when it had gone on for more than a few seconds.

"Kaenarr." Aggie swallowed hard, fighting the ache that filled her. "My brother. My twin brother."

"What are you waiting for, girls? You need to find answers. Your families. It isn't right that you don't know the truth."

"But what if that truth brings our enemies to us?" Lara said. "We don't...remember enough to defend ourselves."

"Maybe when you find out the truth, you'll remember everything." Grace thumped the table with her fist. "I want to help. The two of you have brought more joy to my life than I ever dreamed. I can only imagine the pain your parents feel, not knowing what happened to you—or even thinking you're dead. Tell me what to do, whatever you need."

"A really high-power computer and cable access to the Internet would be a great start," Aggie offered. She made a face at Lara when her friend reacted in dismay. "If we wait until you can buy your own computer, or get enough research time on the library's snail-speed computers, we'll both be grandmothers before we find any answers."

"That's not what we want," Grace said, laughing softly. "All right. When the holiday shopping rush has slowed down, we are going computer shopping. Meanwhile, let's brainstorm. Your brother's name is certainly unusual enough. Do you think he used it like you used yours?"

"No." Aggie shook her head, feeling that uneasiness return as another piece of unrelated information came to light in her mind. "My name is Aguirra. Kaenarr could be twisted around into something more...local, just like my name was."

"Aguirra." Her mother said it slowly, testing it.

"How about your birthmark?" Lara said. She tapped Aggie through her shirt, just below the dip in her collarbone. "Your twin has the same birthmark."

"Maybe it's not a birthmark." Aggie unbuttoned her shirt enough to show the triangular, blackish patch just a little bigger than her thumb. "Maybe it's like...a tattoo. A mark to show...we're...that we belong to someone. Special."

"Well, girls, I think we've made some steps already," Grace whispered, and nodded, smiling.

※ ※

The water in the old quarries froze solid from the last of November and the weather forecasts predicted temperatures staying low enough for the ice to stay solid through the end of the year. The Metroparks opened up two of the lakes for ice skating. The first Saturday of December, Aggie and Lara walked down into the park from Lara's apartment, to meet Greg and Allison for skating. They knew Aggie and Allison would do the skating, while Greg and Lara would sit on the sidelines by one of the old oil drums with a fire burning in it. That plan suited all four of them perfectly.

Aggie, Lara and Grace hadn't been to the store yet to buy a computer. Grace wasn't up to trips by car longer than driving down the street for church. They agreed to lots of brainstorming, refining their search options until they knew exactly where to look and for what. The girls were still talking about it when Greg and Allison showed up.

The usual swirling of blue and green sparks flickered through the air to meet Greg and Allison. Aggie and Lara were used to it. This time, however, the sparks hovered around their friends and didn't fade, and no purple appeared. Greg didn't seem to see the green sparks clinging to his hair and gloves when he got out of the car. He looked around, glancing up at the sky, and frowned.

"Did you hear thunder?" Allison asked, as if she sensed whatever oddness Greg did.

"Doesn't look like a storm moving in, if that's what you're worried about," Aggie offered. She could smell the good weather that would stay with them for several days. One nice thing about being a wolf; she always knew how close bad weather hovered.

"Not that...do they have high-tension wires around here? There's this weird buzzing feeling." He shrugged and rubbed his arms.

*Uh oh.* Aggie grinned as she looked over at Lara. Her friend nodded and jerked her head toward Allison, who had walked across the hiking trail that divided the parking area from the edge of the skating lake. A few tiny, bright blue sparks trailed behind her, like lightning bugs.

*I don't think they've noticed anything except the energy,* Lara said. "I know what you mean." She stepped over join Greg by the car. "Whenever Aggie and I come here together, there's this humming feeling. It's kind of nice. Energizing."

"Yeah, I guess." He looked around once more, his frown fading. "Whatever it is, it's gone now."

*Interesting. They didn't see anything, but at least he felt something. Maybe with exposure...* Aggie trailed off, not quite sure what she meant to say.

Aggie heard the thumping first, felt the rhythm through the ground, accompanied by a whispering hiss of wind. She glanced upwards to see the direction in the movement of the branches and tilted her head back to catch new scents.

No wind. The day was still. No leaves stirred, let alone the heavier branches.

"What's that?" Allison said, turning around to look. They both glanced toward the road, where people who veered off the established bridle paths often rode their horses. They had a clear view of Valley Parkway for hundreds of yards in both directions, but not a horse or even a car was in sight.

It sounded like at least a dozen horses, to Aggie. But nothing came into view even as the sound of riders and massive pounding bodies grew loud enough to drown out the whispering of the wind that never touched them. Aggie shivered, but she felt no fear or uneasiness.

"The hair's standing up on my arms!" Allison said with a giggle. "Feels weird under my sweatshirt and jacket."

"You hear it too?" Greg called, stepping over to join them. Lara was only a few feet behind him.

"Horses? And wind?" Allison shivered, but she grinned as if this was all fun and nothing to fear, too.

*Listen to our instincts,* Lara said. *If none of us are afraid, then maybe we're not in any danger.*

*It's the 'maybe' part that worries me,* Aggie said with a silent growl throbbing at the back of her throat

As they stood and listened, trying to find the direction the sound came from, the pounding faded away far more quickly than it had come. As if the riders had approached and thundered past and were now vanishing into the distance. The whispering rustle of the wind faded, yet not a leaf moved, not a hair of their heads stirred. Aggie smelled nothing. No horse sweat, no manure, no hot leather, no mud churned up by pounding hooves.

"That is so weird," Greg whispered.

"But neat," Allison said almost on his heels. "There are a few times I've been here and I think I hear things or see things, but nothing's there. At least, nothing that I found." She grinned. "It's so neat you heard it too!"

"Yeah," Lara whispered. "Neat."

"Something wrong?" Greg asked. He rested a hand on her shoulder. Lara smiled, blushing at his concern and the touch. Aggie was delighted, counting it a good sign.

"Aggie and I have noticed some...weird things when we're here, too. But never so strong. Maybe it took all four of us being here together to...I don't know...build up enough energy to make something happen?"

"Who knows?"

"Like what?" Allison wanted to know.

*Do they know how we got here?* Lara asked.

*Nope. Subject never came up.*

"Well, about eight years ago, there was a killer storm. July. Do you guys remember?" Lara began.

"Do I ever?" Greg chuckled and settled down on the bumper of his car. "We snuck away on our bikes to have a picnic down by the par course. Allison was so furious when the rain hit. You could almost see sparks coming out of her eyes and fingers when she started yelling at the rain."

"What color?" Aggie couldn't help asking.

"Blue," Allison said, at the same moment Greg gave her a weird look and Lara glared, signaling her to shut up.

"Then the hail started and the thunder and lightning and the sky got pitch black in about two seconds. The wind was so bad, we thought we'd get blown off our feet, right into the river," Greg continued. "Yeah, I remember. Why? Did you create the storm or something?"

"Aggie and I were kidnapped and beaten up by someone when we were children, and dumped in the river during that storm. We ended up at Bonnie Park."

"Wow. Did they ever catch the guys who did it?" Allison half-whispered.

"We can't even remember who we are, let alone who hurt us. Aggie remembered our names, but that's about it. Not a clue." She took a deep breath. "But sometimes, when we go down to where they found us, we...see things. If you hear things too, maybe we aren't crazy."

"Why not?" Greg took hold of Lara's hand and drew her down to sit next to him on the bumper of his car. "There's a whole lot more to reality than what we can touch and see and hear. Maybe it takes a lot of us together to make some things real."

"To open the doorways," Allison whispered. She flushed when the other three looked at her with puzzled frowns. "I just read through the entire *Chronicles of Narnia* this week. It's on my mind."

"Why not doorways?" Lara said, nodding.

"Heck, maybe we're from another world," Aggie added, grinning. She laughed, and the others laughed too, but the sound couldn't drive away the tiny, sharp shiver of *knowing* that ran up and down her spine.

Greg suggested they go to Bonnie Park and see if they got any more strange impressions there. The four piled into Greg's car and drove down the winding park road. No one was at Bonnie Park when they arrived.

They walked down to the river's edge. Greg took Lara's hand but Aggie doubted either he or Lara really noticed. Aggie thought she saw a few blue sparks, a few green, but she couldn't be sure with the angle of the sun on the ice as afternoon turned to dusk.

"Nothing," Allison said after the four stood on the bank, looking down at the frozen edges of the river. "You guys?"

"Nothing."

*The magic's all worn out, maybe?* Aggie asked.

*No. Not that. Not worn out but...* Lara frowned, staring at the water, but from the unfocussed dullness of her eyes Aggie knew her friend saw something else.

Sometimes she teased Lara that she had a computer screen inside her head where she read all the information that just 'came' to her at the oddest times. Right now, it didn't seem so funny anymore.

*It's like a place that's been patched over, once it's been torn. It's stronger than ever because of extra layers. On the other side.* Lara tugged her hand free of Greg's and half-slid, half-stumbled down the bank to the edge of the water. She reached out a hand and bent as if she would touch the ice, but paused there. *It's like the fabric was slashed and somebody patched it from the other side.*

*The weakest place is around the edges,* Aggie offered. She didn't enjoy the *knowing* this time. She hated the feeling of someone putting something into her head from outside.

*Maybe. But what worries me are the people who put the patch on. Why do they want to keep us from going through again?*

"This is crazy." Aggie forced a chuckle. "We're here because some pervert got his kicks from kidnapping kids and torturing them. Maybe the cops were getting close on his trail and he figured the storm and the park were the perfect time and place to get rid of us."

"Maybe," Lara whispered. The focus came back to her eyes. She barely noticed, though, when Greg stepped down to help her back up the incline. Her limp was more pronounced. The sunlight gleamed on the silver bars of her brace where they peeked out from under her jeans at her ankle.

"I believe in magic," Allison said, with a waver in her voice.

# Chapter Ten

"What we have to do is find all the variables for a search," Lara said, when she and Aggie met in the library after school on Monday. "List all the details of how and where and when we were found, then search for people who fit the profile."

"What if our situation isn't the rule?" Aggie had to ask. "What if you and I are the exception? What if we're the only ones?" *What if Kaenarr is dead and they never found his body?* She could barely think the thought—speaking her fear was out of the question.

"We won't know until we look, will we?"

Greg and Allison wanted to help. They made suggestions for how to search the Internet. Allison, it turned out, was a library junkie just like Lara. Brother and sister were fascinated with what Lara and Aggie wanted to do, now that they knew about the friends' mysteriously blank past.

They met every weekend in Lara's apartment to discuss ideas and create a search pattern so nothing would be left out. Allison was nowhere near as proficient as Lara on the computer, using search engines and such tools, but she was good with the physical catalogues and searching books in the library. She volunteered to follow up on any leads Lara found that weren't available on the Internet. Aggie and Greg provided support and ran errands.

Each time the foursome met in the Metroparks for ice skating or just to walk and get some fresh air, a sense of something waiting, an energy, always rose to welcome them. They had no repeats of the auditory hallucinations, however, and that was both relief and disappointment.

"Whatever it is, it only happens when we're together. Like the more of us are here, the more energy is generated," Allison theorized one afternoon in Lara's apartment, as they snacked and brainstormed.

"Or the more of us are here, the more attention we draw," Greg murmured. The three girls slowly raised their heads and put down pens to look at him. He flushed a little. "Hey, what can I say? I started reading some of Allison's fantasies, to get an idea of what she's talking about. You know, we ought to recruit Mike Henderson. He's a computer whiz. When he isn't exercising that horse of his."

"Mike has a horse and you never told me?" Aggie pretended disgust with Lara. Her friend stuck her tongue out at her.

"A big, ugly, yellowy-brown thing. He talks to Omega like other guys talk to their best girlfriend." Lara glanced at Allison. *If he would talk to Allison half as nicely as he does to Omega, she'd do anything for him.*

*Allison deserves better,* Aggie retorted.

"He and Dad Henderson saved Omega from the glue factory when he was a foal," Lara continued. "He keeps him at the Fairgrounds."

"So he'd be some help?"

"He can design a program to help you find exactly what you're looking for," Greg said with a shrug. "He's building a program for me to log all the data on my experiments, all my hybrids and the records of every plant in my greenhouse."

Grace wanted updates on what they had theorized and learned. Aggie enjoyed the evening talks with her mother, the two of them perched on the twin beds in her room with cups of hot chocolate and some cookies, relaxing while Jack worked on business downstairs. She regretted all the years of silence and secrecy, as if she had been afraid to trust her mother.

Grace, Aggie and Lara had agreed from the start of their search that it could take years to find even one person like them. They had to go at it in a roundabout method, never letting people know why they asked. That could lead to dangerous attention and questions.

After all, they had plenty of movies and novels to warn them about what happened to people who were different. From fantasy to B-grade movies when Superhost was still on television on Saturday afternoons, they had a good idea what happened to the gifted and just plain strange. Aggie would end up in a zoo or shot by some fanatic who thought she was dangerous. Or some demented collector of oddities would try to add her to his collection. Or she would end up in a laboratory.

Similar fates waited for Lara, if anyone ever learned about her slowly growing magical talents. Even if people let them live fairly normal lives, they would be watched and studied. Maybe even become the focal point of some odd new religions. The New Age movement made them uneasy enough, without taking the risk of becoming the new deities or drafted as high priests or oracles to give validity to the newest twisted beliefs.

"I know what I am now," Aggie said, after she and Grace had talked themselves out and the cups were empty. "We were talking about..." She mentally slapped herself for almost slipping. Lara knew she haunted the park, seeking the men who shot her mother, but Aggie knew better than to let Grace know what she was doing. "We were talking about using our gifts to get revenge on people who give us a hard time, and I said, I may be a vindictive little Wereling, but I'm not a thief."

"A what?" Grace laughed.

"Wereling. That's an approximation of what we're called, back wherever Lara and I come from."

"And if you have a name, maybe you're a race, a species, not a freak of nature," her mother said with a soft smile.

"Yeah. Not a freak."

"Honey, you were never a freak and you aren't now that I know your secrets. Well, some of your secrets," Grace added with a sigh of mock exasperation as she slid her legs off the side of the bed. "Give me a teenager who tells her mother everything, and that will be the true freak." She stood up and held out her hand for Aggie's cup. "You've done a lot of work today. You two should be proud."

Aggie held on a little longer than usual when she hugged Grace good night. She still had bad dreams where she didn't get back to the car soon enough, and found her mother dead and the thieves long gone.

⚜

March came in warm and rainy. The shorn, spiky remains of Grace's rose bushes turned pale green-brown, as if trying to decide if they would bud early. Aggie liked to stop and study the roses when she came back from her midnight runs, to catch the first whiff of life returning to the prickly canes.

It was nearly four a.m. when she came back, that first Friday in March, reasoning she could sleep in on Saturday and no one would care if she didn't get up until the crack of noon. Aggie felt good about that night's run. She had seen no trouble, despite it being mid-term break for the students at B-W, and warmer weather encouraged trouble-makers to linger in the park.

Still in wolf shape, she stopped to study the rose canes and look for signs of life. Aggie heard a metallic click, looked around and saw nothing coming over the fences from the yards on either side. She stepped up onto the flagstone path around the yard, so her bare feet wouldn't get muddy, then shifted back to Human—just as she heard another click and a gasp.

Aggie turned, looking up the step to the deck. Jack stood in the open doorway, his rifle cocked and raised halfway to his shoulder, his face whiter than weather-ravaged bones. For five long seconds, the two stared at each other. Aggie didn't know what she felt. Her mind slid back to that moment when she had shifted back to Human and knelt by her mother's side, dizzy with the smell of Grace's blood and pain, and her mother had smiled and accepted her differences with wonder.

The back door creaked shut. Aggie blinked and realized she had stood frozen while Jack stumbled back into the house. Now what?

A crash and the sound of breaking glass answered that question. She leaped up onto the deck, through the ajar door, through the kitchen, down the hall to Jack's den.

Her father stood in front of the cabinet where he kept his drafting supplies and his few favorite brands of liquor. The pencils and instruments lay scattered on the floor amid spreading amber pools. The fumes reached up in a cloud to slap at her nose. Aggie flinched back a step in the doorway, watching her father even as a quiet voice at the back of her mind asked how in the world she was going to get that out of the carpet.

Jack raised his rifle by the barrel and brought it down hard on the top of the cabinet. Wood splintered. Pieces flew off the stock of the gun and the top of cabinet. Metal bent as he slammed the gun against the cabinet. Aggie could only stand there, watching, her heart skipping a beat every time furniture and weapon came together with a loud crash-bang. Grace stumbled down the steps from her bedroom but she kept quiet when Aggie signaled her. Jack staggered with each blow, until finally he missed entirely. A sob broke from him and he staggered backwards against his couch. He dropped the rifle. Aggie felt a knot melt out of her chest and leave her throat.

"Dad?" she whispered, startling a yelp out of Jack. He landed on the edge of the cushion, barely balanced there.

"Aggie." He tried to smile, but it crumpled into a trembling travesty that he hid, bowing his face into his hands.

"It's okay, Dad. Really."

"No, it's not okay. I've been drinking too much. Ever since your mother was shot." He collapsed back against the couch. A whimper escaped him when he looked past Aggie and saw Grace with a sad little smile of understanding on her face. He seemed to deflate half his substance. "I almost shot you, Aggie."

"You didn't know it was me."

"No excuse. I'm so all-fired worried about your mother's roses, I was ready to shoot a stray dog that got into our yard and wasn't doing any harm. That was bad enough, but how could I think you were a dog?"

Jack, she knew now, would never accept the truth of what she was. He was already rationalizing it away. What was worse? To let him think he had been in an alcoholic haze, or tell him the truth and possibly break his mind past healing?

"It's early, it's still dark out, you probably just got up and I had no business being outside." She squatted in front of him. With both hands she touched his face and gently raised his head so they could see each other. "Dad, you didn't shoot me. You realized your mistake before it was too late. You're not capable of really bad mistakes like that."

"Oh...Aggie," he breathed, and she caught the sourness of whiskey in his breath. It made her throat close up and her head pound.

"What would we do without you? When did you grow up? My little girl is taking care of me, now."

"She'll have to stand in line," Grace said, coming into the den. She stepped around the puddle soaking into the carpet, and reached down to grab Jack's arm. Aggie caught hold of the other and they heaved him to his feet. "That's still my job, Mr. John Franklin Harsey. And since it's Saturday, you're going to bed and sleep until noon, and then you're going to have a big breakfast and watch the Indians play some of those scrimmage games down in Florida, or whatever they're called."

Aggie muffled a giggle. Grace knew more about the Indians than Jack did, but she constantly pretended to be clueless about baseball just to tease him.

"Love to, honey," he said with a tired smile, "but Dan's coming over at three to talk about that strip of renovations in the Flats that we might get this summer."

Aggie bit back a retort, demanding to know since when did Dan Moon have the right to break in on her father's Saturdays. Dan had expanded Harsey Construction's client list and moved the business into renovation along with new construction. Dan was a hard worker, loyal to her father, totally dedicated to the company. He loved construction; she could tell that just by the sweet spicy scent that came from him and the light in his eyes when he talked about the challenges of putting together a building, taking it from concept and blueprints to three-dimensional, solid reality. But did that give him the right to take Jack's Saturday away from him?

Aggie knew she might like Dan just because of his drive and ambition, but she didn't like the way he talked about plans for the company's future as if it were *his* company. Just like she suspected he thought she would be his someday.

Dan was never rude or demanding, and he could actually be good company. Aggie just didn't like the feeling that she didn't have a choice in the matter. Was it all in her imagination? Did he take one look at her, one look at her father's business, and decide his future lay in marrying his partner's daughter?

Still, there was nothing she could do about it now. Aggie and Grace guided Jack upstairs to his bed, helped him take off his shirt and shoes, and guided him to his bed.

"It won't do any good to tell him," was all Grace said on the matter, when they returned to the den to clean up the mess.

They shampooed the carpet three times, but the fumes were still strong when Dan arrived. He said nothing about the dents in the cabinet, the visible absence of bottles. He suggested a pet odor remover he had found useful in 'similar situations.' Aggie stumbled through her thanks, feeling guilty for the thoughts she had entertained for the last few hours. Dan cut her off with that smile that could be so warm, so friendly, and started talking about the next Indians' game, Sunday afternoon. He just happened to have four tickets—would she and Grace like to go with him and Jack?

Somehow, Aggie agreed to go. She actually enjoyed dinner. Dan carried most of the conversation, steering it away from business. Even Grace was charmed. Dan talked about movies and the last few books he had read and a marathon he considered running in the fall.

"You ought to compete," he told Aggie, getting up to pour coffee for him and Jack.

"Me?"

"You're a runner. You do the mile without breaking a sweat, and that takes endurance. You're a natural athlete. The discipline and the sense of accomplishment will be great. Unless you're going out of town for college?"

"Nope. Aggie's staying in town and getting more involved in the business. She's a big help to her Mom and me," Jack said. He cradled his fourth cup of coffee between his hands and glanced out through the bay window of the dining room. "She'll work for me this summer, like usual, graduate next year, then go to Tri-C until she figures out what she really wants to do."

"Smart. Costs less money and you can experiment with programs without feeling like you wasted a lot of time. I like smart girls." Dan toasted her with the cup.

Aggie felt odd. She wondered if she liked this new, considerate side of Dan Moon. He hadn't made her feel that he looked at her body only, like the guys at school did. Maybe the oddness came from knowing that if she were a few years older and Dan a few years younger, she might have enjoyed his attention, Grace wouldn't have objected, and marrying Dan Moon would keep the business in the family.

*Isn't that a horrifying thought?* She reached for Lara's mind and showed her the events of the evening.

*Dynastic marriages happen all the time,* her friend responded.

*I'm not a princess or an heiress.* Aggie shivered and she heard echoes of someone, long ago, calling her Princess. Who? And why?

⁂

"I found a name," Lara said the moment she opened the door of her apartment late in March. She laughed when Aggie's mouth dropped open. "I just knew you were going to look like this. I couldn't just tell you; I had to see you."

"One name? Where?"

Aggie's mind spun at the thought that someone, somewhere in the world, matched the criteria they had set up in their search program. Someone, somewhere, had appeared out of nowhere under mysterious circumstances, during a massive, freak storm. Someone with no identification. Speaking a foreign language.

Lara led the way down the hall to the little room that was too small for a bedroom and too large for a closet. It was just right to hold her computer and hutch and one full wall of bookshelves for all Lara's precious reference books. Aggie settled down on the edge of Lara's desk and gripped tight until her knuckles turned white.

"They found a boy in Pennsylvania in a freak storm on the same day we arrived. Allegheny National Forest."

"That's a few hours away, at least."

"Get this—they estimated he was eight or nine years old. The list of birthmarks, to try to trace his identity, lists an unusual, dark, triangular one right under his collar bone."

Aggie had never felt faint before in her life, but she was sure she was close now. She held on tighter to the edge of the desk until the plywood creaked. She couldn't say the name, but it rang through both their minds.

Kaenarr?

"That would make him sixteen, going on seventeen. They named him Brody Cooper."

"Okay, so how do we get hold of him?"

"No idea."

"Lara..." She swallowed hard, fighting an urge to shift shape just so she could vent the twisting emotions inside herself with a good, long howl.

"I'm lucky I got this information. I think it was released to me by mistake. His foster family is supposed to be kept out of the public records, to protect him."

"From what?"

"You hate those gossip rags in the grocery store, right?"

"Anybody with half a brain should avoid them. Why?"

"Brody tried to escape from the hospital, and there was a wolf running around at the same time. The fact that he didn't speak English and he kept trying to bite everyone who came near him...the gossip rags near Pittsburgh had a field day. They keep dragging the story out of mothballs every couple years, trying to find the Wolf Boy." She tipped her head to one side and studied Aggie. "Now do you see why I want you to quit being the Wolf of Wallace Lake? What if somebody gets a picture of you? We'd never have any privacy. I'm surprised we didn't end up in one of those magazines, listed as survivors of a UFO crash or something equally stupid."

Aggie opened her mouth to ask a question, but Lara stopped her with an upraised hand. She bent over and dug under her desk, coming up a moment later with an envelope folder that strained its elastic loop closure.

"I did some research while I was waiting for the official records to come through. Take this home and read it, show it to your mom, get some ideas from her on what we should do. I think this guy is going to be a tough case whenever we do manage to contact him."

Aggie took her time walking home, her mind spinning with impli-cations and images of happy and bitter reunions and fragments of memories. She felt guilty and sick over it. She could have done some-thing, searched for Kaenarr, maybe found a way home if she had only pushed past her fears and remembered him sooner. Why hadn't she been able to remember?

She kept the envelope closed as she walked, knowing that if she slid the elastic band aside just to take one glimpse, some errant gust of wind—a miniature tornado, with her luck—would blow up and tug precious pieces of paper from her hands.

# Chapter Eleven

Brody Cooper was found in the Allegheny National Forest, close by the canoe livery that served the main branch of the waterway. Lara and Aggie had been found in the water, too. Aggie wondered if that had something to do with their survival, or with their appearance in the storm itself. Brody was found half in the water, clutching a smoldering limb of a tree.

One of his rescuers described the tree later as having a purplish tinge to the wood, and leaves shaped like no leaves he had ever seen. By the time someone thought to investigate the place where the boy had been found, the branch had been split up for firewood and burned.

He had four broken ribs and a broken leg, and the right side of his body was bloody and torn from what several people described as claw marks. Despite his weakness from blood loss and shock, Brody fought off everyone who tried to help him. His main line of defense was to bite everyone who got close enough.

Aggie laughed quietly when she read the dozen reports of people whom Brody had bitten during the rescue attempt and his first few days in the hospital. If her jaw hadn't been wired shut, she knew she would have bitten every chance she got. It was a natural reaction for her.

The boy was sullen and silent, refusing to cooperate with the hospital staff and the social workers. When he had healed enough to be released from the hospital, the Coopers took him. The social workers predicted disaster. Surprisingly, though Brody had a tendency to escape outdoors whenever possible and an uncanny talent for taming the meanest dog, he never tried to run away. He liked his foster family.

That, Aggie knew, was the key to why Grace and Jack had such an easy time with her. She had liked them, had been willing to do what they asked. If they had separated her from Lara, that might have been a different story.

If Brody was her twin, Kaenarr, perhaps he had tried to run away to find her?

Brody became ill a few weeks after the Coopers took him, ran a high fever and talked in his delirium. Then they realized the boy didn't speak English. Everyone assumed his silence was because he was uncooperative, perhaps mentally deficient. When he recovered from his illness, everyone treated him better. But by that time, the damage had been done. He trusted no one but the Coopers, and the social workers knew better than to transfer him away from them.

They did their best to seal Brody's records and keep the Coopers' name out of the records, but there were leaks. Every once in a while, someone with a camera and a nasty sense of imagination managed to get a picture of Brody running, barefoot in the woods, often accompanied by the wild dogs that inhabited the woods and open fields in that part of the state. The story got coverage, then died away when nothing sufficiently strange happened. Aggie was relieved to see Brody was careful to stay in the background, otherwise. How hard had these last eight years been for him? Did he fight back? Was running his only way of releasing the pressure?

She remembered the need to run that often shook her when she was younger. If she hadn't latched onto Grace and her adopted mother hadn't loved her so easily and quickly, Aggie wondered if she would have become a tabloid item like Brody. She admitted she had a nasty sense of humor and a need sometimes for revenge, no matter how petty. How many times over the years had she shifted to wolf shape and invaded the backyards of schoolyard enemies, to dig up plants or terrify their pets, tear apart a play fort or wreak some tiny bit of inexplicable revenge? Aggie had lost count.

Brody maintained a B-minus average in school, preferring sports and carpentry over all other subjects. With his talent for animals, Aggie was surprised he didn't want to go into veterinary work. Then again, she didn't enjoy the bookkeeping work she did for Jack even if she was good at it. If she didn't want to take business courses and become an accountant, why would Brody subject himself to years of studying?

According to the last file Lara had printed out, he was in a carpentry apprenticeship program. He didn't have a driver's license or cell phone or any other necessary items for a junior in high school. He worked hard and put every spare penny into his savings account. He did have a library card and used it regularly.

Aggie wondered, if she hadn't had Lara to look after and to look after her, what would she have been? A total loner, enduring the daylight hours until she could shift shape and run all night through the parks? Aggie made a mental note to look up the area where Brody had grown up and see what park systems were close by to offer release and cleansing.

"Wonder how you feel about chocolate?" she muttered, with a grin she shared with her mother. There were times she and Lara indulged themselves, sharing a king-size Hershey's Special Dark on special occasions, like other people split a bottle of wine. They never let themselves go beyond that. With all the questions and mystery in their lives and the certainty someone had tried to kill them, it just wasn't smart to lose control, even for a few blissful hours.

Grace and Aggie were still reading, slowly trying to digest what Lara had found, when Jack got home from work that night. He whistled, which made mother and daughter share a smile. Any time Jack Harsey came home from work in a good mood and not dragging his feet or muttering about 'that elected moron' or 'those in-bred excuses for architects,' was a special occasion.

"Wow, what's that?" her father said with a chuckle when he came into the kitchen, slung his jacket and tie onto one chair and his brief-case with the ever-present, dog-eared roll of drawings into their usual corner. "Homework? Going for valedictorian?"

"This is some work Lara and I are doing on our own." Aggie started gathering up her papers while Grace got up and went to the refrigerator to start pulling out the rest of their dinner.

"Work? Looks like you're shredding the gossip rags." He read over her shoulder as she shuffled through the printouts of newspaper articles and police reports. "What's this about a—" Jack choked. "What kind of joke is this, Aggie? Wolf boy? That kind of stuff only runs on TV."

"Unfortunately, it's very real," she said a little breathlessly. Her heart skipped a beat when the word 'wolf' left her father's lips and his voice cracked.

"Aggie, I don't like this stuff. It's...I don't know. It's sick, talking about werewolves and things like that. People are obsessed with death, seems like nowadays with all the vampire stories and movies and horror movies and—"

"Jack! Be serious," Grace said as she opened the oven to check on the chicken. "It's a supermarket gossip piece about a boy who ran away from home a lot and was good with dogs. That's all. You know how they distort things like that."

"I don't read that trash and I know you don't, either." He shook his head as he crossed the kitchen and kissed Grace—a ritual he had begun after she was shot.

Aggie finished gathering up the articles and headed for her room. Something felt heavy in her chest when she saw how much relief Grace's explanation brought to her father. His shoulders straightened and the sour scent wafting from him cleared within a few heartbeats.

Did her father suspect, even subconsciously, that he hadn't mistaken her for a big dog in the shadows and moonlight?

*   *   *

Their research hit a brick wall. They had no address to use to contact Brody Cooper and determine if he was Aggie's brother.

Mike thought of writing to the hospital that originally treated Brody when he was found. That yielded the address of the first office that handled his case, which put them in contact with another office. By the second week of April, a large envelope arrived unexpectedly at the Berea Library. Lara had made it her return address, to make her request for information legitimate. People seemed more prone to give information to a research librarian at a public library than to someone searching for their own enlightenment.

The envelope excited them. Lara tried to call their group together. Mike had gone to Youngstown State for a computer seminar. Greg had evening classes he couldn't miss and Allison was sick with the flu. Grace and Jack had tickets at Playhouse Square. That left Lara and Aggie to ceremoniously slit the big neoprene envelope and catch the thick packet of papers and reports that fell out.

"His school transcripts," Lara whispered, her voice rising in disbelief. "They sent us his doggone school transcripts!"

"Isn't that against the law?" was all Aggie could say.

"I think so." Lara sat down and gathered up the papers into her hands. She got that pink tinge to her nose that came when she was embarrassed or angry. Aggie suspected it was both this time. "Since we have the reports and nobody is being very helpful... I mean, it's their fault we got the information, and we'd be idiots not to use the information handed to us..."

"You'll never make a politician. You can't even talk yourself into something that smells the slightest bit wrong." Aggie hugged her friend and slid the stack of papers neatly out of her hand. "Since Brody could be my brother, I'll do it." She settled down on the other side of the coffee table and started to read.

Lara looked at her a moment, mouth open. Then a wry chuckle escaped her. She got up and stepped into the tiny kitchen, her brace creaking more than usual, and left Aggie alone to read. Soon, the faint aroma of fake crab filtered through the apartment. Aggie grinned and kept reading, trying to make sense of abbreviations and terms that were insider lingo. They had to be insider lingo. Otherwise the schools in Pennsylvania were in sad shape.

They nibbled on seafood salad and freshly baked corn muffins for dinner while Aggie kept reading and Lara made notes. It amazed Aggie that someone who had so much written about him could be so hard to find.

"That's it," she muttered, feeling rather stupid not to have seen it before.

"What's it?" Lara stretched out her bad leg on the couch and tugged on the buckles to remove her brace for the evening.

"Brody's in hiding. Those gossip sheets latched onto him and his foster parents and social workers are doing everything they can to keep him hidden." She tapped the city maps Lara had spread out for her, to find streets and neighborhoods to get a feeling for where Brody had grown up. "He has all those reporters sniffing around, just begging for signs of someone who doesn't fit in, so they can write more lies about him." Aggie choked. "Lies that are half true, but not the half they want!"

"If anybody cares about him, they're not going to admit they know where he is and they're certainly not going to pass a message on to him, asking him to call us."

"Do you blame them? Do you blame him, for wanting to hide? Where would either of us be if we hadn't stuck together? Despite my folks, I'd probably be a loner, skipping classes whenever I could, spending all my free time in the park and driving myself crazy trying to figure out things. And you, well, you'd probably be all right."

"I'd be a loner, too," Lara said, nodding. She sighed as she started massaging her leg through her broadcloth pants. "I'd have my computer and my job at the library and school, but nothing else. Maybe not even Greg."

"Speaking of Greg—" Aggie began with a smile.

"We're good friends. We want more, but we're both so busy with school and work and our schedules hardly ever coordinate."

"And the times both of you are free, we're working on this search of ours. Sorry. Never really considered that."

"Our time will come," she said with a smile and a shrug.

"I think a summer wedding would be romantic." Aggie burst out with a bark of laughter when Lara blushed bright pink. "You could go camping for your honeymoon."

"Don't start talking that way. You'll probably scare Greg off forever."

"Okay. Back to Brody Cooper."

"We'll find him," Lara assured her.

"Oh yeah? This pile of papers is a dead end. It tells us he's smart, but he doesn't care about school. Doesn't care about anything but running track and playing with dogs."

"And carpentry." She held up a thin sheaf of papers held together with a paperclip. "He's in the carpenters union apprenticeship program, remember? And the main office address is right here. Right under our noses."

"Lara, you are a genius."

The letter was easy to write because they had been talking about it, planning it for months. General enough not to frighten Brody, but enough details to catch his interest. They sent it in care of the union local overseeing his apprenticeship and sat back to wait. Greg calculated that with the mail system being the way it was, bills were always delivered the day after they were mailed, but important things like the clue to a lifelong mystery would take at least a week. They allowed a few days for Brody to read the letter and think about it and come up with some kind of answer, then another week to get back to them.

At the end of that time, there was no reply. Lara sent the letter again, keeping the library as a return address and using her first initial, so no one would know if the inquirer was a man or woman. The anonymity might add to the mystery and pique Brody's curiosity more. They hoped.

No response to the second letter. Aggie wondered if maybe the union hall wasn't passing on Brody's mail, so the second week of May, Greg volunteered to call. Having a man call might make it sound more official and important. Lara didn't like making phone calls. Aggie knew she would freeze up if someone started asking questions she wasn't prepared for. If she could be face to face in a confrontation, she could read her opponent's scent and body language to help her navigate. The phone was a barrier she couldn't get past.

The union official said Brody did get his mail and volunteered more information when Greg asked. Brody did his work well and quickly and kept to himself. Supervisors competed to have him because he listened, he didn't cause trouble and he had a knack for eyeing his assignment and knowing exactly how much material he would need, down to the last nail. Brody got in trouble several times for cutting lumber without measuring first. When he constantly proved himself right, word got around and no one bothered him about it again.

"Interesting," was all Lara would say. She shared a meaningful glance with Aggie, who also had that knack for knowing distances and volumes and such, but who had no liking for carpentry or building things of any kind.

They sent a third letter. And two days later, a fourth.

A response came three days after that; a terse note from Brody, typed and unsigned, using the union hall as return address. He demanded that L. Monroe leave him alone. He knew despite the address that L. Monroe was another 'arrogant creep reporter' and obviously hadn't done enough digging or 'he' would know that Brody was working with a lawyer to sue every single magazine that ever published another story about him again.

"Not good," Allison said, after their quartet had read and re-read Brody's letter and tried to think of what to do next. Mike was out of town on family business and Grace and Jack had taken a two-day trip to a construction conference in New York.

"What do we do, short of driving down and cornering him?" Lara asked. She glanced at Aggie and fought a grin. *You could go wolf, hunt him down and scare him into cooperating.*

*What if he's something bigger and nastier than a wolf?* Aggie returned.

*What's bigger and nastier? A lion? An elephant?*

"Can't," Greg said, taking her off-the-cuff remark seriously. "That's too much time away from school and work."

"We weren't suggesting you do it," Lara said. "Aggie and I could probably go down once classes are over for the summer—"

"Dorayn," Aggie said. "We'll tell him what we're trying to do. He can figure out what we did wrong."

"He knows lots of union people, working for your Dad," Greg said, nodding. "Maybe he could go down there and get someone to tell him where to find Brody."

"Not now." She shook her head. "We're gearing up for a really busy building season. I couldn't ask him to go out of town until this fall, when things slow down again."

"That might be good," Lara said, nodding. "Give Brody time to calm down, maybe even forget. Where's he going to go, anyway? He's a junior in high school."

◦◦◦◦

Brody's eyes gleamed as he read the latest bulletin, handed him by the union man in charge of the apprentices. He didn't worry about anyone noticing his interest. He always stayed in the shadows, turned so others couldn't see his face. It was so ingrained in him to avoid notice and the prickling sensation of staring eyes, it was unconscious now. Sometimes when he thought about it, he speculated that he couldn't catch people's attention if he wanted.

If only he could go completely invisible. Then so many of his problems would be solved.

But here was one problem solving itself, right in front of him. He had a nagging feeling that he had been wrong in answering that nosey letter from Ohio the way he had.

Ten summer apprenticeships had opened up at Harsey Construction, just like Mr. Dorayn had said in his last letter. He would get construction experience and get completely out of Pennsylvania for the summer. He could put a good hundred miles between him and those tabloid writers who thought they could get a retirement bonus out of him. Berea was close enough to Cleveland he could get there by bus. He could find the library in Berea, scout around and find out just what L. Monroe really wanted from him.

*Would* a reporter use a library as a return address? The more he considered the query letter, Brody doubted himself. Sometimes he thought the letter wasn't about him at all, but someone searching for people with big blank pasts and lots of question marks filling up those blanks, like him. Not him in particular, but only the places where he fit a 'shopping list.'

Brody kind of liked that idea. He wasn't a freak, but someone who maybe belonged to a larger group of nobodies with a lot of bad luck behind them. Maybe some others who understood why he never felt comfortable anywhere, why he had dreams that made him wake in a sweat, blank on every detail two seconds after he opened his eyes.

Why he knew he belonged to someone, yet couldn't find that someone.

"Sign me up," he said, slapping the paper down on Chad Hasselflach's desk. The union man looked at the announcement circled in pencil and Brody's calm face, almost missing the excitement dancing in his eyes.

"Kind of thought you'd be interested, kid." Chad nodded, his big, perpetually sunburned face breaking into a grin. "You're really aching to get out of town, huh?"

Chad had helped fend off a few reporters who tried to hunt down Brody at the union hall on a lucky tip. He hadn't waited long enough to find out what the gossipmongers wanted before he sent them packing. Brody had felt compelled to tell the whole story, just to pay back the big, soft-spoken man. He had been a friend ever since, without giving Brody preferential treatment. Chad had told him, 'You can't change your past. Not what you did or what happened to you. But you can sure do a heck of a lot about your present and your future. Don't have no sympathy for a guy who won't straighten out and walk right.'

For Brody, the easiest way to walk straight was to avoid reporters and answer some nagging questions about L. Monroe at the Berea Library.

# Chapter Twelve

"Hi."

Aggie identified the slightly breathless voice as 'the new guy.' That was how her father referred to him all weekend. No name, just 'the new guy.' She had heard him call to someone from across the construction site when she arrived that morning for her first day of summer work. His was the only voice she didn't recognize out of the usual morning babble. His scent preceded him into the trailer; spicy clean despite the ninety-eight degree downtown Cleveland June weather and the sweat that glistened on his bared arms and forehead even in the shadowy cool confines of the office trailer.

"Hi," she said, glancing at the door hanging open behind him. Her father and Dan were both out for lunch. The refrigerator next to the door was for anyone to use, and he reached for the handle as he smiled at her.

Big, blond, gray-eyed, muscled, with that type of fair skin that refused to tan no matter how many gallons of tanning lotion he bathed in. She felt sorry for the red glow covering him.

"Abbey, right? I'm Jake." He reached in for a clear plastic bag with two cartons of yogurt and a bag of raw veggies that rivaled what she usually brought for herself.

"Aggie."

"Hmm? Sorry. Must not have heard Dan clearly." Jake grinned.

Aggie sensed he had a personality to match his scent—clean, honest, no false crud to interfere. Then she saw the book he pulled out of his backpack as he turned to leave.

"Is that the new Honor Harrington?" She would have pounced and yanked it out of his hand, but fortunately she was on the other side of the trailer, sitting at her desk.

"Sure is. You like reading Weber?"

"He doesn't write nearly fast enough."

"I'll loan it to you when I'm done, if you want." Jake turned so she could see the black tasseled bookmark three-quarters of the way through. "I read fast."

"Thanks. I'd really appreciate it."

"No problem." He grinned as he stepped outside.

Aggie knew she should have guessed something was going on when Dan commented on her having met 'the new guy.' She was busy typing a letter to the building inspector that her father wanted to take with him to his meeting in twenty minutes. She barely heard what Dan said. Later she wondered how he knew Jake had been in the trailer, unless one of his cronies was watching.

Watching the new guy, or watching her? Obviously, it was time for Grace to have another talk with Dan and remind him that her teenage daughter was off limits, even in his future plans.

Two days later, Jake brought the book to her as promised. Dan watched the exchange with a sneer and muttered something about 'useless bookworm' only a few seconds after Jake stepped through the door.

"You read just as much," Aggie couldn't resist saying. She hoped Jake was far enough from the trailer door he hadn't heard. She didn't mind being called a bookworm, but there was something in Dan's tone that made her bristle.

"Yeah, but I read to make myself smarter." He flashed that grin that could make her heart skip a beat no matter how much he irritated her. "The guy's always got his nose in a book. One of these days, he's gonna get hurt. We sure don't need any zombies on this site, getting some innocent guy in trouble."

"I wouldn't call the guys who work for you innocent," Aggie muttered. That earned a chuckle from Dan.

"Don't you worry. I've got them under control. Nobody around here bothers the boss's little girl. That's the order from your Dad and from me."

Aggie smothered a groan, even as a tiny smile caught one side of her mouth. Yes, her father was definitely a little over-protective. She didn't mind. The ones who didn't respect Jack Harsey were afraid of Dan Moon. The smart ones were friends of Dorayn, which made them her friends, too.

Some of Dan's usual crew were roughnecks she preferred to ignore instead of having to put them in their places. Last summer, there were two men who didn't care that she was Jack Harsey's daughter and underage. One followed her to an unfinished upper floor of that summer's building, when she went up to get some fresh air during the lunch break. He tried to talk her into a few kisses. Aggie gave him a black eye. He didn't come back to work the next day and his buddy seemed to get the message, because he quit after two more days. Grace suspected that Dan had frightened them away.

On Friday, Aggie waited for Jake at the end of the day so she could give the book back to him. They chatted for a few minutes, standing by the gate while the other workers got into their cars and left one by one for the weekend.

"You gonna stand and gab all night?" Smithers called to them as he stomped across the gravel yard to the cage holding his guard dogs.

"In a minute," Aggie called to him. She knew he wouldn't release the dogs, because Dan and her father were still in the office trailer, finishing up a few details.

"Would it make any difference if he did release the dogs while we were in here?" Jake asked with a chuckle, lowering his voice a little. "I've seen them. They're all bark but no bite."

"Their bark is bad enough. And their breath—yuck! What happens if one of them falls on you? Or worse yet, piddles on you? It'd take years to get the smell off."

Aggie hated the aging Doberman Pinschers Smithers used to guard her father's construction sites. He never had any fewer than four, and he never seemed to have any young ones when he replaced the ones that died. Did the whiskey-soaked old guard go to the pound and specifically ask for aging dogs to replace the ones he lost? The more they drooled, the better?

None of those dogs dared to make a sound or move when she walked by their cage. Aggie had asserted her dominance in that regard years ago. All it took was a quiet moment when no one was around to slip into the cage and change to wolf. The dogs were terrified either by the transformation or the flow of magic it required, and groveled at her feet. Every time there was a new dog added to the bunch, Aggie repeated the ritual. She would have felt sorry for the decrepit, half-mad beasts, but Smithers babied them and the dogs enjoyed it. They had no dignity.

"Hey, you want to catch the game? I have a buddy who works at the stadium, and every time there're a few unclaimed seats, he lets me know and we get in for discount. Of course, that's if you like the Indians."

"Aggie!" Dan appeared almost out of nowhere. The timing made Aggie think he had been listening to her and Jake talk. He stomped across the yard toward her, smiling despite the tension and sour scent he radiated. "Emergency dinner party. How fast can you get home and into your prettiest dress?"

"Emergency?" she echoed. Something sounded wrong, but she couldn't figure out what.

"Some bigwigs need their feathers smoothed." Dan flashed Jake a false grin and hooked his arm through Aggie's to lead her over to her car. "Your folks need you to help impress them."

"Okay," she sighed. Impressing and entertaining was Grace's domain, and if it was important enough to need her help, Aggie knew better than to hesitate.

Later, she wondered if it had been a set-up. The board members didn't seem all that upset or in need of smoothing. They laughed with her parents and congratulated Jack on the progress of his latest project.

Had she really been needed? She was rather bored by all the business talk.

She sat next to Dan and he didn't try anything. He barely looked at her. Despite his heavy cologne, she caught the rich, sweet scent of triumph.

〜〜

Monday morning, Aggie arrived at the site and saw Jake in the yard. She stopped to say hello and ask about his weekend. She meant to ask him when the next discount seats were available for the Indians, when he frowned a little and looked around before addressing her.

"So, I hear congratulations are in order."

"Huh? For what?" She thought he meant the dinner meeting Friday night, which had turned out to be a false alarm.

"Some of the guys say you and Moon are engaged."

"Only in their imagination. I'm still in high school!" She shrugged it off and went on to the office.

Less than an hour later, she stepped outside to find Dan to take a phone call. She saw him and Jake glaring at each other, then suddenly turn and stomp away. Dan headed straight for the trailer. He saw Aggie watching and a tiny smirk caught up one corner of the hard, flat line of his mouth.

"Do yourself a favor and stay away from Jake," he said as he slid past her through the door. "The guy's nothing but an accident waiting to happen."

Just after lunch, Jake walked up a temporary ramp to the second floor when it suddenly came apart at the seams. He went down, landing on his side hard enough to crack two ribs and dislocate his shoulder. Two falling boards clobbered him, requiring stitches on his forehead and across his cheekbone.

Aggie shuddered when she heard about it, because she used that ramp not an hour before. She liked to climb up to the highest point at lunchtime for some fresh air and sunshine. She had even considered asking Jake if he wanted to join her at lunch that day.

While the others clustered around the paramedics who worked on Jake and prepared him for transport to Lutheran Medical Center, Aggie went to check out the remains of the ramp. She barely started before one of Dan's goons chased her away.

"I don't know that much about construction," she told Lara and Greg later that evening, "but I do know what wood looks like when a nail's been pulled out with a tool and when it's been pulled out by force. The holes were clean on more than half the boards I saw. And there were supposed to be six C-clamps holding the boards to the I-beams that supported the ramp. I only saw three on the ground, and when I went under the I-beam, I didn't see any clamps still holding on."

"Set-up?" Greg whistled, shaking his head. "Were they out to get Jake, or just to cause trouble for your dad's company?"

"I don't know. There's been some grumbling about the supposedly historic buildings that were torn down for this new project, but they were demolished before Dad was hired to do the job. I mean, if you're going to get all excited about a building being of historic value, you do it before demolition starts, right?" She shrugged. "There's a lot of crazies in this world. Unfortunately, some work for my Dad."

Her mind kept going back to that almost-argument she had seen that morning, and Jake's comment about her being engaged to Dan. She knew some of Dan's loyal gang had a tendency to get rough with people who didn't snap to when he gave orders. There were always a few fights at the beginning of a project when new hires had to be taught their place in the pecking order.

She sometimes wondered how fanatical Dan's 'guys' were about supporting him and his orders. What if someone had decided to teach Jake a lesson for infringing on what they considered Dan's territory? It was funny when they were protecting 'the boss's little girl,' but what if they set out to hurt someone to keep him away from Dan Moon's woman? Even when she and her mother both denied Dan's claim?

ᗡᖘ ᖘᗡ

Aggie concentrated on enjoying her summer and ignoring the specter of her senior year of high school. She exorcised her frustrations by planning nasty tricks to play on Dan. She daydreamed of luring him into the park, at night, so she could shift to wolf and frighten him into leaving her alone. Aggie knew she couldn't do that. Her father depended on Dan, and Dan was devoted to the company. He made sure the business thrived. As long as he didn't print an engagement announcement in the paper, she thought she could handle him.

Grace was at the site the day Jack and Dan went over the apprenticeship applications and chose who would work at the site for July. She went to work specifically to keep her husband calm. Jack took the apprentices for PR purposes, but Dan always complained about the problems the 'outsiders' caused. Aggie hoped the apprentices would keep Dan busy and away from her.

Jack decided to only give five positions to out-of-state applicants, reserving the other five for local boys. For the out-of-state apprentices, he had to provide housing. As Grace told Aggie later, with a sigh and a resigned smile, it was the cost rather than loyalty to the local union that prompted Jack's decision. Harsey Construction would provide housing in a boarding house only a few blocks from the site. The apprentices had to take care of their own food, laundry and entertainment after hours. Grace put together the information packets to send to the out-of-state offices. When she left to come home for dinner that evening, Jack and Dan still hadn't decided.

⋙ ⋘

The new accountant's first name was Joe. Aggie didn't know his last name because Jack couldn't remember. Joe worked mostly afternoons, working part-time at three difference construction companies, and he had been with Harsey Construction two weeks before Aggie met him.

The Monday after her father sent off the apprenticeship packets, Aggie worked the entire day, making the housing and transportation arrangements. Joe came in at lunchtime.

He was tall and skinny with thick lenses that couldn't hide crystal gray eyes and a mop of black hair that an entire jar of gel couldn't tame. Joe's presence changed the tone inside the office trailer the moment he stepped through the door. He never shouted or got angry. Aggie liked how the sharpness in the atmosphere mellowed when he smiled indiscriminately at everyone as he made his way to his desk in the corner. He tossed a plastic bag of cookies down on the central table, twisted the wire closure off, snagged three cookies and left the bag hanging open in clear invitation to snackers. Dan walked in five seconds after Joe got settled. He saw the cookies, grabbed a handful, sighed and shook his head. He never once glanced toward the corner where Joe was turning on his computer.

"Hi, Joe," Dan called. He stomped out of the trailer with a backwards wave of one cookie-filled fist.

Aggie muffled her laughter behind her hand. Glancing around, she saw Joe watching her. Those eyes sparkled even more and he winked at her. For some reason, a man who brought cookies to work to share irritated Dan, but Joe wasn't insulted.

Then again, Aggie thought, maybe Joe brought the cookies simply because he knew it would frustrate Dan. She decided she liked him for that. Maybe she should get to know him better.

They exchanged comments during the rest of the afternoon, when he wasn't untangling a problem or she wasn't on the phone or her father wasn't in loud, sometimes laughing conference with different people. Joe seemed a nice enough guy. Aggie thought he might be fun to spend time with, but how could she find out? She cringed at the thought of simply telling him she wanted to get to know him. How often had Grace warned her about making a man think he was being hunted?

"The thing about men is, you have to make them chase you until you catch them," her mother had said when Aggie had come home broken-hearted because her first crush had ignored her.

This was in the days before adolescence started to work its unfriendly, smelly magic on the boys around her.

Aggie had never tried to catch the interest of anyone since that time. She wasn't sure how to approach Joe without scaring him away or encouraging him too much. Why couldn't this come as naturally to her as shifting shape or hunting in the dark? She was rather frustrated by the time she walked out to her car at the end of the day.

She needed to unwind. Aggie looked around and grinned. With nearly everyone gone, now was the perfect chance to climb up and get a good view of the city and some fresh air.

Joe walked out of the trailer, heading for his car as she headed for the elevator. He called out to her, asking where she was going. When she pointed up and slapped the spare hard hat on her head for emphasis, Joe went ghost white and failed miserably at summoning up a smile.

"What do you know?" she murmured, as she stepped into the elevator. The old warehouse was being converted into office space on the top five floors, boutique shops on the next three, and a bar/comedy club on the bottom two floors. "Poor Joe is afraid of heights."

Aggie laughed as she stepped out of the elevator and toed her shoes off before she stepped out onto the grid of I-beams and planks that made up the top floor. The old warehouse needed so much reconstruction, it was more economical to take the entire building down to its skeleton and start over, rather than figure out what needed replacing and reinforcing. Some people stayed very carefully on the big, thick, slightly rusted I-beams, near the support ropes strung everywhere throughout the building. Aggie scooped up her shoes and danced along the boards in her bare feet, racing to the furthest edge of the building. The wide open spaces commanded a wonderful view of the Flats, the water and bridges and other restored buildings up and down the river. She needed this taste of heights and wind and bright open spaces before she headed back to Berea. She spent far too much time indoors lately, and she felt stifled.

When she came back down twenty minutes later, after dangling her toes over the edge whenever possible, she found Dan waiting for her. He leaned against the bumper of his truck, arms crossed, head slightly bowed, idly toeing at the gravel in front of him. He didn't look up until she was almost to her car. She couldn't read his expression; even his eyes had that veiled look that meant he hid how he felt. His scent had a bitterness from anger past, a spicy tang from amusement, and something under it all that confused her. She couldn't define the smell, what it reminded her of, what it might mean.

"Joe thinks you're going to break your neck," he said, as he stood up straight. "Thought he was going to throw up, he was so worried about you."

"I'm the last person here who'd fall." She sidled past him and unlocked her car.

Dan sighed. "The geek has a point. It's not all that safe up there. Bullet nearly fell last week."

"Now that would be a catastrophe. Warn the earthquake watchers at Case." Aggie grinned as she said it.

Bullet was a mountain of a man with only one speed in life: amble. No one could unbalance him or knock him off his feet. For him to develop unsure footing meant something, but Bullet wasn't a Wereling who could almost fly if the winds were strong enough.

"Just be careful up there, will you? Think about your Dad and me, how we'd feel if you broke your pretty little neck." A smile flicked across his face that made Aggie shiver.

She knew exactly what Dan would like to do with her neck, and then move on to the rest of her body. She could smell it on him, and she had overheard several workers speculating on what a wild time she and Dan would have their first night together. She had only been slightly mollified to realize everyone knew she hadn't done anything with Dan.

"Thanks for worrying, but I'm able to take care of myself. I don't need or want anyone's help or interference. Least of all a guy who probably gets sick climbing the stairs," she added, raising her voice to fight a growl that wanted to leap out of her throat. "I have to head home, Dan."

"Okay. Fine. I just wonder why Joe's so worried about you all of a sudden." He jammed his hands into the back pockets of his jeans and stepped back as Aggie slammed the door and shoved her key into the ignition. He was still watching her, that frown of deep thought darkening his face, as she pulled out onto the street.

To Aggie's surprise, Joe suffered no injuries or accidents during the next few days. Did she really think some of Dan's goons would attack the skinny accountant just because he showed interest in her? Maybe Dan had let his loyal followers know that Aggie didn't encourage Joe, and with his fear of heights, he wasn't worth the trouble. Aggie felt a moment of relief. Joe was a nice guy. But that was the problem. He was just nice.

⁂

Brody stepped off the bus at the Cleveland terminal and shivered, despite the humidity. There was something in the air here. An energy, a presence he hadn't felt since he was on the other side of the dark wall created by the storm when he was eight. He hunched his shoulders and slung his duffel bag over one shoulder, his backpack over the other, and hiked toward the long, low-slung building.

The other two apprentices were far ahead of him. They had started out together, but he had stayed in his seat and napped when they went exploring, testing their forged driver's licenses at the truck stops along the way.

L. Monroe's letter flicked through his mind during the long ride, despite his certainty this was just another reporter looking to beef up tabloid sales. Something hinted in the letter, something trying to get his interest, but also a promise of information that he hadn't been able to find yet.

Brody stepped through the doors, out of the reek of fuel exhaust and people who had been too long without washing, into the synthetic clean of air conditioning and disinfectant. Paco and Herb had already found the snack machines and were plunking in quarters like they were playing a slot machine.

The instructions that came with their tickets said there would be taxis outside the station, and gave directions how to get to their boarding house. They would have a day of freedom to get used to Cleveland before they had to report to work at Harsey Construction. Brody saw maps and brochures with tourist information in a rack just a few steps from the door. He filled his hands with those while his companions snagged candy bars. Dorayn waited for his call, ready to help him get settled, but Brody wanted to do things for himself. There was something about this town that made him shiver in anticipation.

# Chapter Thirteen

The taxi driver smelled like he had been awake several days without brushing his teeth or showering, and looked like he hadn't combed his hair in all that time, either. Brody sat on the right in the back, to get as far as he could from the smell. The other two didn't care. They asked the driver about bars and places to pick up girls. They finally stopped talking long enough for Brody to ask where they could find a Laundromat and convenience stores, just before they disembarked in front of the grimy red-brick building that had probably been there during the first Wall Street crash. Brody had a horrid thought, as they climbed the half flight of stairs into the lobby full of much-mended furniture and peeling green linoleum. Would he have to share a room with these two?

Fortunately, not. An hour later, Brody stretched out on his back on his narrow, lumpy bed, and stared out the greasy gray window at the grimy brick wall opposite him. He was here in Cleveland, far from the reporters. Chad had promised no one would find out Brody had gone to Cleveland. He had a job and a temporary reprieve from trouble, and he was one step closer to solving the mystery of L. Monroe.

⁓ ⁓

Paco and Herb decided to go bar hopping. Brody couldn't understand why, since they had to report for work the next morning. Just because it was Sunday didn't mean they could do whatever they wanted. He explored, walking around the Flats, getting a good idea of how to get to and from the construction site. He walked up to the fence and nearly burst out laughing when the drooling, decrepit Dobermans lunged at him, bashing their faces against the chain link fence. It took only a few seconds of looking them in the eyes to assert dominance and send them running, yipping, back to the old man in a faded blue uniform, who lounged in the shade and reeked of whiskey even from fifty yards away.

Brody decided there was too much concrete in Cleveland to enjoy it. He thought about visiting the zoo. The lure of Wolf Wilderness was strong, but he didn't have much cash in hand and the fee to get in

could feed him for the whole day. The similarities between the wolves
in their recreated habitat and himself were just a little too close.

Maybe Cleveland at night, even a Sunday night, would be more
interesting. He had a far better way of exploring when night came.
Brody was glad the other two apprentices ignored him. He didn't have
to worry about someone coming to invite him for a nighttime outing,
and the resulting questions when they couldn't find him. He didn't
need any more awkward questions for the rest of his life.

&#x2766;&#x2767;

The wolf was black, a solid blur with gleaming ivory teeth and
claws among twenty shades of black and gray shadows. He stepped
out from the darkness under the arches and flat lines of concrete,
rust and steel of the Veterans Memorial Bridge. He strolled across the
pavement and grass to the edge of the Cuyahoga River, appearing and
disappearing in the shadows and watery streaks of light from the full
moon cutting through dissipating clouds.

Settlers Landing Park was unusually empty, even for nearly midnight on Sunday. Cleveland slept, gearing up for another workweek
and recovering from an afternoon of rain. A soft breeze riffled through
the thicker fur around the wolf's neck and played around the sharp
tips of his ears, making them twitch. He paused at every sound and
became a statue until the disruption ended. Then he moved on.

In the direction of the Terminal Tower, horns blared as two late-
night delivery trucks swerved around each other, trying to beat the
change of a traffic signal on Ontario and St. Clair. The wolf lowered
his head and glared, green-brown eyes glowing a little brighter in the
black mask of his face.

The breeze shifted, coming off the river now. The Cuyahoga River
smelled of mud and dead weeds and the last dirty drips from the rain
that had washed the streets momentarily clean. The wolf minced down
the steps to the river's edge and lowered his head to drink. He jerked
back from the first taste of the water and whined. Salt and grit, oil and
ashes borne on the air from the Ford Plant made the water bitter and
thick.

The wolf tipped back his head to vent a purely Human howl of
frustration. Then stopped. Footsteps echoed off the piers of the bridge
and the stone steps of the park. A woman giggled. The breeze brought
a faint whiff of beer stink. A man laughed. The woman let out a shriek,
ending in laughter as an engine roared into life and headlights blazed
down at an angle the parking lot's designers never intended.

"What the—" The man stopped and swore, accompanied by the
plop-crack-tinkle of a bag of empties hitting the pavement.

"Huh?" another woman said.

"Look at that!"

The wolf turned and stared at the beam of headlight that had nearly scorched his flanks a moment before.

"What is it?" the first woman said. Feet shuffled across the parking lot, accompanied by more giggles.

Three figures silhouetted by the headlights appeared at the edge of the parking lot, looking down at the wolf. He held still and tried to melt into the pavement under his feet. His ears flattened back against his skull and his fur stood on end as muscles tensed, ready for fight or flight.

"Just another dumb dog," the second woman said after a moment.

Released by the scorn in her voice, the wolf took a step, partially forward, partially out of the beam of the headlight. The first woman gasped and lunged forward and spewed.

"Never seen a dog like that before," another male voice said, as the wolf melted into the darkness under the bridge. Then everyone's attention fastened on the puking woman.

*⁜*

"Aggie, what are you eating?" Jack leaned over his daughter's shoulder and stared into her bowl.

"Oatmeal. Don't sneak up on me like that, Dad." She didn't look up from the newspaper spread across the picnic table.

"Since when could anybody sneak up behind you, Miss Sharp-Ears?" He patted her head and read over her shoulder.

"It's the principle of the thing, Dad. With all those rough-necks you hang around with downtown, you could sneak up behind the wrong person and end up in the hospital."

"Well, that's why I bring you to work. You do a great job protecting your old man." Jack pressed a kiss into her dark curls, where a curve of ear peeked through the tangle.

Aggie turned the page before reaching up and behind herself to tweak her father's nose. He snorted and sighed and stepped away. Jack had long ago given up trying to figure out how she could execute that move without looking. He paused again and checked his reflection in the door, frowning at the increasing bulge of his waistline over his new blue leather belt.

"Most people cook the oatmeal before they eat it," Jack murmured and stepped back into the house.

"You don't know what something is like until you try it." Aggie stuck the spoon into her mouth to keep from laughing, and sucked the last few gritty drops of milk off the edge.

The floor creaked in front of the dishwasher in the kitchen in place of an answer, followed by the thud of Jack putting his economy-size travel mug down on the counter to fill with coffee.

"Anything about the zoning debate in the paper?" Jack asked

"I'll check." Aggie scanned the headlines. The Monday paper was almost as thick as the Sunday edition and slid from her grip as she flipped through it. Sections D, E, and F hit the deck and opened up as they spread apart.

A photo of a wolf, silhouetted against the moonlit Cuyahoga River, sat in the top right corner of the right-facing page. Aggie stared, her mouth dropping open. She slid down to all fours and leaned over the paper to get a closer look.

What was a wolf doing in downtown Cleveland in this day and age? Was it a real wolf, or a Wereling? What if it was someone hunting her? An enemy? What if the person who had tried to kill her and Lara was coming to finish the job?

"Any luck?" Jack said, coming back out onto the deck. He bent down to snatch up the closest three sections. Then he saw the wolf photo too. "What in the world is that?"

"Somebody saw a wolf down in the Flats last night, Dad," she said in a soft voice. Aggie sat back on her haunches and managed a lopsided smile. "What would a wolf be doing in downtown Cleveland?"

"I don't want you wasting your time finding out," he snapped. Jack's hands shook as he gathered up the scattered sections of the newspaper.

"Dad—"

"It's probably someone's idea of a joke." He tried to slide the page with the photo out from under her knees. Aggie slapped both hands down on the sheet. "Aggie, honey—I'm going to be late for work."

"Let me cut out the photo and you can have it." She got up and darted into the kitchen, trailing the page like a tail.

"Sure. Just don't ruin the cartoons on the other side. I haven't read Beetle Bailey or Hagar yet." He sighed and followed her into the kitchen. His forced laugh wobbled a little.

"Darned scissors are never where I leave them." Aggie nudged the junk drawer closed and stepped over to the dishwasher to see if the scissors were in there. "I wish I'd been there last night."

"You know, this fascination of yours with wolves could get you into trouble."

"Oh, Jack, don't be ridiculous," Grace said, coming into the kitchen. She picked up his travel mug and stepped over to the refrigerator to pour in cream for him.

"I can take care of myself," Aggie mumbled. She settled on a paring knife in place of the scissors. In a few seconds she had the picture and caption neatly cut out of the paper, and handed the rest to her father. "Wolves are like good-luck charms for me."

"I don't know..."

"Daddy, have you ever met a wolf you didn't like?" Her saucy smile faded when she looked up and saw her father pale a little. "Sorry." She went up on her toes and brushed a kiss across his forehead.

Grace sighed and shook her head. At least she was amused by

the exchange.

"I just don't like the idea of you going anywhere near a real wolf."

"Scared you pretty bad when I tried to pet those wolves at Cedar Point, didn't I?"

"Scared isn't the word. You're the reason half my hair is falling out. You know that, don't you?"

"Just half?" She wrinkled up her nose at him. Grace muffled a snort of laughter. Instead of relaxing at the teasing, Jack just grew more intense.

"Wolves—real wolves—are dangerous."

"Daddy, that's just stupid folklore. Wolves are very social animals. Territorial, yes, but timid around people. They won't attack unless they're cornered or sick."

"Oh?" He slapped the photo. "Any wolf caught wandering around downtown Cleveland has to be sick or desperate."

"Or lost," she whispered.

"Hmm?" Jack studied her suddenly neutral expression. "Aggie, promise me something." He waited until she looked him in the eyes. "Promise me you aren't going to go downtown tonight to look for that wolf."

"Dad—" She turned to her mother, but Grace raised her hands in a gesture of surrender. It was the fear gleaming in Jack's eyes that broke down the wall of irritation. "I'll stay home tonight, Dad. I promise." She brushed another kiss across his cheek. "You'd better get going. You don't want to hit rush-hour this morning."

"Neither do you." Jack's color returned to normal and the sickly-sweet odor in his sweat began to fade. He smiled and the expression reached his eyes. He swatted her behind with the edge of the paper as he snatched up his mug and left the room.

"I just have to get washed up and I'll be on my way." Aggie waited until she heard the front door click shut, and then the sound of her father's boots on the flagstone walk leading to the driveway.

Aggie sighed and sank down on the stool in front of the breakfast bar, staring unseeing at the newspaper photo of the wolf. Her father worried about her too much, and it was her own fault. If only she had been a little more careful, that evening when he saw her shift from wolf to Human.

"I'm sorry, Daddy, but..." She met Grace's gaze. "There's a wolf in Cleveland," she whispered.

"Silly girl," Grace said. "There always has been. Now, there are two." She gestured down the hall. "Scoot. I think you'll probably want to talk to Lara before you go to work?"

Aggie laughed, feeling much better. What would she do without her mother to speak common sense and guide her around these rough spots?

๛ ๛

Lara had little advice to offer. She promised to spend the morning doing an Internet search to see if anyone else had seen the wolf. She had a friend at the Cleveland Public Library who could call some friends at the newspapers and police for more information. Other than that, they would just have to wait. Neither of them were happy with Aggie's promise to her father not to go looking for the wolf.

Wracking her brains for ideas and explanations got Aggie through the boring, sometimes frustrating drive downtown. She even managed to ignore the haze from the smoking stacks along factory alley, and the rising din of traffic, horns and rattling jackhammers echoing off the endless concrete. Her sensitive hearing usually gave her a headache that battled with the nausea from her hyper-acute sense of smell. Why people thought civilization and progress were so wonderful, Aggie had yet to figure out.

In the Flats, the smells and sounds weren't so bad. There was even the aroma of freshly turned dirt to give the air some life, plus the smells of the river so close to hand. To gain enough room for the owner's profit, on this particular job Jack's company had to build a cantilevered deck out over the Cuyahoga River. Whenever Aggie managed to climb up there, the view was spectacular enough and the fresh air strong enough to make up for other discomforts.

Why the Planning Commission had agreed to the cantilevered deck, Aggie couldn't figure out. Only a fool would make it easier for some drunk to make a leap into the river. Still, the challenge kept Harsey Construction busy, and conquering the tricky details would help their growing reputation.

Dan stepped into the trailer doorway when Aggie reached the parking lot, and watched her get out of the car. She pretended not to see him as she snatched up her insulated lunch bag, then turned, nudging the door closed with her hip.

"Morning, Aggie," he called.

She felt the hot pressure of his gaze moving up and down her body. If anyone else gave her a 'check it out' look, Aggie wouldn't have minded. She worked to keep her body trim and in top athletic form, and if other people admired her peak condition she wasn't embarrassed.

Dan, however, added a new dimension to his admiration. Possessive. He looked at her the way she looked at the Corvette she wanted to own someday. As long as he didn't get nasty, she was able to ignore him. To be truthful, Dan could be good company when he wasn't trying to pressure her into seeing the world his way. He was a good leader, a good businessman, and Jack honestly needed his help. His possessive attitude did keep the grunges on the crew from bothering her— like a flea collar kept away the nuisance of bites and diseases and scratching.

Aggie also knew better than to face Dan with the cold hard facts of her disinterest, because he would take it as a challenge.

Dan stepped down from the trailer doorway so she could go in ahead of him. The smell of scorched coffee competed with the harsh chemical tang of fresh blueprints in the confined space of the trailer. Aggie hurried to open the three rickety aluminum frame windows, earning puzzled frowns from the Federal Express courier and ten young men, strangers, in jeans and blue work shirts. They all held scratched and dented construction helmets and work gloves so new Aggie smelled the stink of the indigo dye when she walked past them to her desk.

Her father was on the phone, doing his nodding, 'uh huh, right, gotcha' routine. He met her gaze, tilted his head toward the now-open windows and grinned an apology. He knew how sensitive her nose was and usually remembered to open the windows before she got there. He must have had a busy morning already.

Aggie realized one stranger watched her. When their gazes met, he tilted his head toward the window, shrugged and gave her a lop-sided smile. He was grateful for the somewhat fresh air. She nodded and returned the smile and turned her back to the group to sink into her chair. She had to pretend to be busy, to get Dan off her back.

"What do you think?" Dan said, stepping up behind her and resting his hand on the back of her chair.

He leaned close enough for the bacon and coffee on his breath to reach her. She hated that combination. Aggie contemplated for two seconds his reaction if she twisted around and bit his hand. After all, how many times had she threatened just that when Dan got too close? He never seemed to learn.

"Think of what?"

"The kids." He nodded back toward the young men dressed for construction work.

Aggie turned her chair, effectively removing Dan's hand and making him stand up straight. Pretending to notice them for the first time, she studied the identically-dressed group.

"The new apprentices, I hope?" Aggie found her gaze lingering longest on the one who had smiled at her.

His hair was longer than the others, covering his collar. She couldn't tell if it was black with glossy streaks, or dark brown. His shoulders were wide, his torso tapering down to hips almost too narrow. He leaned his weight on his toes, not resting on his heels like the others. His nose was long, almost sharp; his jaw squared. From that angle, she couldn't tell what color his eyes were.

She shook her head and turned to her work. The last thing that apprentice needed was to get on Dan's bad side from the beginning, just because she showed some interest in him. She looked for the paperwork she had left on her desk Friday.

"Busy tonight?" Dan perched on the edge of the desk, towering over her.

Now Aggie really did want to bite him. She spotted the files just seconds before Dan sat on them. There was no way she would put her hand anywhere near his rear end. Not with all those strangers in the office—especially not with her father around. If Jack got the idea she really was interested in Dan, even in the lowest physical way, he would have wedding invitations in the mail before the ink had dried. Jack thought Dan was the greatest thing to come their way since the revitalization of Cleveland began.

"I'm going out with Lara."

"Jeese Louise! You see her practically every day." He slid off the desk, nearly taking the files with him.

Aggie heard the distinctive click of the phone settling into its cradle. "Dad's done."

"Give me a chance, will you?" he said, as he started across the office to take his place next to Jack for the orientation lecture.

"When you learn to howl at the moon," she murmured. Aggie glimpsed that apprentice looking at her, and bent her head over her paperwork. Something about him made the hair stand up on the back of her neck.

# Chapter Fourteen

"What do you think?" Dorayn paused in crossing the yard when Aggie stepped out of the trailer for a breath of air. He gestured with his chin at the apprentices.

"Haven't seen them in action yet." She shrugged and realized that she looked for the one who caught her attention. What was wrong with her?

"That one's fast and a hard worker. Sure to make enemies for himself if he keeps it up." The white-haired man chuckled. "I think we'll get along just fine. You should get to know him. Name's Brody Cooper." He winked at Aggie and walked away before she could do more than gape.

*Brody?* Aggie called with everything in her soul.

She didn't feel any response, but neither did she get the emptiness that meant no one was there. It was more like the dullness in the mental atmosphere that she sensed when Lara was too busy to talk with her. Mind-to-mind talking wasn't a constant thing, the girls had learned. They had to be listening for each other. Maybe Brody wasn't listening?

If he was *her* Brody Cooper, Kaenarr, her twin brother.

*Lara?*

*What's up? You sound unraveled,* her friend responded instantly.

*I found out who the wolf was last night. I think.*

*Aggie?*

*Kaenarr's here. Working for my Dad!*

*Well? What did he say when you talked to him?*

*I haven't yet.* Aggie closed her eyes, took a deep breath to calm herself, and wrapped up her memories of the last few moments to send in a lump to Lara. All her thoughts, her impressions, her images of Brody the few times she had seen him.

*Oh. We have a problem, don't we?*

*Fix one problem, get another.* Somehow, despite the lump in her throat, the heaviness in her gut, Aggie grinned.

꧁꧂

During the lunch break, Aggie climbed up to the second floor to check out the progress of the cantilevered deck and work off the nervous energy she had built up while planning how to approach Brody. She needed a higher perspective and fresh air. She didn't take the elevator, but climbed a conveniently placed I-beam leaning against the side of the building. She carried a hard hat, per regulations, but didn't put it on until someone let out a squawk. Grinning, she stepped out on the nearest girder and scurried across the open space to reach the side of the building facing the river.

The soft breeze coming off the water tugged at her hair. Aggie smelled waterweeds, mud and wet stone, the stink of burned fuel from the cabin cruisers. She closed her eyes and tracked the flight of a flock of gulls by their creaking screels. The elevator creaked and squealed as the gate folded open. Heavy, hurrying feet stomped across the boards and I-beams, approaching from behind her. Aggie smelled salt and stale coffee and a faint residue of bacon in the man's sweat.

"Aggie Harsey," Dan snarled, "how many times do I have to tell you—" He stopped short when she brought up the hard hat and settled it on top of her head. "Very funny. It's dangerous up here without any rails. You shouldn't be playing around."

"I only come up here when nobody is working." Aggie knew better than to fight a doomed battle. She turned and skipped her way across the beams to reach his side.

"That's beside the point." Dan reached out to grip her arm, but she sidestepped him and scurried across the plywood platform to the elevator. It would do her no good to go down the leaning I-beam and give Dan more fuel for his lecture.

"Dad knows I never lose my balance. He doesn't mind if I come up here," she said as he joined her in the elevator.

"Yeah, well your old man doesn't know everything. What I say goes here, got it?" He leaned close, trying to tower over her. It didn't work, since he was only four inches taller.

"Got it." Aggie slapped the 'down' button.

The elevator's cage door snapped closed, nearly taking off his back pocket. He let out a yelp. Aggie held her breath, fighting laughter the whole day down to the ground. At the bottom, she ignored the grinning, whispering construction workers as she walked across the lot back to the trailer.

⁂

"Hi, Aggie?" Brody thought his throat would close up before he could get the words out. Something about the owner's daughter drew him and made him tense. He got the same feeling from dreams where he thought he could break through the darkness but never did, and woke with a headache, covered in sweat and his sheets wrapped around himself from tossing and turning.

"Hi. Brody, right?" Aggie smiled and her face lit up and for a moment he had the feeling nothing else in the world mattered to her but him. That took his breath away.

"Uh—yeah—I'm..." This was not starting out right. "Is that your car?" He pointed at the dusty gray Cavalier sitting next to Jack Harsey's silver Lincoln. Of course that was Aggie's car. He had seen her drive it on a dozen errands already. "Where's Berea? I mean, how do I get there?" He pointed at the lettering on the back of the car, discretely small, that read 'Merrick Chevrolet, Berea, Ohio.' His heart had skipped a beat when he saw it for the first time.

"Well, fastest way is to ride home with me tonight." Her eyes sparkled, but it wasn't nasty laughter. It was like she shared a joke with him, but he couldn't remember what it was. "Come on in the office and I'll get on the RTA site for the bus routes. Or you could hike on up to the Terminal Tower and take the Rapid to the Brookpark station, and a bus into Berea from there... Lost you already, huh?"

Brody nodded and grinned and followed her into the office trailer. This was going to be easier than he thought. He wouldn't head into Berea to find the library and L. Monroe tonight. Or any night this week. There was too much to get used to in Cleveland, just for starters. He would wait until this weekend, when he knew the territory a little better.

Gil Doyne waited just a few feet away from the trailer when Brody stepped out, his hands full of computer printouts explaining the different routes for the bus line and a long sheet of paper with notes in Aggie's handwriting. The paper even smelled like her, clean and open like the wind.

"Word of warning to you, kid," Doyne growled. "Stay away from Dan Moon's girl. Lots of guys smarter and more important than you got real sorry they went where they weren't wanted."

"Dan Moon's girl?" For two seconds, Brody was completely lost. Then he remembered the way Moon watched the boss's daughter. He also remembered the numerous little ways Aggie's body language shouted 'stay away,' whenever Dan came near.

He bit his lip to keep from saying something that would probably get him in trouble. Aggie already struck him as a smart girl who knew how to take care of herself. If she didn't drive Dan Moon away, that was her choice. Maybe she liked him, but she made it hard for him so he appreciated her more.

"I'm too busy getting settled to go poaching," Brody said with a shrug and a grin.

"Smart boy." Doyne nodded and favored him with a wintry little smile, then turned leisurely on his heel and walked away. Brody watched him for a few seconds.

What would Doyne do if a wolf visited him in the middle of the night? A moment later, Brody knew and he almost laughed aloud.

Doyne smelled like a man who drank his supper. By the time Brody visited him in wolf shape, the man would be too blasted to notice or even remember what happened. And if he did realize what danger he was in, he would probably wet his pants. Not a pleasant prospect for someone with a hyper-sensitive nose.

❧ ❧

Aggie couldn't talk to Lara to report on her first encounter with Brody that evening. Her friend was at work and besides that, Dan came over for dinner to decide what projects to take after the Flats renovation. Aggie wondered what was up when both men asked her to stay and talk and give her opinions once dinner ended. When Grace reminded her to do the dishes, all the while watching Dan, Aggie knew. She was almost seventeen, and obviously her father thought she was old enough to accept Dan's interest. Did they plan to arrange their dynastic marriage this summer?

Aggie took her time doing the dishes. She thought about the atmosphere in the house recently. Had her parents been arguing? Or had Jack decided to encourage Dan's interest in her without persuading Grace?

Maybe, Aggie conceded, she had been so busy trying to contact Brody she had ignored all the subtle signs. Maybe it was time to stop being subtle with Dan Moon. Maybe a visit from a black wolf in the middle of the night would help scare him off. Maybe shifting from wolf to Human and back again would unsettle him enough to at least slow him down.

Maybe, if Brody really was her brother, she could transfer to a school in Pittsburgh and live with his foster family for her senior year?

Grace went outside to work in her garden, with the backyard lights turned on. Jack and Dan were still talking in the den when Aggie finished the dishes. She went upstairs, moving as silently as the shadows, just in case they tried to waylay her. She heard Grace come inside and say goodnight to both men. She hoped that meant Dan was leaving.

Aggie settled in the window seat, to watch the moon and breathe the night cool and relax before going to sleep. If she went to sleep. Maybe it was time for a moonlight run. She listened to the insects chirping and a few barks from the neighborhood dogs. She thought she caught the distinctive acid-sweet stink of cats on the wind and the smell made her stomach churn for a few seconds. No wonder the dogs were restless.

Grinning in the darkness, Aggie slid the screen aside and waited for the first slinking shadow of a cat. No slimy, spitting, scratching feline was going to leave its scent mark in her backyard.

Aggie concentrated so hard on the moonlight and shadows in the tree-filled back yard, she was startled when a truck engine started with a roar in the driveway. She grinned and imagined Dan seething with frustration all the long drive home to Brook Park. She suspected she didn't confront him about his ridiculous plans because it was fun exasperating him.

"Aggie?" Jack's voice drifted up the stairs.

She sighed and tried to force her concentration back into the yard below. Any minute now, those miserable cats would come creeping in.

There! The hairs on her arms and down her neck stiffened to attention as she caught a furtive, silvery-gray movement at the corner of her eye. Aggie glanced over her shoulder at her closed bedroom door. Was that creak in the roof, or a stair tread as her father came upstairs?

It would only take a few seconds to leap down from the balcony, shifting to wolf long enough to scare that cat into a screaming lightning bolt of fur, and then jump back up to the balcony. Long enough for her father not to see? She couldn't risk that again. Not ever.

"Aggie?" Jack tapped on her door. If she didn't answer, he would assume she was asleep or just being stubborn.

The sound caught the ears of the cat—no, two cats creeping in tandem through the neighbor's peony bushes lining the left side of the yard. Aggie hoped the ants living among the roots of the bushes swarmed and crawled all over the cats. They paused now, listening for another sound. She grinned in the darkness and forced her breath to stay slow.

*Just two more steps,* she silently begged. *Please, Dad, go away.*

Her door opened, spilling light into the room. The sound of the copper bells hanging on her doorknob and the sudden streak of light falling into the yard alerted the cats. They lifted their heads, staring up at her window.

"Aggie, can I talk with—" Jack stopped when he realized there was no one in the bed. He turned.

She snatched up a handful of stones sitting in a corner of the window seat—souvenirs from half-forgotten vacations—and flung them with needle-fine accuracy into the darkness.

"Not again," Jack grumbled.

"Ha!" she crowed softly, as the stones shrieked through the air, arching slightly, unhampered by the minimal night breeze.

Twin yowls of shock broke the relative stillness of the night. Two silver-gray streaks sped back through the peony bushes. Aggie leaned against the windowsill and tracked the cats' progress by the renewed barks and yelps and howls of the neighbor dogs. She giggled and imagined the cats' fur standing straight out from their bodies.

"Proud of yourself?" Jack asked.

"Yep. You taught me, remember?"

"I taught you to use a slingshot to hit paper boats on Wallace

Lake, not to torment defenseless kitties." He stepped up to the window and leaned against the wall beside it, his back to the now-quiet yard. He smiled, so Aggie wasn't worried.

"No such thing as a defenseless kitty. Besides, the new animal laws say all household pets have to be kept on their owners' property. If dogs have to be tied up, so should cats."

"I can't understand why, the way you love dogs, you don't have half a dozen around the house."

"I'm friends with every dog in the neighborhood. I can play with any dog I want, and when it's time to feed them and clean up after them, I can just send them home." She grinned and turned around in the window seat to face him.

"I know that line." He chuckled. "I used it when people asked how come your Mom and I didn't have kids. Then your Mom brought you home and the line became just that—a line."

"Dad, there's a difference between kids and dogs." Not much, in Aggie's book, but she wouldn't admit it aloud.

"Maybe. Dogs you can housebreak a whole lot faster than kids. Or husbands," Jack added after a few seconds.

"What?" Her mouth dropped open.

"What have you got against Dan? The man's in love with you."

"Really? When did he tell you that?"

"You couldn't find a better husband than Dan Moon. He's dependable, he doesn't sleep around—"

"How do you know?"

"Aggie!" Jack winced when his voice echoed around the backyard.

"Oh. Is that the guy talk you never want me to hear?" She grinned and stuck her tongue out at him.

"I'm just saying you could do a whole lot worse than Dan Moon. He's more than willing to wait for you to get out of school. He's dependable, smart, he knows how to get the men to work hard, and he knows the business like the back of his hand. I want someone around to take care of you and your Mom, if something ever happens to me."

"Dad, you're as healthy as a horse. If anything ever did happen to you, Mom and I will take care of each other. Don't worry."

"It's a father's job to worry. The only way you'll hold onto the business is with someone else holding the reins. You manage the books just great, but just because you're my little girl is no reason for the next owner to keep you on."

"Why don't you just adopt Dan and let me off the hook?"

"He wants you just as much as he wants the company, Aggie. If he had to make the choice between you and the company, I'm putting my money on you."

"Flatterer." She decided this conversation had gone far enough. "Does Mom know you're planning on marrying me off?"

Jack flinched, his eyes widening in fear. Then he realized she was teasing, and grinned, shaking his head.

Aggie stood and slid the screen back into place. "Go to bed. You have those apprentices to babysit tomorrow and you'll need all your rest to handle them." She caught hold of his hand and pretended to drag him back through her room to the door.

"You're the babysitter." Jack smiled and sighed and retreated gracefully.

⚜ ⚜

Aggie-wolf stepped out of the shadows streaming out behind the closed and locked concession stand at the end of Wallace Lake. She closed her eyes and took deep, snuffing breaths of the night breeze. The moon hung low on the horizon, which had a pinkish-silver tinge as dawn prepared to ease into the sky.

A soft, sighing whine escaped her as she minced her way across the crumbling pavement of the parking lot and started down the side of the asphalt road, moving from the lake to the river. At this time of night, not even the rangers patrolling for illegally parked lovers would come down this section of South Quarry Lane. Aggie-wolf stayed on the soft, muddy grass, separated from the asphalt by gravel berm, and broke into a trot. The gentle night breeze toyed with the thick, dark ruff of fur around her neck and teased the curved plume of her tail.

The parking lot gleamed like silver in the moonlight. The bathroom building and the first stations of the exercise par course cast long, soft-edged black shadows. She ignored the silent obstructions to the wind and continued down the curving road to the ford where the road dipped down as it crossed the Rocky River.

Sitting back on her haunches, she let out a soft howl that barely rose above the edges of the trees and echoed faintly off the curved arch of the pedestrian bridge a few yards away. Loneliness weighed down the sound, threatening to break it. She hoped, wherever he was, Brody heard her cry and started listening with his soul.

⚜ ⚜

Aggie watched for Brody all day Tuesday, every time she had to leave the office to find her father or Dan to answer phone calls or sign papers.

Brody was a hard worker. Maybe too hard. She noticed he seemed to do more than his share of the lifting and carrying. It was normal to give the apprentices the drudge jobs, carrying boards and tools up and down ladders or shifting debris, loading wheelbarrows, hauling pipes and conduit out of the current work path. Brody seemed to do his own and half the other apprentices' carrying, too. Every time Aggie turned around, she found him on the ground, carrying something somewhere, handing loads up to the men on the upper level or taking something off a pulley. By lunchtime, she had yet to see a tool in his hand.

"He's strong and he's fast," was Dan's only response when she mentioned it to him. Then he gave her a second look. "What are you worried about him for? Something I should know about?"

"I'm worried about all the apprentices." She turned her back on him and stepped over to the refrigerator to pull out her lunch bag.

"Rabbit food again?" He chuckled, leaning over her shoulder as he watched her unzip the green and blue bag. "When are you going to eat some real food when I'm around?"

"Raw food is the only real food." Aggie wondered what he would say if she brought in a slab of the fresh liver intended for dinner, and ate it raw in front of him. "I always keep a watch on the apprentices just to make sure your gorillas don't deliberately drop something on one of them."

"Hey, my guys are always careful. Ow!" Dan jerked his hand out from under her nails and dropped the inch-thick ring of zucchini he had tried to steal. "You are one fast, mean lady."

"Thank you." She batted her eyelashes at him. The next moment, she regretted that. They were alone in the office trailer. Dan smiled and leaned closer.

"Aggie—"

"I don't like being interrupted when I'm eating, Dan. I might bite you, and I'm late for my rabies booster."

A shout out in the construction yard stopped Dan with his mouth open and nothing coming out. Aggie decided she liked him best that way as they both ran for the door. She reached the door first, in time to see Brody leap up from a seated position and put himself between two red-faced men with sunburned arms and dusty T-shirts. Both men were part of Dan's 'team.'

Fights between the team members usually meant someone tried to work his way up the pecking order, or defend his position from someone he considered a threat.

Aggie sighed and wished people could handle things like the animal societies. Like wolves. Once a position was established, it stayed that way until illness or injury intervened, and the wolves accepted the change as the natural order.

Brody didn't seem to understand that this was just another lunchtime show of physical politics. He held both men apart, their shirts caught in his fists, his arms locked stiff. It was almost funny, watching the two men swinging their fists, trying to get at each other and Brody standing immovable.

"What the heck is going on here?" Dan shouted, and stepped past her. He jumped down from the doorway and jogged a few steps into the gravel-strewn yard.

Brody turned and saw him and let go of the two men. They both leaped to resume their fight, and smashed Brody between them. He let out a shout and spun, throwing them off. They landed on their backs and slid a few yards, sending up clouds of dust and gravel. Aggie winced, imagining how it felt on their backs, through their sweaty clothes. Then she stared at Brody, who had dropped into a crouch and watched the two men. She suspected he was too used to being attacked when the odds were weighted against him.

# Chapter Fifteen

"What's with you and that Cooper kid?" Joe said halfway through the afternoon. They were alone, both Jack and Dan gone on errands.

"Cooper...Oh, Brody. Nothing. Why?" Aggie turned from her perch in the open trailer doorway where she watched the activity in the yard. Dorayn had taken Brody as his assistant and she was glad. He let people prove themselves by their actions, instead of trying to immediately classify and judge them before they did anything wrong or right.

"You've been watching him every chance you get."

"I watch out for all the apprentices. What's bothering you about Brody?"

"That kid... You don't have anything in common with him, that's all." He huffed and turned back to his computer screen.

"Oh, great...you're jealous." Aggie swallowed a bark of laughter when Joe stiffened and his face turned red. "Listen to me, Joe. If there was anything between us, even for two seconds, even if it was only in your wildest dreams, Dan's goons out there would know. Half the guys working for us think I'm Dan's property, when they're able to think at all. They take it really personal when they think someone is infringing on Dan's territory. And you wouldn't like how they tell you to get lost. Get the picture?"

She turned away and went back to her desk, but not before she saw Joe's expression freeze. She was glad the breeze moved toward Joe instead of her. She didn't want to smell his terror.

Besides, she had her own new problems to consider. What kind of trouble would Dan's goons make for Brody? If Joe thought she was interested in Brody, what would the muscle-heads out on the job think?

*Lara?*

*I'm here. What's up? You feel...I don't know. Tight.*

*I need you to do me a favor. It's really important.*

⁂

Brody liked building things. He was good with tools, cutting, hammering and making sure the angles were tight, sharp and perfect. He had a knack for eyeballing a broken brace or a sagging door and know-

ing exactly how to fix it without ever using a measuring tape or marking the lengths before he cut or drilled. The smell of sawdust was his
favorite perfume, the even rhythm of hammered nails his favorite
music. When the chance came to help his career and find out what L.
Monroe really wanted, Brody had jumped at the chance. Now, though?

He sighed and looked up at the afternoon sun, half-hidden in the
haze of the Cleveland skyline. He didn't like the smells here. He didn't
like the people he worked with, other than Anton Dorayn. He didn't
like the hotel-cum-boarding house where the apprentices stayed. He
didn't like the rancid smell of half-cooked food and the thumping music
that stabbed through the walls and woke him in the morning, just
when he had finally fallen asleep after a restless night.

What he wouldn't give for a moonlight run in the woods. If he
could find the woods. Just him and the dew on the grass, raccoons,
and owls gliding through the trees. Fresh, clean air and no people, no
cars zipping past with their radios or stereos set on 'chop and liquefy.'

He would take off his heavy, hot, constricting shoes and just stand,
feeling the ground soak up into his feet for at least half an hour. He
would let everything flow away, out of his body. Then he would shed
every encumbrance and just run. Hard and fast and flying through the
forest until the trees looked like they fled away behind him. He could
run without stopping or losing his breath, run for hours with nothing
to hold him to the ground, nothing but air between him and the forest
and the animals.

He couldn't do that here. The only face of Cleveland he had seen
so far was a forest of concrete, smog and noise. The only animals were
the Human kind and they fought with crazy words before they threw
their bodies into the battles. The battles were always over strange,
useless things that had to be fought over again on the next working
day.

"Brody." Dorayn looked up from the bracing they had to build
before the studs on the existing wall could be cut. "We're out of nails.
Go on down and get us another box, and four of the eight-footers,
okay?" He smiled and went back to wrapping insulating tape around
the exposed wires for the makeshift power system.

Brody nodded and headed for the ladder down. Dorayn was probably the biggest reason for sticking it out at this miserable job. He
liked Dorayn. Not just because the big, weathered, white-haired man
didn't stink of beer when the day's heat sweated the poisons out of his
body, but because Dorayn actually let him do something. He liked it
that Brody climbed faster and picked up on what he was supposed to
do before his mentor finished an explanation. The other construction
workers thought he was a smart-alec. The other apprentices thought
he was showing off. Dan Moon let the other workers order him around
and give him a dozen conflicting orders until Dorayn stepped in this
morning and permanently took Brody under his wing.

Besides, there was that sense that he had known Dorayn before. Like an old friend. From the 'before' time.

Brody had already learned the workers were divided between Moon's 'gang' who smelled of beer, smoked during breaks and told stupid stories full of foul language and too much sex, and the men who looked to Dorayn as their leader. Dorayn didn't have to prove anything to anybody. Brody labeled him the alpha male of the pack sharing territory with Moon's pack. He always came running when a fight started and intervened in the matter. Anyone who refused to listen was a beta male in Moon's gang.

Brody slid down the ladder, taking every other step and jumped off six feet from the ground. He landed running and skidded across the gravel to the storage shed. It was dark, but he smelled the sharp stink of warm metal on the left side of the shed and reached for the closest box. It was open. Through his gloves, he felt the length from head to point. It was a quarter inch shorter than the nails Dorayn and he had been using. He felt along to the next box and found the right length.

The door slammed open, squealing in protest on its rusty hinges and a man-shaped shadow blocked out what little light poured into the shed.

"What the heck are you doing in here with the lights off?" a froggy voice demanded, followed by a belch.

Gil Doyne. He smelled so consistently of beer, Brody wondered if the man bathed in it, besides drinking three bottles at lunchtime. After his second bottle, he had started talking about his distant relatives, highly placed in politics in the suburbs around Cleveland, mayor and councilman and other important figures. Halfway through the third bottle, he bragged how he was going to run for office pretty soon. Brody decided he hated politics, if people like Doyne could get elected.

"Getting nails," Brody said, and picked up the box. He took a step for the door, but Doyne didn't move.

"You're weird, kid. You know that? You trying to tell me you can see in the dark?" He belched.

Brody leaped, sliding through the gap between Doyne and the doorframe. His hands clenched into fists, squeezing the box of nails until it threatened to burst all over the ground. Brody took a few quick breaths and told himself not to fight. He had learned the hard way that fighting, even in self-defense, always brought a reporter running.

It didn't matter that the fight was always instigated by the other guy. Brody was always labeled the villain, no matter what the outcome. He was too fast, too accurate with his fists and feet. He liked the acid stink of their pain, the sweet-sour smell of fear when his opponents realized he beat them. It was like a drug and if he didn't stop himself quickly, he always ended up pounding his opponent almost to the edge of losing consciousness. That was fine when he defended himself, but not here at work, when his attackers only used words as weapons. Not when his enemy was a beer-stinking idiot.

"You are too fast to be believed," Dorayn said when Brody climbed up and tossed the box of nails onto the boards next to him. Then he frowned at the place where Brody had climbed up. "I thought the ladder was over there," he said, pointing at a spot ten feet over.

"It is." Brody shrugged and tried to grin as he set down his armload of two-by-fours.

He had that queasy feeling in his stomach again. Dorayn wore that odd, slightly amused look that Mom Cooper wore when he was younger and did something totally strange. When she wanted to both laugh and cry and couldn't quite figure out how to tell him what he had done wrong. Like the time Brody put his shoes on and then his socks. He hadn't learned enough English yet to explain that he was used to going barefoot.

"You got something against ladders?"

"Too slow." He opened the box and pulled out a handful of nails and went over to the spot where they had stopped working on the bracing framework.

"I remember when I was your age," Dorayn said with a sigh. He ran one gloved hand through his hair, leaving a streak of muddy dust along his sweating scalp. His sigh turned into a chuckle. "I used to love a challenge, too, when things got boring. Don't you go making speed so important you get yourself hurt. We're a long way up."

"Don't worry." Brody accented his words with fast, sharp thuds of the hammer. He grinned and nodded a little in time with the blows. "I never lose my balance."

"I'd like to see what you'd do on the edge of an I-beam thirty stories up," Dorayn muttered. Then he chuckled and picked up a handful of nails and settled down next to Brody to resume hammering at a slower, measured pace.

Through the hammering, Brody heard a car drive into the construction yard. It was an older engine, with a rattling undertone, and its tires crunched in the gravel. Brody felt a shiver run up his back, like an icy fingernail had stirred the hairs, pushing them the wrong way. He lowered his hammer and turned, looking over the edge of the building into the lot.

It was an old, rusty blue Chevy, and it pulled into the spot next to Aggie's car. Brody watched, feeling a building sense of pressure.

He felt almost disappointed when a tall, fair-haired young man climbed out of the driver's seat. Dressed in jeans and T-shirt, there was nothing special about him. The girl who climbed out from the back seat immediately after him had to be a sister, they looked so much alike, willowy and wheat-haired. Brody felt a tingle like electricity race down his back and thought he saw a few blue sparks dance around her hair. It and the sensation fled in a moment. He wondered if his lunch milk was a little closer to the expiration date than he thought.

Then the redhead in faded jeans and white eyelet shirt climbed out of the passenger seat in front. The illusion of blue sparks stayed, dancing around her glowing curls and fingertips and suddenly spinning up like a tiny tornado. Brody sat back on his heels when it seemed the sparks aimed straight for him—then vanished.

"You okay?" Dorayn asked, barely glancing at him.

"Yeah. Fine." Brody took a few deep breaths and watched the three head toward the trailer office. The redhead wore a leg brace and limped. He swayed, overwhelmed for a moment by an image of an elfin, red-haired child tumbled about by cosmic forces and battered by brutal powers.

"You don't get paid for sightseeing," Dorayn said, and reached over to nudge Brody with his hammer.

"Who's that?"

"Hmm?" The big man leaned over the edge, frowning a little. "Oh, friends of Aggie's. Nice kids. That's Greg and his sister, Allison and Lara." He gestured with his hammer, pointing out the three just before they stepped inside the trailer. "They come sometimes to meet Aggie and go do something downtown."

"Like what?"

"How should I know? Go ask them yourself." Dorayn chuckled when Brody just shook his head. "You're their age. What's to stop you from being friends? You might be surprised what happens. But later, okay? Better get back to work before one of Moon's boys catch you gawking."

Brody turned back to his hammering, but left a corner of his attention waiting, watching for the trio to step out of the trailer office. Allison emerged only a few seconds later. She stepped out into the yard, looked around and came right over to the side of the building where they were working. Brody looked down and met her gaze and felt another jolt run through him when she smiled as if she knew him. As if she knew all about him and liked him anyway. He managed to smile back, but for the life of him he couldn't think of a single thing to say.

"Mr. Dorayn?" She had a soft, sweet voice with a rock-hard strength under it.

"Hi, Allison. What can I do for you?" Dorayn stopped hammering and nodded to Brody that he could stop too.

"Have you seen Aggie? We're supposed to meet her, but she's not in the trailer and her car's still here."

"City Blue didn't make its delivery this morning and she had to run out and get the new prints. She took the truck. Shouldn't be gone much longer."

"Thanks." Allison's gaze flicked to Brody. Her smile widened. "Hi.

Are you one of the apprentices for the summer?"

"Brody Cooper," Dorayn said. "Allison here's a librarian for the summer. Brody likes books, don't you?"

"Yeah. Love 'em." Brody fought a growl of frustration, for his frozen tongue and for Dorayn's presence. He couldn't exactly jump down to where Allison was standing and spend the next two hours just looking into her eyes, but that was exactly what he wanted. He felt a trembling move through him when he realized Allison didn't seem at all uncomfortable with his silence or the way he kept staring at her. She stared back, and smiled.

"If you're looking for anything special, I could try to find it for you," she offered.

"Thanks. Um...you live in Berea by Aggie?" A little of the pressure filling his head and chest dissipated when she nodded. "Is it nice?" That was a stupid thing to ask, but Allison's smile didn't fade and she just nodded again.

"Hi." Suddenly Greg and Lara were there too, looking up at him and Brody felt that prickling sensation that meant he was under intense scrutiny. "I'm Greg," the young man continued.

"This is Brody Cooper," Allison said. "He's one of the apprentices Aggie was talking about. She was worried about all of you staying in that roach trap where the company—"

"Allison!" Lara blurted.

"Oops." Allison put both hands over her mouth, but her eyes danced and she didn't look at all contrite. "Anyway, if you want someplace nice to go on the weekend, the Metroparks are really close."

"Is that by you?" Brody managed to say without letting too much eagerness show. Allison nodded, blushing a little.

The appearance of the company truck pulling into the gravel yard stopped any further conversation. The three turned as one to go meet Aggie, saying the usual nice, meaningless things people said when they had just met a stranger they probably would never meet again. All except Allison. She looked back a few times and smiled at Brody.

"Be careful," Dorayn said under his breath, ending in a chuckle.

"Huh?" Brody picked up the hammer that sometime during the encounter had slipped from his fingers.

"She likes you, but take it slow."

"I wasn't—I wouldn't—I just met her," he finally spluttered and turned back to his neglected hammering. Brody knew the heat in his face and neck had nothing to do with the blazing sun.

Still, when the four walked back over to Greg's car to talk for a few moments, he risked pausing to turn and look for Allison. She waved to him and smiled and he smiled back.

Maybe he was wrong. Maybe coming to Cleveland had been the very best, most right thing he could have done.

"Hey, Brody, no daydreaming on the job." Dorayn nudged him

again with the head of his hammer. He chuckled. "Better not let old
Dan see you staring at Aggie too much. He thinks he owns that girl
and he can be nasty when his territory is invaded."

"Does she know that?" Brody asked without thinking. He was too
busy watching Allison.

"Aggie doesn't miss much of anything around here. Don't know
what that girl is up to. She doesn't encourage him, but she doesn't tell
him to go chase his tail, either."

"Chase his tail?" Brody almost dropped his hammer on the up-
swing. A shiver passed over his whole body. That was a familiar phrase
from long ago, but it certainly didn't belong here in Cleveland, Ohio.

"Aggie says that all the time. Good choice of words, huh?"

"Yeah." He went back to his work and echoed Dorayn's grin.

Where had he heard someone else use that phrase? Why would a
girl in the middle of the concrete jungle of Cleveland use a phrase like
that?

Maybe she had a lot of dogs back home. Or she hung around with
people who had a lot of dogs. That had to be it. Maybe that was the
reason for the odd, pleasant scent Aggie gave off. Clean but with a
touch of wildness and mystery, nothing Brody could identify. And now
that he really thought about Dorayn's words, he doubted he should
ever get close enough to Aggie to catch the scent again to unravel it.

Still, he had nothing to worry about on that score. Brody sat back
on his heels and watched Greg's car drive away. Allison leaned out the
window and waved to him and he knew he was perfectly safe from
Dan Moon's jealousy. He had disliked Dan from the moment he walked
into the trailer office Monday morning and the man raked the apprentices with a look that clearly said 'Don't you even think about making
friends with me.' Brody had felt a strong sense of danger come off
Moon and vowed to stay as far from him as possible. He wondered
why Aggie put up with him.

Aggie Harsey was none of his concern, Brody reminded himself.
Finding L. Monroe and finagling a way to see Allison again was top
priority in his life. Although, now that he thought of it, not exactly in
that order.

Grinning, Brody went back to work.

✍ ✌

*He's got something,* Lara thought to Aggie as Greg's car turned
down the street and pulled away from the construction site. *I don't
know what it is, but for a few seconds I felt that tingling we get
when there are a few of us in the park. It didn't last very long.*

*Yeah, I know.* Aggie settled down into her chair and stared unseeing
at the screen saver on her computer. *I felt something when I pulled
in, even before I saw Greg's car. What's with Allison? I thought she
was going to burst.*

*Remember how we've been worrying she's going to break her heart over Mike?*

*Yeah. He finally paid attention to her?*

*Nope.* Laughter made Lara's mental voice rich. *Allison fell for Brody. They looked into each other's eyes and I swear completely different sparks went flying. Didn't you see it?*

*I didn't see anything. How do you think he feels about her?*

*If we hadn't spoken up, he never would have known we were there. If you're worried about keeping him here once he knows the truth about us, Allison will take care of that easy.*

*I hope so. Just because Brody doesn't give off colored sparks like you and Greg and Allison doesn't mean he's like me. It doesn't mean he's Kaenarr.*

*Still...*

*Still, nothing. It's only Tuesday. He's passed inspection with you guys. If we need to find out more information, we can always sic Allison on him.* Aggie picked up a pile of papers and pretended to be engrossed in them as Dan stomped away from Jack's desk.

# Chapter Sixteen

Brody thought if he didn't find some place where he could take off his shoes and feel life and clean soil under his feet, he would go out of his mind. He had found a few isolated patches of grass and trees, but the smells of truck exhaust, the sterile hardness of concrete and the blinding glitter of glass destroyed what little relief those patches of nature created. Brody wanted a place where he could lie full-length in the grass and not worry about someone stepping on him; where he could look up at the stars and not have them obscured by smog and the burn of lights from buildings and vehicles; where he could hear crickets sing uninterrupted.

A raucous burst of laughter broke into his thoughts. Brody looked up from contemplating his hot, heavy boots and turned around. He was last in line to put away his tools for the day. There was no one to take his place away if he left the line.

Four apprentices gathered around Dooley Harper, one of Moon's gang. Brody caught a glimpse of light on slick paper and a momentary flash of a bare, pale leg. Some girly magazine, probably. Wasn't there anything for them to think about after work besides sex and beer?

"Yeah, she's hot," Ryan Taylor said. He rocked back on his heels and stuck his thumbs in the loops of his belt, just like Dooley. "You know who's really hot? Aggie Harsey."

"You shut up," Dooley growled.

"Oh, come on." He grinned and slapped the older man's shoulder. "Don't try to tell me you don't notice every time she walks by. The way she moves, all that hair. You can spend hours just thinking how she'd look without—"

"I said, shut up," Dooley repeated, dropping to a whisper. "One thing you got to learn around here, boys." He looked each apprentice in the eye in turn.

Brody almost dropped the hammer and Yankee screwdriver cradled in his arms. Dooley was terrified, if the sudden pallor under his tan and the tremor in his voice were any indicators.

"Don't even think about Aggie Harsey that way, much less say it out loud. She belongs to Dan—"

"Not from what I've seen," another apprentice broke in.

"She belongs to Dan Moon," Dooley repeated, "and if you even think about touching her or seeing what you shouldn't see, he'll know. I've seen guys put on permanent disability just for asking her out."

Whether the apprentices were impressed or frightened, Brody didn't bother to look or listen long enough to find out. He put away the tools he and Dorayn had been using and headed for the time clock and the gate. Smithers had one of his decrepit Dobermans on a short chain and stood at the gate with one hand on the lock. The dog growled at Brody. The sound was mush by the time it got through the gaps in the dog's teeth. A tiny puddle of drool lay between the Doberman's feet.

Brody spared one disgusted, pitying glance for the dog and stepped out through the gate.

Maybe tonight he would try the Cleveland Zoo. He doubted anyone would be too upset if he took off his shoes and walked on the grass. Maybe he could even climb a tree if the zoo was open past dark, and the shadows were thick enough for hiding.

❧ ❧

"There's something wrong with that kid," Dan muttered as Aggie brought big glasses of iced tea and slices of chocolate cake out onto the deck for him and Jack.

He had come over after dinner to talk about the problems at the construction site that had plagued them that morning. Jack's den was stuffy in the day's heat. Grace had suggested they go outside to enjoy the cooler air and promised them some dessert.

Now, Aggie wished her mother had left them to suffer indoors, when Dan smiled at her and brushed his fingers down her wrist before taking the plate of cake from her. She gave him the quelling look she had learned in junior high that worked equally well on angry dogs and hormone-driven bullies. Dan winked at Jack. Aggie glanced at her father, just in time to see that satisfied smile on his face.

Aggie played with the idea of shifting to wolf, just for one delicious moment of imagining their shock. Dan wouldn't want anything to do with her ever again. But, on the downside of that freedom, Jack would hit the bottle big time and Dan would leave the business. And she might become a target of tabloid reporters, like poor Brody had been.

Thinking about Brody brought her back to the conversation she had come in on.

"What kid?" Aggie suspected she knew. Dan had complained about the apprentices non-stop since they arrived.

"The Ehrnreich kid. Can't hold onto his hammer more than five seconds before he loses it. When I get hold of Paponetti down at the union hall, he's going to be sorry he sent that kid over here to give us trouble. I told Dorayn to take him. He can get anybody to straighten out without us getting hit with a harassment suit. He said he wouldn't, he was perfectly happy with that Cooper kid."

"All the other apprentices are slugs. Why make Dorayn suffer because he's a good teacher? He picked Brody, so why can't you leave them together as a team?" Aggie said before she could stop and think.

"First name basis already?" Icicles dripped through Dan's voice.

"Better watch out, hon," Jack said, his mouth full of cake. "Old Dan here's getting jealous."

"He has no reason—and no right, either," Aggie said, glaring at them both. Dan's smile returned, with an edge to it. "I'm no more interested in Brody than I am in Dan. Besides," she tossed over her shoulder as she reached for the screen door, "Brody met Allison today and the way they were looking at each other...I'd better give him her number before he bursts."

"Oh, absolutely," Dan sneered, his words accented by the clicking of the sliding door shutting. "Can't get in the way of young love, can we?"

"The more you protest, the more interested Dan will be," Grace said softly, at the kitchen table. She picked up one of the cupcakes she had just iced for the children at summer church camp, and held it out to Aggie. "Need some chocolate?"

"I need about half an hour of pure privacy with Brody and a big stick to hit him with until he listens to me." Aggie took the cupcake and licked all the frosting off.

"Maybe it's a good thing you aren't scheduled to work tomorrow," Grace said. "Let Dan cool down, give yourself some time to think, let Brody get settled so when you do talk to him, he'll be more comfortable."

"I hope you're right, Mom. But if he really is my brother..." Aggie caught her breath, torn between laughter and tears. "I remember...I used to yank on his ear, when he was stubborn and wouldn't do what he was told. We used to scratch and bite like little monsters, but we always ended up laughing."

The only cure for what she felt, the only way to stop the tears from bursting out, was a long, hot, fast run in the park. She hugged her mother, slipped out the front door, and was on all fours the moment she slid into shadows.

⁊⊱⊰⁊

The parking lot stretching out behind the Colony Inn lay in darkness. Only two of the ten parking lot lights worked. Brian Thomas belched and glared as he stumbled out of the bar. It was only part of his bad luck that he had parked his car in the deepest, darkest part of the shadows. After the lousy day he had at work, that weird kid who kept him from beating Mulcahy to a pulp, and now feeling dizzy-sick from his evening of beer and whiskey, he didn't need to get lost on the way to his car, too. He sighed and shrugged his shoulders and started across the dark lot.

Something growled in the shadows to his left. He kept walking and tried to look for movement without turning his head. What had that self-defense instructor told him once? Something about never letting enemies know he knew they were there. Try to get an element of surprise and knock them off their feet as soon as possible.

"Yeah, right," he muttered, and tried to convince himself he had heard his own stomach growling.

Something sharp scratched on the pavement just to his right and a few yards ahead. Thomas looked and thought he saw a dark, low-slung shadow dart under a car.

He read a story once about carjackers who hid under the car and when the owner came to unlock the car door, reached up, grabbed his ankles and threw him to the ground. Then they climbed out, searched the dazed victim and took money, keys and anything else that caught their fancy. Thomas vowed to look under his car before he approached it.

A sound like nails on a chalkboard tore through the quiet parking lot. Thomas winced and stopped short and pressed his hands to his ears. Glancing up, he saw a low-slung, dark shadow dart between two cars.

He had to fight to take the next three steps. He stumbled over to the car the shadow had just left.

Four long, deep gouges in the glossy red paint stretched from just under the door latch to the front tire on the left side of the car. It was a Thunderbird, too. That kind of sacrilege made Thomas more nauseated.

He didn't want to know what kind of weapon made that kind of marks. Anything that could gouge through paint and primer into the fiberglass could just as easily shred flesh. He had never been a runner in high school, but he beat the school record for the hundred-meter dash getting to his car.

Halfway there, Thomas realized he only went deeper into shadows. The smart move would be to turn around and head for lights and witnesses. His feet weren't listening to his brain, and kept running for his car.

He didn't have the breath to cry out when something large and solid and *furry* knocked him down from behind. It hit him just above his knees and made him fold up like a jackknife. One flailing arm reached out and his hand connected with something wet and hot, furry in spots and jagged in others. Then Thomas rolled across the pavement, picking up bits of broken beer bottles, crumpled wads of paper, weeds and dust blown into the parking lot during the day.

Something growled in his ear when he fetched up hard against his own car's bumper. It licked his ear and took a mouthful of his hair and yanked, hard.

He screamed, sobbing every time he stopped to take a breath. He was hoarse, but didn't stop screaming even when the police showed up more than forty-five minutes later. The onlookers were amazed that a grown man could scream and cry and manage to blabber the entire sordid story all at the same time. He did it six times in a row before the paramedics arrived and gave him a shot to calm him down.

An hour later, a sleek black shape slid out of the darkness around Dan Moon's house in Brook Park. Leisurely, the wolf moved through the shadows and bushes around the base of the little bungalow, first depositing scent markings, then methodically digging at the roots of every bush. She didn't dig up the bushes themselves, but exposed the roots and slashed them.

That accomplished, sharp teeth flashed and uprooted every marigold, every day lily, every gladiolus. Aggie-wolf then got up on her hind legs and with her forepaws pulled away at the badly-anchored rose trellis. The fall crushed the four fragile, newly-planted rose bushes at the trellis' base.

The sound of the crash echoed through the neighborhood. A dog barked a few houses down, but the wolf let out a soft growl, ending in a whine. The dog stopped barking abruptly.

When silence returned to the street, she scratched out divots bigger than her head all across the yard. The front yard was barely larger than a handkerchief and when the wolf finished, there was more bare dirt than grass remaining attached to the ground. Sharp teeth flashed in a tongue-lolling grin. She trotted around to the back yard and repeated the process all over again; flowers, then divots.

Dan had a new, redwood deck he had bragged about for the last two weeks, trying to coerce Aggie into coming to see it. Aggie-wolf saw it now and wasn't impressed. She trotted up the steps and was just starting to squat and leave the final insult when a truck roared down the street and squealed into the driveway. Headlights flashed, narrowly missing her as she darted into the darkness of the neighbor's yard.

Dark eyes sparkled and the panting of canine laughter throbbed through the night, underscoring the anguished scream that only a man who worshiped his yard could make.

# Chapter Seventeen

When Brody got back to his room at the boarding house Wednesday night, after a long walk to avoid the bus and the other apprentices, he found his room strangely clean.

Everything was missing, down to the sheets on the bed and the dust curls under the bed. Including his duffel bag, every scrap of clothing, his books and the diary Dr. Gorman had started him keeping when he was eleven. Brody wasn't too worried about anybody reading the diary because it was in a language from the Before-Storm-Time. His handwriting was bad enough to make plain English a cipher. It was the fact that someone had taken it that bothered him.

He walked slowly around the room, checking out the spots where he had left his possessions, looking for signs on the floor, taking slow, deep breaths to catch any scent that might give a clue.

The smell of English Leather led him to Dale Carpenter. Something about the way Dale talked about himself, the few times Brody listened, made him suspect the other apprentice had things to hide too.

Brody walked down the hall and listened at the door until he heard enough movement to indicate Dale was alone in the room. He knocked on the door, softly, like he had heard the other apprentices knock on each other's doors when they were being secretive.

"Yeah?" Dale said, yanking the door open. He saw Brody, his eyes went wide and his mouth dropped open. He hesitated just long enough for Brody to grab him by his collar and lift him up high enough his toes didn't touch the ground.

"Where's my gear?" Brody asked in that quiet, reasonable tone of voice that always seemed to frighten people more than shouting. It worked best when people only knew enough about him to make stupid assumptions. Dale, judging from the stink of fear pouring out of his sweaty skin, was one of those people.

"At—at the—the job," he said through the slow choke.

"Why?"

"Mr. Moon said—" Dale got no further.

Brody had heard enough. He threw him backwards, hard enough

for him to land on the bed, bounce and flip heels over head and land on the other side. He wisely stayed there on the floor until Brody stalked away down the hall.

The gates were locked around the construction site when Brody got back. He walked along the fence for a couple hundred feet, looking for the best place to climb over while attracting the least attention.

From the river side of the site, he heard the barking of the drooling, tottery old Dobermans and the creaky voice of their keeper. They wouldn't hear or scent him for at least ten minutes if he moved carefully and stayed out of the breeze. Brody kept walking, checking the edge of the fence for the place where the barbed wire at the top had broken away.

There! Grinning, he peeled off his boots and left them tucked behind some windblown rubbish caught against the fence, then leaped and grabbed hold of the links of the fence with fingers and toes. In seconds he had skinned up and over and dropped lightly to the ground. Now to find his gear. Why hadn't he thought to ask Dale where they had left his things?

Brody tried to think like the childish idiots who had been pestering him. If they were consistent, wherever they put his gear would have a few pathetic booby traps around it.

Two could play those games.

He looked up. Somewhere among the girders and I-beams and precarious perches sat his gear. Brody avoided the ladders and elevator and limited himself to climbing the scaffolding he had seen men clambering up and down all day. That had to be safe. There was no time for anyone to loosen bars and joints between the end of the workday and when the gates were locked.

At the river side, one grizzled Doberman lifted its head and pricked up one drooping ear. It whined. The others didn't hear, too busy inspecting the carcass of a gull that had expired some time that morning and cooked all day in the hot sun.

The first dog whined louder. The Doberman with the cropped left ear raised its head and looked back toward the construction site. A third dog looked at the other two, then took a few hesitant steps toward the shadows and crossbars of the building.

"Hey, guys, whatcha hear?" Smithers looked over his shoulder once at the building, then back out to the river. He thought he could see a girl in a black bikini sitting on the edge of a pleasure boat on the other side of the river.

At least, he thought it was a girl in a black bikini. It didn't occur to him that no girl in her right mind would be in a bikini this late in the day, on the river in the cooling breeze. He only hoped if he waited long enough, she might move. He waved in the general direction of the building.

"Go get him, guys. Eat him up."

Released from attending their leader, the dogs scampered a few yards toward the open end of the building, then slowed to a more sedate trot. One tripped over a tangle of electrical cord someone had dropped from the upper stories and never retrieved. The dog whimpered and hurried to catch up with its mates.

All four stopped, skidding on the sandy concrete when they reached the edge of the shadows surrounding the building. An unfamiliar, tantalizing odor stopped them like they had run up against a brick wall. Instinct told them what the scent meant, but their ancient brains didn't want to believe. The grizzled Doberman whined and lowered its head, stretching out its neck to test the air. The crop-eared one sneezed and shook its head, jangling the studded collar that was almost loose enough to slip off. It whimpered, nudged the first dog, then took two tentative steps toward the dark blot of shadows at the base of a pile of concrete rubble.

A sleek black, white-fanged shape emerged from the darkness inside the building and grinned at the dogs. For two long heartbeats, all four dogs froze. The wolf yawned, revealing dripping fangs and red tongue and the deep expanse of its throat. It tipped its head back, green-brown eyes sparkling maliciously. The breeze off the river ruffled the fur around its neck and a low whine emerged. Then the wolf lowered its head and took a single step toward them.

The dogs whimpered and looked back over their shoulders, expecting Smithers to come rescue them.

The wolf took another step and the third dog piddled, its back legs trembling.

Another whine escaped the wolf. All four dogs lowered their heads and stretched down on their forelegs, submitting.

The whine turned into a growl, lips writhing back further from the wolf's fangs. With a loud snarl, the wolf leaped.

Yelping, running into each other, claws scrabbling on the uncertain footing, the dogs raced toward their keeper, faster than any of them had moved in years.

The wolf grinned and skidded to a stop at the edge of the late afternoon sunshine. He listened with perked ears as the dogs yelped and squeaked and scrambled across the rubble-strewn ground, bumped into each other and bounced off piles of lumber and metal and stone.

"What are you lunatics so upset for?" Smithers groused when they skidded around the six-foot-high cable spool and nearly ran into him.

The old guard stood, gave one more glance at the girl in the black bikini—who still hadn't moved—and turned around. Trotting on his bowed legs, he held his gun in one hand and his whiskey bottle in the other and headed toward the building with the four dogs cowering behind him.

The bottle hit the concrete and shattered with a chiming splat.

The wolf yawned again and let out a little 'whoof.'

"Wa—wa—wa—" Smithers closed his eyes and tried to lift his whiskey bottle to his lips. It wasn't there. That galvanized him into action. He opened his eyes—upset to find the wolf still there—and raised his gun.

In a fraction of a second, the wolf turned and fled back into the shadows, vanishing without a sound.

"Why can't you move like that?" Smithers groused. Then he gasped. "Gotta call the police. Gotta call the animal warden. Gotta call the Marines!"

He kicked up sand and pebbles as he ran around the side of the construction site for the gate and the office. No way was he going to take the shortcut through the building. Slipping and sliding, he kept changing direction every few steps, unsure where to go, what to do.

Brody sat on the sidewalk with his back against a telephone pole, putting on his boots, when the old man slid up to the gate and dropped his keys four times before finding the right one to unlock the gate and let himself out. The four dogs huddled around his legs, impeding every step.

"Did you see it?" Smithers spluttered. He bent over, hands braced on his thighs and gasped for breath. "There's a wolf back there." He waved a shaking hand toward the construction site, then gaped when he realized the gate hung open.

"A wolf? In Cleveland? Naaaah." Brody leaped to his feet, scooped up his duffel bag and backpack, and started down the sidewalk. He glanced back once at the clang of the gate slamming shut, and grinned.

The day wasn't a total loss, though he would probably spend the evening finding a new place to stay. He suspected moving out would get him in trouble with Harsey Construction, but right now, he was in too good a mood to care.

≈≈

Brody was just stepping out of the trailer as Aggie drove onto the construction site Thursday morning. He had probably just put his half-gallon carton of milk in the refrigerator. That was all he ate for lunch, or for the whole day, besides four refills of the water bottles everyone wore clipped to their belts.

Dorayn had brought him over on Tuesday and asked if Brody could put his lunch in the refrigerator in the office, so he wouldn't have to drink warm milk at lunchtime.

She wondered where Dorayn was. Aggie closed her car door and started across the gravel yard to ask Brody. Then she heard the angry voices coming from the office trailer. Her father's, pre-eminent. Dan's a close second. Dorayn's voice fought to break through the other two's strident tones. Aggie couldn't make out individual words and as she drew closer to the dusty white trailer, she suspected she should be grateful. She smelled the bitter, burned acid stink of anger. Its energy traveled through the flimsy metal walls of the trailer like cracks in parched ground, threatening an earthquake. She stepped up into the doorway and held her breath until her father noticed her.

Jack stopped with his mouth open, face just starting to turn red, his thinning hair sticking out from his head like a corona of static. He had a bad habit of running both hands through his hair, sometimes yanking handfuls if the situation was particularly bad. Aggie didn't see any strands on the shoulders of his blue shirt or dusting his trout tie, so things hadn't gotten too bad. Yet.

"There's no way any of the apprentices can be blamed," Dorayn said, overrunning Dan for a few seconds. "They don't do anything without somebody double-checking it during and after. You're not putting this on any of those boys."

"What's wrong?" Aggie broke in.

"Nothing, honey." Jack tried to grin. He only managed to look nauseated.

"Somebody's trying to blame the apprentices for something," she said, and continued into the office.

"We're not *trying* to blame anybody," Dan grumbled. "Those kids messed up some key work in preparing the support braces. We have to re-do it all before we can go on to the next phase."

"We're just lucky the building inspector is a good buddy of good old Dan," Dorayn said. "Could have been a lot worse. Fines and bad marks on our record. Right, Jack?"

The underlying sharpness of his tone and the burning look he cast Dan made the hairs stand up on the back of Aggie's neck. She stared at the three men. Lightning nearly flashed between Dan and Dorayn before the older man turned and left the office trailer. Dan and her father watched him go. Aggie wished she could read minds, but she suspected what she read in the air and saw in their faces told the same story. Then Dan left.

"Dad?" She watched her father go back to his desk and sink down into his chair.

"Nothing to worry about, honey."

"Dad, that building inspector was supposed to just pass over some big mistake, wasn't he?"

"Why would an inspector ignore something dangerous?" Jack didn't look at her, but started fussing with papers on his desk.

"He's a good friend of Dan's, so he shouldn't have even come out here?"

"Sweetheart, there's an awful lot you don't know about the construction business and codes and all that silly legal work." He smiled, but didn't meet her eyes.

"Are we in trouble, Dad?"

"No. Not at all." Jack shook his head, making more hair stand out. With a gusting sigh, he pushed up from his chair. "It's a good thing Dan calmed him down, though. A really good thing." Shaking his head, he stepped out the door.

Aggie didn't want to sit around the office if Dan came back in and tried to convince her he was right. She wanted to talk to Brody. If she touched him, would that break through the barrier between their minds? What was wrong with him, that he couldn't hear her? They were twins, after all.

*If* he was Kaenarr. It had been nine years since she and Lara landed in the river. They had grown up, changed from the battered children they were. There was so much they couldn't remember—maybe Brody had forgotten everything, through the trauma of the storm and physical abuse? Maybe that blocked his ability to hear her call?

The problem right now, though, was how to touch him without giving one of Dan's followers an excuse to harass Brody. If she showed the slightest interest, they would think she was interested in him.

Aggie laughed as she came up with the perfect plan. She needed some backup, though, just in case people asked questions. That was easily handled with a mental call to Lara. In moments, it was arranged. Aggie scribbled down Allison's phone number and address and fought not to laugh as Lara showed her the younger girl's blushing excitement.

Brody and Dorayn were on ground level, sorting through a tangle of tools and scrap, when Aggie found them. Brody glanced up when she was still halfway across the yard. She wondered if he sensed her presence as clearly as she could sense his now.

"There you are," she said, and waved the piece of paper. "Allison asked me to give you her number. If you're free tonight," she added with a little shrug. Dorayn caught her eye and grinned, shaking his head as if he knew exactly what she was up to. Aggie held out the folded paper, a short enough length that Brody's fingers had to touch hers when he reached—eagerly—to take it.

Nothing happened. No zap or sting of power, no blue sparks of magic. Aggie bit her lip against a growl of disappointment. Brody grinned and jammed the paper deep into his pocket.

Aggie caught Gil Doyne and a couple other members of Dan's gang watching. She hoped they had heard what she said.

⁂

Aggie came back from running errands just before lunch. She got out of her car in time to catch the sparkle of sunlight on water as it fell from the second floor in a glistening stream, straight down on Brody's bare head. The sipper-bottle followed and bounced off Brody's shoulder with a hollow, echoing thud. Aggie winced, even though Brody didn't flinch.

Brody didn't react at all, neither picking up his pace to get out from under the water nor looking back at the bouncing bottle nor looking up to see his tormenter. He continued across the yard to the storage shed and went inside and came out ten seconds later with a red metal tool box tucked under his arm.

From Aggie's vantage point on the ground, it seemed like half the working gang stopped and moved a few steps closer to the ladder Brody had to climb. He and Dorayn were on the second floor, putting together a support system for the power cables to keep them out of the way while the flooring was being installed. Aggie clenched her fists, positive there had to be some nasty trick waiting. Should she warn him? Would that only draw more attention to him?

*Brody? Kaenarr? I know you're there!* She shouted with all her mental strength, but Brody didn't pause or look around. *I swear, you're suffering brain damage from testosterone!*

He never tipped his head back to look up at the ladder, never looked left or right or even flinched as the cement truck roared into the lot almost on his heels. He could have been the only one in the entire construction site.

Aggie slowly walked to the trailer door, watching, not caring if anyone saw her. She suspected they were so intent on watching Brody, waiting for something, they never noticed her.

He avoided the ladder. Four running steps took him to a length of rusting, galvanized pipe as thick as his waist that had been removed from the side of the building. It leaned against the wall, out of the way until somebody came to cart it away to the junkyard. Brody jumped up on it and ran lightly up to the second floor without hesitating or slipping, despite the steep angle. Aggie knew from experience how heavy that toolbox had to be, how it had to throw off his balance. It wasn't easy walking those pipes when they lay flat on the ground. She had seen enough construction workers fall and tear their clothes and hands when goofing around on similar pipes. Brody climbed it as easily as if he were barefoot and going on all fours.

Smiling, Aggie paused on the steps into the office and studied the faces of the men who had gathered to wait for Brody to climb the ladder. She caught a few disgruntled looks pass between some of the higher level jerks in Dan's gang.

It just wasn't fair that by beating his tormenters at their game, Brody earned more trouble in the future. Aggie tried to plan how to warn him. Maybe she should try to confront him this evening when he went to visit Allison. Maybe she should offer him a ride to visit Allison, and keep him prisoner in her car until they had that long-overdue talk.

~ ~

Brody took off his helmet, wrinkling up his nose at the sour smell of sweat on hot plastic and the metallic bite of the reinforcing bands. The metal had itched against his scalp all morning. Working in the full sunlight had been worth it just to keep away from the other apprentices and Dan Moon's gang.

Now, the gauntlet awaited him. Dorayn went to his truck to get his lunch bucket, leaving Brody alone in the lunchtime noisy yard. Squaring his shoulders, Brody fastened his gaze on the door of the office trailer and headed across the gravel yard. He felt every piece of stone through the soles of his boots, every brush of the breeze across his shoulders and face, heard every intake of breath, felt the gaze of the other workers raking him from head to foot.

It was almost as bad as his first day of school. He had insisted on going the day the teachers certified he had caught up with his age group. Dr. Gorman had tried to talk him out of it, to wait until fall, but Brody had insisted. How was he supposed to know that being the new kid was bad enough in sixth grade, but coming in the middle of April not only marked him as different, it make it impossible to make any friends before summer vacation?

This was worse than sixth grade, Brody knew. These were grown men with years of nasty tricks. He had already dodged enough missiles to know the throwers were getting angry and moving up from water and bottles to tools and stones.

The shade of the office trailer was welcome, the air cool even without air conditioning or fans. Brody paused in the doorway to let his eyes adjust and looked around. Jack Harsey was on the phone, with Dan Moon hunched over the desk, watching him. They seemed to be carrying on a silent conversation with hand signals and grimaces. Aggie had her back to the door, working on her computer.

"Hi." She turned around, smiling a little, not at all startled to see him standing there, watching her.

Brody still didn't understand how she could feel the presence of others in the trailer when they made no noise coming in. Nobody he knew could have that sensitive hearing. At least, nobody he could remember since waking up in the hospital.

"Lunch," he said, and pointed at the refrigerator. He waited until she nodded, then walked across the carpeted floor to open the door.

"Thanks for reminding me. I've been kind of caught up in all this." She stood and came around the drafting table full of blueprints to join him at the refrigerator.

Brody knew which bag was hers; despite the cold her clean, warm scent still clung to the plastic. He handed it to her.

"Thanks," she said, and rested a hand on his arm. "Be careful out there, Brody. You can't keep dodging those jerks forever, and the more you do, the angrier they'll get. You could get hurt badly."

How did she know what was going on out there? He looked into her eyes for a long moment and forgot what he had been thinking.

Somewhere in the shadows of his memory, beyond the forest and the storm and the pain, he had known someone else with the same dark, deep eyes. Someone who laughed with him and raced through the forest and snuck treats to him to eat under his blankets when they both should have been asleep. Someone who pulled on his ear to stop him when he wanted to do something that would get him into trouble.

"They think you're breaking the law if you don't let their stupid jokes bother you," she continued.

"Aggie?" Dan's voice made her flinch.

Brody fought an urge to turn around and clip his boss one across the chin. Only a blind man could miss the flicker of distaste in her eyes.

"What is it, Dan?" She squeezed Brody's arm and stepped past him toward her father's desk.

Jack was still on the phone, but Dan had turned to face them. He glared at Brody, then smiled when he turned to Aggie.

"Why don't we go get some lunch?"

"I brought mine." She hefted her bag and thermos.

"I know, sweetheart, but—"

"I'm not your sweetheart, Dan." Aggie sounded more tired than upset.

Brody headed for the door. He had heard the gossip from both sides. Dorayn said Dan didn't know up from down when it came to Aggie Harsey. Dan Moon was a big bag of hot air, blustering and threatening and telling everybody else how to live, but he couldn't control Aggie. According to Dan's gang, he was on the verge of marrying Aggie and taking over the company.

"So, how are you and Aggie getting along?" Dorayn asked, when Brody settled down on a pile of boards next to him. He sighed when Brody could only give him a shrug for answer. "You two really should talk."

"Why?"

"You're a foster kid, right?" Dorayn waited until Brody nodded. "So was she. Harseys adopted her."

"If I make nice to Aggie, her father'll adopt me?" Brody didn't know why his heart started thumping so fast and hard, banging against his ribs.

"You're a little old for that, kid." He shook his head, his crooked grin making Brody think the older man knew everything there was to know about him, and things he had forgotten about himself, too. "You know, Aggie had it rough when she first got fostered. You met her friend Lara, right? Well, the two of them were kidnapped and beat up something awful, and then just dumped. Right in the middle of a freak storm. In the middle of the park. It was July, nine years ago." He didn't seem to notice when Brody choked on a mouthful of milk and sat up straight and stared at him. "I was there. That's how I got my job with Harsey. I helped fish the girls out of the river. Jack Harsey and his wife were there. They took charge of Aggie while the rest of us were trying to keep Lara alive. They fell in love with Aggie. Jack remembered me and he gave me this job." Dorayn tilted his head to one side and frowned. "You okay, kid?"

"Yeah. Fine. A freak storm, in July, nine years ago?" Brody looked at the office trailer as if he could conjure Aggie and make her tell him...tell him what? She probably didn't remember any more than he did.

How could he broach the subject with her, anyway? Should he? What good would it do? The past was better left buried. Several times, he had tried asking questions, getting information from the people who had been there when the Coopers found him. It had only led to trouble. Questions only brought reporters onto his tail. He didn't need that.

Aggie certainly didn't need that kind of harassment, either. She had been nice to him. He wouldn't do that to her.

※ ※

Brody knew he was in trouble when he stepped onto the plank across a gap in the second floor grid and felt the board move. It should have been held tight with C-clamps at both ends. His gaze shot to the C-clamps and even from ten feet away he saw the half-inch gap between the clamp and the wood.

The smell of mud, oil and wet metal filled his nostrils. There should have been dry, sterile dirt and the scent of concrete dust in the air directly below him. The jackhammers had torn up the foundation on Tuesday, threatening his ears to the bursting point. It hadn't rained since then, so where did the mud come from?

That moment of distraction cost him. Brody finished lifting his foot for the second step, intending to move backwards off the unsteady board.

Something hit the board under him, hard and solid and fast enough to jar his footing loose. Brody shifted forward and had to put his other foot down to steady himself. His boot slipped on the board.

The smell of oil came from the wood. He felt the grit that covered the layer of oil on the wood, then the slickness. He tried to shift his weight back onto his other foot. No such luck. Brody dropped to his knees, planning to grasp the un-oiled sides of the board to regain his balance.

"Brody?" Dorayn, only four steps behind him, had finally realized something was wrong.

He didn't have time to answer. Brody hit the board with his knees and realized as he bounced that this board didn't belong there. It was too thin. It creaked and groaned and swayed in the middle. It shifted in its loose moorings at either end and cracked under the impact of his falling weight.

The ground was only twelve feet below. Brody rolled off the board and twisted in mid-air so he wouldn't impact the ground with his side.

His move knocked the board loose from the C-clamps. Brody heard the rattle, the clang of loose C-clamps falling and hitting the girders and support bars, the hollow clatter of the board hitting at one end and then twisting through the air, directly above him.

A sparkle in the air distracted him. Silver sparkles. Vague memories lashed him, driving the breath from his lungs. He froze, remembering the pain, the terror, the anger. The black patch in his memories tried to expand and swallow him whole.

No. He refused to remember. He had put it behind him. It was the only way to survive.

Then he couldn't concentrate on anything but landing. Wolf instincts took over, wiping all else from his consciousness. He relaxed his ankles and rolled forward to absorb the impact. Head over heels in a loose ball, in mud and oil, dead fish and river weeds. Now he knew where the water came from to make the mud. The board hit him a glancing blow across the side of his face and knocked his hard hat loose. Then one C-clamp tumbled down and clanged against the back of his skull.

# Chapter Eighteen

Somewhere far away, Brody heard the honking of horns, the rumble of mid-afternoon traffic, a police siren, the sounds of someone laughing and talking above the shriek of some stupid rock song in a bar further along the riverbank.

He took a deep breath and choked on mud filling his mouth and nostrils. Brody cautiously lifted his head, checking for broken bones and twisted muscles. Silver sparks filled his vision for a few seconds.

Feet thudded on ladders. The elevator clanged and rattled its way down to the ground floor. Men shouted. Brody lay still, on his side, breathing cautiously through the mask of mud, and thought he heard laughter through the shouts of surprise. Would they be relieved or angry when he stood up and walked out of there unhurt? He felt bruises forming from the impact, but the mud had softened his fall and he still knew how to fall without getting hurt.

"Brody?" Dorayn's voice echoed off the metal beams and the remnants of concrete and brick.

"I'm okay." He rolled onto his hands and knees and pushed himself upright. Brody moved slowly, just in case he wobbled. He wouldn't let his enemies see any weakness in him. Not now.

"You are incredible, kid. You know that, don't you?" Dorayn said. He came to a stop five feet away and jammed his gloved fists into his waist. He stared Brody up and down, slowly shaking his head.

"Get out of my way, you rock-heads," Aggie growled, and pushed her way through the gathering crowd of men.

She stomped her way across the rubble, hands clenched, shoulders hunched. Brody smelled her anger and fear, sweet and hot and clean even through the mud and oil and filth filling the air and clogging his nose. Then she stepped around the last man. Her mouth fell open as she looked him up and down.

"Are you okay?" She barely waited for him to nod before she turned sharply on one heel and surveyed the workers. "I know none of you have the guts to admit which one of you geniuses thought up this trick."

"Trick?" someone gasped from the back of the crowd. Brody

thought it was an apprentice.

"I was standing in the yard and saw what happened." Aggie stalked over to the board and nudged it with the edge of her moccasin, wiping away the grit and revealing the gleam of oil. "This isn't an accident. That board isn't thick enough for walking. The moron who put it on the bridge is either too stupid to work here, or did it deliberately, to hurt someone. Which excuse is it?"

Her voice cracked. The men gathered around recoiled. Aggie was the boss's 'little girl,' and it suddenly became clear that if she wanted, she could get them fired. Brody heard her anger, but he also heard the fear.

Fear for him?

"Come on, Brody." She held out her hand for him.

"I'm just—"

"You're going to the hospital to get checked out. I don't care if you're a stunt man from Hollywood, nobody takes a fall like that without getting hurt." She raked the crowd with her gaze again. "I'm going to insist on X-rays and every bit of evidence necessary to *hang* the jerk who did this to you." Aggie grabbed his hand and led him away at a fast trot.

"But Aggie—" He coughed and spat up more mud.

The hot sun immediately started drying the outer edges of the mud caking his hair and sticking his clothes to his flesh. Brody felt twenty pounds heavier.

"I know you're okay. I could tell just watching you move. And Dorayn wasn't worried. He'd insist on coming with us if he thought you were hurt." She let go of his hand but kept moving toward the office trailer. Brody stayed with her despite an urge to run in the other direction.

How long had it been since it was fun to get really icky, sticky, grossly dirty?

"You deserve the rest of the afternoon off after what happened, and you need to change your clothes." She didn't go into the office and Brody was glad. Then he saw her pull keys from her pocket and head for her car.

"Not good." He stopped short and gestured down at his muddy, oily clothes.

Aggie grinned and he thought she was the most beautiful person he had ever seen. The sparkle of fear still lit her eyes, but she started to relax now. He sensed the crackling tension leak out of her muscles and her sharp scent softened.

"Wait just a second." She darted up the steps into the office.

Brody didn't hear her speak to anyone and he decided there was no one in the office trailer. That was a relief; he didn't look forward to hearing Jack's reaction to what happened to him. He knew Dan would either chew him out or laugh.

"Here." Aggie jumped down the steps with a clean, faded blue flannel shirt in her hands. She waited until he turned his back, peeled off his sodden shirt and T-shirt and put on the flannel shirt. He swam in it until it stuck to the oily mud that covered his chest in black streaks. "That's Dad's, for when he feels like taking off his business suit and climbing around with you guys like in the old days. He won't mind at all," she hurried to add, when Brody opened his mouth to ask.

She opened up the trunk and pulled out a car blanket, then wadded up his muddy shirts and put them in the trunk.

"Wrap the blanket around your pants, take off your boots and put them in the trunk, and we're set." She moved around to open up her door, clearly assuming he would do as she told him.

Brody obeyed. It was either that or stand there and argue until they gathered a crowd of witnesses.

The smell of warm vinyl and lemon air freshener enveloped him, subtly woven with Aggie's clean, musky scent. Brody relaxed into the seat cushions and wriggled his stocking feet into the carpeted floor matt. There were worse ways to spend the afternoon. Maybe he had earned some free time. He refused to think of the razzing he would get in the morning.

"You sure you're okay?" Aggie asked as she slid into the driver's seat and put her key into the ignition.

"Fine." He nodded, and winced when the lump on his head made itself known with a sudden, sharp throb. Brody pressed his hand against the spot and told it to shut up.

"What's that, then?" She smiled and reached over to feel the slowly rising lump. "No blood, at least. Something clobbered you when you fell, or after?"

"After." Brody felt a little foolish, remembering how the C-clamp and board had tumbled down, as if he were the Coyote in the old 'Road Runner' cartoons.

"Want to tell me what happened?" she asked, and started the engine.

Brody told her. He didn't think it would do him any good to try to avoid the truth. She asked questions that surprised him with the attention to detail. When did he notice the C-clamps were loose? When did he realize the board was too thin? When did he notice the oil spread under the dirt? He described every sensation for her, from the first wobble of the board to the taste of the oily mud in his mouth. He didn't pay attention to his surroundings until the car drove past the Greek society college buildings on Bridge Street, then turned up the flagstone driveway next to the white wood-frame Century house.

Mrs. Harsey was in the front yard, weeding the flowerbeds. She stood up, shading her eyes with one hand, and a frown of concern crossed her face when she saw Aggie's car. Something inside Brody ached, catching an echo of another woman who frowned and worried about him. Not Mom Cooper. Someone before that. Someone with dark brown hair touched by flames, and gray eyes, who laughed and scolded and held him. Someone who smelled sweet, like rain-drenched soil, who loved him more than anyone else in the world.

Brody shook his head, almost welcoming the ache that came with the unwise move. He had to push those memories of his mother far into the darkness of the past. She had to be imagination, not memories—because if his mother loved him that much, how had he ended up in Pennsylvania, battered and alone?

He envied Aggie her mother, who worried when she came home unexpectedly in the middle of the afternoon.

❧❧

Aggie paused in the hallway between the laundry room and the kitchen and listened to the muffled pattering of the shower upstairs. Brody's clothes were more mud than oil, fortunately. She had used extra soap and swished his clothes through a strong solution of pre-wash treatment before dumping everything into the washer.

Now for her headache and whatever aches he had discovered while washing up. Peppermint tea to soothe, with a few other herbs thrown in. She turned on the back burner, filled the teakettle with water and put it on to boil before she fixed their cups. She never used bagged tea and refused to use the assortment of strainers to keep tea free of bits of leaves and bark and twigs. Aggie suspected Brody wouldn't be one of those men who could handle road-kill without blinking, but gagged at a few bits of dried leaves floating around in his cup. Besides, the herbs themselves were good for him, not just the liquid steeped out of them.

Aggie flinched when the background humming of the shower upstairs stopped. It occurred to her that if Dan found out she had brought Brody home, he might take a hand in his followers' nasty tricks. Maybe this afternoon would finally bring on the confrontation where he would give her an ultimatum and she could slam the door in his face once and for all—and he would finally leave her alone. How many times did she have to tell him she wasn't interested before he actually listened?

"You're a coward, you know that, don't you?" she murmured.

"Aggie?" Brody called from upstairs.

"Down here. Come down the back steps at the end of the hall," she directed. The kettle started rumbling and she took it off the burner and poured into the mugs before the water came to a full boil.

"Are you sure this is okay?" He appeared at the bottom of the stairs, barefoot, hair slicked and still dripping a little, wearing blue sweatpants and a green oversized shirt.

"Positive." Aggie hoped he didn't realize she had given him her extra sweatpants. Jack's were far too big, even with a drawstring. "If you're worried about being alone with me, Mom is in the back, watering her flowers."

"Huh?" He let her push him down into the chair at the end of the butcherblock table. Brody waited while she brought the mugs to the table. "Dan Moon's a real jerk, isn't he?"

"Unfortunately, Dad thinks he's the greatest thing since sliced bread, and he wants me to marry Dan."

"What about your Mom?"

"She wants me to...find my own way, my own place. And she doesn't think Dan's anywhere near good enough for me."

"You think Dan told someone to ambush me?"

"Even though I've told him about twenty times already that you're interested in Allison." Aggie choked back a giggle when Brody's face lit up.

"What does she think?" He grinned, and Aggie had the awful feeling Brody was willing to forgive the knot on his head and his bruises just for the chance to talk about Allison.

"She couldn't shut up about you, after that one meeting." She paused to sip at her mug. Not quite strong enough yet. "Today is my fault, I guess. Dan doesn't know when to let go."

"He's a jerk and you're too nice to give him a black eye like he deserves." Brody shrugged and picked up his mug. He sniffed the rising steam. "Is this ready?"

"You're awful calm about this."

"You can't stop a guy from being a jerk, no matter how long and fast and loud you talk." He cocked an eyebrow at her in lieu of a grin and sipped at the tea. Unlike most men she knew, he didn't wrinkle up his nose at the herbal healing concoction.

"All done?" Grace came in through the porch door. She cast Aggie a questioning look before turning back to Brody with a warm, concerned smile.

Aggie knew what her mother wanted to know—had she confronted him with her theory that he was her brother? She knew she was a coward. She had been working up to it, honestly, but how did someone just come out and say, *I think you're a Wereling and my twin brother?*

"Let's take a look at that bump of yours," Grace continued, when Aggie shook her head in answer to her silent question. She stepped up to the sink and washed her hands, then picked up the gauze pads and antibiotic wash she had brought down earlier.

Brody winced when she parted his hair enough to get a good look at the back of his head. Grace patted his shoulder and dabbed on the antibiotic.

"Broke the skin, but I don't think it's any worse than that. Just a few more seconds—there." She stepped away to toss the stained gauze in the wastebasket, then settled down at the table with them. "So,

Brody, you're from Pennsylvania?"

He gave Aggie a wide-eyed look, which she couldn't answer. What was her mother doing?

"What's your family like?" she continued.

"I don't have any." Brody shrugged and bent his head over his cup of tea.

"What, you were raised by wolves?" slipped out of Aggie's lips, earning a sigh from her mother. Brody raised his head and met her gaze with a grin for a few seconds. "Sorry."

"Wolves are a lot nicer than some people I've met." He shrugged again. "I'm a foster-kid. I don't know where my real family is or who they are or anything."

"Then your name—" Grace prompted.

"My foster-parents gave it to me."

"But they didn't adopt you?"

"Mom," Aggie muttered.

"I'm sorry, Brody. I'm just trying to understand where a nice boy like you comes from. How did you lose your family?"

Now Aggie understood. She wished she could tell her mother the tactic, to lead Brody into talking about their similar circumstances, wasn't working. The tension in the air felt like a guitar string tuned so tight it would snap at any moment.

"More like they lost me." His forced smile was more a grimace. "Somebody wanted to get rid of...doesn't matter. I don't know and I don't want to know. Any sugar for this?" He picked up his cooled mug of tea.

"Aggie was abandoned, too," Grace said. She slid the pot of honey across the table to him. "The worst day of her life was the best for Jack and me, when we found her."

"Mom..." Aggie closed her eyes. She didn't want to see if Brody got disgusted by Grace's sentimentality.

The doorbell rang. Grace bestowed a sunny smile on them and got up to answer it.

This was Aggie's chance, but she wasn't quite sure what to say. It would all be so much easier if Brody's mind was open to hearing her. Or maybe she should shift to wolf and take her chances that he was Kaenarr and not an unreasonable facsimile?

"From the way they were talking," Dan said, striding into the kitchen ahead of Grace, "I thought I'd find you at the hospital getting a neck brace and a hundred stitches."

"He's bruised and sore, a few cuts, but nothing serious," Grace said. "The worst of it was his clothes, thank goodness."

"Just enough time for a tea party, huh?" He pulled out Grace's chair, to settle down next to Aggie.

"Why don't I go check on your clothes?" Aggie said, and got up to hurry down the hall to the laundry room. The moment and opportunity had been lost.

Brody's clothes were still damp. The four of them sat there for another twenty minutes, making small talk. Rather, Dan chatted with Grace, tried to drag Aggie in the conversation and ignored Brody. It was a relief to everyone when the dryer buzzed and Aggie could give Brody his cleaned clothes.

That relief died quickly when Dan insisted on driving Brody back to the work site. Aggie decided since she had already destroyed Dan's yard and garden, she would dig holes in the tires of his truck and ruin the paint job.

She forgot all that when she and Grace walked Brody and Dan out to Dan's truck, parked along the curb. Brody hadn't buttoned up his shirt and when he turned to climb into the passenger seat, the angle of the sun was just right to highlight the V of skin under his collarbone.

Aggie lost her breath and stared at the triangular, dark mark the size of her thumb. Birthmark or tattoo? How many times had she been asked the same question? A hoard of memories raced through her mind, like cats released from a closet where they had been imprisoned.

Then Brody pulled the truck door closed, Dan gunned the engine and they were gone, speeding down the street above the speed limit. Aggie took a stumbling step into the street, as if she could grab the bumper and drag the truck back to her.

"Brody...please...come back," Aggie whispered. She couldn't seem to get her breath.

She rubbed her thumb against the corresponding mark on her chest, just below her collarbone.

One of her oldest memories was a story her mother—Aggie thought it was her birth mother—had told her. An ancestor had been burned there, marked by a tiny amulet she wore around her neck. Whether the story said descendants were born with the mark or descendants had to be tattooed there, she couldn't remember.

"Aggie?" Grace slid an arm around her shoulders. "What's wrong?"

"Did you see it, Mom? In his collar?" Aggie tugged down on the collar of her T-shirt, showing her matching birthmark. "It really is him. My brother. Kaenarr."

"Next time," Grace murmured. "Next time, it'll work out."

*Brody, can you hear me?*

Silence. She was sure she felt that heaviness in the mental air that meant the person she tried to call wasn't listening. Like the times Lara had blocked Aggie out because she concentrated on something else.

Brody wasn't listening, that was all. For all Aggie knew, he didn't know he could hear her. Maybe he had forgotten there was anyone to hear.

*Aggie?* Lara's voice sounded thin, as if distance or a thick wall separated them. *What's wrong?*

*Brody is Kaenarr, and I completely screwed up my chance to talk with him.* She felt sick to her stomach, caught between frustration and anger and laughter at the idiocy of the whole situation. *Lara, I ruined everything!*

*Show me,* her best friend said, her voice and mental touch soothing. A single spark of blue emerged in the air in front of Aggie's nose.

In moments, all Aggie's memories of the entire disastrous day spilled between their minds.

*He probably doesn't know he can hear you,* Lara said after a few moments of silence to think. *You have to convince him who you are before he can hear you thinking at him.*

*Duh. What do I do?* She followed Grace back to the house. *You know Dan couldn't have cared less if Brody broke every bone in his body. He just showed up to get in the way. I'm going to get Dan Moon for that, if it's the last thing I ever do.*

*If it weren't for Dan Moon, it might have taken us a few more weeks to have this proof that Brody is Kaenarr. His goons wouldn't have gone after him if Dan didn't disapprove of him.*

*They tried to kill my brother!*

*Let Dan know. If he's really serious about you, he'll be turning himself inside out to make it up to you.*

*I'd like to turn him inside out permanently,* she growled. *But what do I do about Brody?*

*Talk to him tomorrow. Ask him to help you with errands. Buy him lunch. Food always works with Greg.*

*This is my brother, not my boyfriend.*

*Men are men. They either think with their hormones or their stomachs. Look at it this way—once everybody knows Brody is your brother, all those jerks who've been harassing him at work will have to be nice to him.*

*We have to convince Dad, first.* Aggie shivered at the thought. What exactly would Jack Harsey's reaction be?

*Worry about that once you talk to Brody. Oops, got to go. The summer reading program just let out.*

"Thanks," Aggie whispered. She continued through the house, out the back door, and shifted to wolf. She didn't care if any of the neighbors were home at that time of the afternoon. She ran fast enough that nobody saw more than a blur. If the police department got more calls than usual about a big black dog running loose of its chain, Aggie didn't care. She had to get to the park, where she could breathe, where the hidden energy of the land vibrated up through the ground, through her paws and helped her think. Her mind spun with fragments of memories, bits and pieces of images that threatened to make sense, if she could just get enough of them together. Maybe once she had her brother back, he would remember things that would help put that picture together.

. .

"How do I get to Olmsted Falls from here?" Brody asked, as the truck pulled out onto Bagley Road, heading east toward the highway entrance.

"Why?" Dan grunted.

"There's a girl I want to see." He shrugged and nearly suffocated from trying not to laugh. The stink of relief coming from Dan Moon was almost nauseating.

"What's her address?" Dan did a quick turn into a driveway, barely glanced in both directions, and backed out, sending the truck back the way they had just come.

"Don't we have to go back to work?"

"You had a rough day," he said with a shrug. "By the time we get back there, you'll be able to get in—what?—an hour of work? What's her address?"

Brody pulled the paper out of his pocket. He had barely remembered to retrieve it before Aggie took his clothes to wash. There was something wrong with Dan Moon, that he wouldn't believe Aggie wasn't interested, but he'd believe his supposed rival when he expressed interest in a different girl. Brody knew there was a place where people just didn't act that way, where doubting a woman's words was considered an insult worthy of a battle to the blood. He wished he could be sure it existed somewhere real and not just in his dreams.

Wishes like that always got him in trouble. He scolded himself yet again to concentrate on something solid and real—like finding out if Allison was as interested in him as he was in her. Forget about the sparks, the dreams of running through the forest in wolf shape, of finding others like him. Maybe from this moment on, he would stop shifting to wolf and concentrate on being an ordinary guy. If he could have a girl like Allison on his side, would it be so hard?

. .

"So you're Brody." Mr. Terrel nodded slowly, looking Brody up and down as if he had never seen anyone like him before.

The crest fur of Brody's wolf body stood up stiff, irritating the Human body he wore now. Brody wanted to lash out, but he couldn't do that because Allison stood next to him.

Or rather, Allison bounced on her toes next to him, smiling so brightly those blue sparks dusting the air around her turned to gold. Her hand kept twitching, like she wanted to hold his hand. Brody would have grabbed hold of her hand and never let go, but Allison's parents stood on the front steps, two steps above him, and frowned as if they were afraid of saying something wrong.

"Greg and Allison have told us—" Mr. Terrel began, and got a nudge in the ribs from his wife. "They mentioned meeting you the other day at the site. So, you're in construction? How old are you?"

"Seventeen. Give or take." Brody wondered why everybody's parents were so interested in him all of a sudden.

"Still in high school." Mrs. Terrel nodded.

"Mom, can I borrow the car?" Allison said.

Brody almost laughed as a sudden sharp, citrus smell of panic filled the air from both parents. He would have grabbed Allison and kissed her right there in front of them if he dared, in pure gratitude for taking their attention off him.

"The car?"

"Let the girl show off her new temp license," Mr. Terrel said, relaxing visibly. "Where do you plan on going?"

"Just along Columbia. Maybe down Bagley to the Dairy Queen," Allison said with a shrug.

A new, slightly sour tang in her excited, sweet scent told Brody she had lied, even if he couldn't read her body language, the sudden evasiveness in her glance.

"Ah. That's fine." Her father dug in his pocket and pulled out the car keys, tossing them to her. "But no ice cream. Dinner's in an hour."

"Brody, you'll stay for dinner?" Mrs. Terrel asked, earning a muffled squeak of delight from Allison and a new frown from her husband.

"Thanks. That'd be great."

Then Allison grabbed his hand and dragged him down the driveway to the dark green Saturn.

"They don't like it when I go through the park. I don't know why," she confided as she pulled out of the driveway. "Except maybe that Aggie's mom got shot in the park. But that was at night and in the winter. The park is what I want you to see. It's the greatest place. Aggie said you'd probably...well, she said you seemed like a guy who likes wide open spaces and lots of green, and you can't get that where you're staying. So, I'll show you the park and you can go back there to run or whatever when you're off work."

"If you meet me there," Brody said. He muffled a chuckle when Allison blushed bright enough, he could feel the heat from the passenger seat.

He nearly laughed aloud when he realized Allison was taking him back the way Dan Moon had brought him. The urge to laugh strangled when Allison turned down a road bracketed by trees and Brody felt a strange jolt in the center of his chest. He had felt it, riding with Dan, but had attributed it to the conflicting scents coming from the man and his longing to shift to wolf and just run, hard and fast—after leaving a few claw marks in the man's arrogant face.

"Like it?" Allison said as the road turned to blacktop and the car slowed around the first bend and slid into shadows.

"Great. It smells different already." Brody didn't mind the smug little grin she gave him, as if she had just given him the greatest gift of his life. The way his life had been the past few days, this visit to the park might just be that.

He hunched forward in his seat, drinking in all the greenery, and rested his hands on the dashboard so he could feel the shadow-dappled light resting warm and soft on his skin. Allison drove slowly, in silence, along the gently curving road, past the shallows where the ducks congregated and old willows with corrugated trunks leaned over the road and high grass baked in the afternoon sun. Brody rolled down the window and tilted his head so the wind hit him in the face. He had always envied dogs, who could get away with such behavior.

"Aggie says she comes here a lot when things get hectic and she can't take the concrete and noise any longer," Allison said.

"This is great." Brody leaned back in the seat and closed his eyes against the bright sunshine.

He took deep breaths and grinned. He didn't know what he wanted to do more: slide over closer to Allison so he could drown in her sweet, clean scent and bask in her smile, or curl up in the sunshine and sleep away his troubles and let the poisons of city living bake out of his skin. The tension between the two needs was invigorating; nothing like the tensions that had torn at him since he got on the bus last week.

Something tingled and tickled on his fingertips. Brody opened his eyes just as the car went down a slope and crossed a shallow ford. Blue and green and purple sparks spun and swirled above the river. He watched them dart away, following the bank.

"Where does that water go?" he asked.

Allison barely glanced at the river as the car went up the slope on the other side of the ford. "Bonnie Park. Which is where we're headed. There's probably a dozen kids in the wading pool, but it should still be a great place to sit and relax."

"Sounds good."

"Do you like it here?"

"It's great." He traded grins with her.

"There's just something about this section of the Emerald Necklace...sometimes I can believe there's a hidden doorway somewhere around here. That a bolt a lightning will hit and the door will burst open, and we'll be able to jump through to another world."

"What kind of world?" Brody sat up straight. He watched the road winding in front of them, instead of Allison. His fingers ached when he dug them into the upholstery.

"Like this one. Less cars and houses and people...but the same feel, I guess." She shrugged. "Like you could put our world over the other one, and they'd fit together. Like plastic chairs that are made to stack. Dumb way of explaining it, huh? But that's the way I see it. Or feel it, anyway."

She started to slow as they came to an intersection where the park road crossed a major road. The light turned green when they were a half dozen yards away, and the only car in front of them turned right. Allison went straight through. Brody caught glimpses of a wide meadow with tall, sun-scorched grass and more trees, but he was too lost in the images Allison had sketched with her words to really see anything.

"Why do you—I don't know—what makes you think about things that way?" he finally asked, as they turned right at an intersection marked with four stop signs and an arrow that pointed to Bonnie Park.

"It's really Aggie and Lara's fault, I guess. Their lives are such a mystery." Allison's smile had dimmed and seemed tight now. With the wind tugging her scent away, Brody couldn't read her scent to tell how she felt. "They...landed here, I guess. For all anybody knows, they were thrown off a spaceship."

"What?" He had to laugh, because the only alternative was to howl and shift to wolf and run, to shake off the creeping, prickling feeling under his skin.

"It's nine years now. There was this killer, freak storm. I remember because Mom and Dad were so upset by it. Greg and I snuck off for a picnic and our folks were frantic. Like they thought we'd vanish or get hit by lightning." Allison pulled into a parking spot facing the river, what little could be seen over the raw stone wall that bordered it. She sighed, letting out a long, deep breath.

"Anyway, they found Lara and Aggie right here, in the river. Beat up something awful. That's why Lara wears that brace. They thought she'd never walk again. Somebody kidnapped them and beat them up. Burned and cut and Aggie had broken arms and her jaw and...we met Lara after she was put with the Hendersons. They're foster-parents. That was after she got out of the hospital, and she still looked awful. Why would somebody do anything like that to little kids?" She turned to Brody with sad, beseeching eyes, as if he could give her the right answer that would fix everything.

Brody thought he would suffocate. He scooted back in the seat so his back pressed against the door. He felt his fur begging to break through his skin, a howl clawing at the back of his throat, and an ache deep in his bones. Memories of falling and fire and knives through every nerve suffocated him, tried to reach inside him and turn him inside out.

"A freak storm? Nine years ago?" He shook his head, hoping this was just a bad dream and he could wake himself.

"Just like the one that dumped you in Pennsylvania." Allison's eyes widened. She clamped both hands over her mouth and blushed bright red.

"How do you know that?" he whispered. All the pressure inside him shattered, leaving him feeling hollow. He sat perfectly still. He felt as if everything around him elongated and Allison sat miles away, with tears filling her eyes.

"Aggie and Lara are looking for other kids like them. They just want some answers. You wouldn't answer their letter."

"What letter?" Suddenly, he knew. Didn't Dorayn say Lara was a librarian in Berea, just like Allison? Didn't that reporter have a return address at the Berea Library? His fingers went white, clutching at the door handle and the gearshift between them. "What's Lara's last name?"

"Monroe."

"All this time, I thought some jerk reporter was going for a new angle."

"Brody, we're serious! We have to find answers. Don't you want to know what really happened to you?"

"What kind of answers? There's a bunch of sickos out there, maybe some cult that practices child sacrifice? That our own parents don't care enough about us to find us? I have enough problems without hooking up with a bunch of crazies trying to make something out of all this."

"Don't you want to know the truth?" The tears glistened even brighter and bigger in Allison's eyes, and blue sparks danced along their edges.

Blue sparks and purple sparks and green sparks. Brody summoned up the fury of raking claws and fangs dripping blood to push away the guilt he felt over her tears. Anger was the only way to shield himself and survive.

"No. I want to go somewhere nobody points fingers and makes up crazy stories and they don't care that I don't have a name or a family. I want to find a nice girl and get married and have a bunch of kids and fall asleep in front of the TV and get fat and worry about my retirement fund. No mysteries. No reporters. Nobody asking questions and trying to make something mysterious out of a really, really bad part of my life. Okay?"

He glared at her until her sorrow turned to the anger of stung feelings. Brody smelled the tears salt in the air give way to the spicy, sour scent of Allison's anger, and he was relieved. She wiped her tears away with the back of her hand and turned the key in the ignition so hard and fast he thought she'd break it off. They drove back to her house in silence. He slouched in the seat and closed his eyes. The wind ruffled his hair and brushed against his face, but he couldn't enjoy it. He couldn't even breathe deeply enough to catch the thousands of scents and read the world around him.

Mrs. Terrel was at the end of the driveway, checking the mailbox when Allison pulled up in front of the house. Brody only said good-bye and tried to smile because he knew Mom Cooper would be disappointed if he was rude. It wasn't Mrs. Terrel's fault he was furious with Allison.

"You're not staying for dinner?" the woman asked. Brody almost believed she wanted him to stay, but he remembered the discomfort both Allison's parents showed when he first arrived at the house. Were they in on the scheme to dig into his past, just like Allison and Lara and Aggie?

"I have to do things. Thanks anyway." He tried to smile, and took a few backwards steps toward the street. If she would just stop looking at him, he could leave.

"Can I give you a ride to the Rapid station?" Greg called from the side of the house. He stepped out, pushing a wheelbarrow full of plants. The smell of freshly-dug soil and healthy, green growing things billowed out from him in an intoxicating wave. Green sparks spun around him like fireflies in a spiraling dance.

Brody remembered *a man with golden hair and blue eyes, green sparks cascading off his fingertips to create images in the air.* He remembered *laughing with a red-haired, green-eyed girl, laughing so hard they rolled on the ground, tickled by the green sparks, entranced by the images of dancing animals.*

Pain shot through his bones on the heels of that memory. Brody remembered why he tried so hard to forget during the day, when he was awake. The good dreams only came at night. Daylight brought the bad memories.

"I need to walk. Thanks," he called over his shoulder as he headed down the street.

At the first bend in the road, trees grew thick enough to offer him some cover. Brody barely remembered to look in all directions before he leaped the ditch and stepped into the shadows and shifted to wolf. A low whine escaped him as he choked off a howl, and ran.

In his mind, images dug against the wall he tried to hold against them. *The red-haired girl screamed and writhed under an onslaught of purple sparks. A red-haired woman flung herself into the storm, fury brightening her face like lightning. Arms spread, blue sparks erupted from her in a wave that enfolded the girl and Brody and...there were others, but he couldn't remember who. The blue sparks soothed the pain and picked them up and flung them all into darkness.*

Brody ran, letting his nose choose his path, while his pain and fury pushed him to speed that threatened to tear his muscles from his bones. He dug his claws into the soil and smelled blood, instead.

⁂

"How should I know where he went?" Dan Moon's voice snapped through the phone lines.

Aggie sighed and knew she had just committed a major error,

calling him to ask where Brody was. She was just grateful she was on the phone and not in the same room with him. The stink of his anger and jealousy would probably make her sick.

"I'm just—Mom's worried about his head. He banged it pretty hard. The last thing we need is Brody getting dizzy on the fifth floor and falling."

"Let me take care of Brody. That's what your Dad hired me for, right? To worry about all the problems." Dan's little chuckle, obviously meant to be reassuring, just made the hairs stand up on Aggie's neck.

She knew if she pressed the matter any further, it would make Dan more determined to give Brody a hard time. Aggie didn't need her brother driven away before she could break through that wall in his mind and convince him of her identity.

Maybe Brody didn't remember?

No. He had to remember. Where else would that picture of a wolf in the Flats have come from, except her twin brother running as a wolf, exploring his temporary home?

"Well?" Grace asked, after Aggie thanked Dan, fended off an invitation to go to a movie, and hung up.

"Dan says he took Brody back to the site and Brody left early to get some aspirin and go to bed. I didn't tell him I called Brody's boarding house first, and that creep at the front desk said he wasn't there."

"Maybe he's taking a long walk," Grace offered.

"Can you imagine Brody telling Dan anything he planned to do?" Aggie sank down at the kitchen table and snatched up two freshly baked chocolate chip cookies off the cooling rack. Thank goodness her mother understood what she was going through.

"If he wanted to get away from there and not have anybody question him, why not?" She turned back to scooping more dough onto the cookie sheets.

Aggie knew that had to be the answer. She ate four more cookies, then forced herself away from the table and went outside. She curled up on the old wooden swing hung from the ancient oak tree, took deep breaths of the fresh air, and tried to calm herself enough to think.

What should she do about Brody?

Kaenarr, rather. She had to keep reminding herself that Brody was her brother. Her twin brother. Her younger twin brother. By twenty minutes.

How she knew such things with such certainty, she had no idea. But she and Lara had learned over the years that when such flashes of knowledge came, they were true and reliable.

Aggie was Aguirra, the elder, the responsible one. She was pledged to support and protect Lara. No, her name was Alaria. Laramon, which the nurses had changed to Lara Monroe, was...Aggie couldn't quite remember who. Someone important.

Maybe someone involved in the attempt to murder Lara, nine years ago this month? Someone had tried to kill Lara. Aggie and Brody had been caught in the whole ugly mess. How and who, Aggie had no idea. If it had taken nine years to regain that much memory, how many more years would she have to wait until she remembered everything?

The ringing of the phone barely intruded into her swirling, tangled thoughts. Aggie paused every once in a while to call Brody with her thoughts, until her head hurt. It was like she banged her head against a stone wall.

"I'll do more than yank on your ear, little brother, when we finally get all this straightened out," she whispered.

Somehow, that cheered her up. Aggie looked forward to racing and tumbling and mock-fighting with her brother, like they used to do as children, both in wolf shape and Human. Funny how she hadn't missed it until she remembered doing it. What was wrong with her mind, her heart, that none of this worried her until she remembered something she had forgotten?

"Aggie?" Grace stepped out onto the deck. "Dorayn just called." The gentle breeze brought Aggie the scent of sun-warmed roses and the tang of her mother's worry. "He heard Dan talking to you. Dan came back to work alone. Dorayn heard Rodriguez ask about Brody, and Dan said Brody had already left our house when he got here."

"What did he do with Brody?" Aggie leaped from the swing, shifting to wolf before her feet hit the ground.

"Anybody home?" Jack called, his voice boisterous with good cheer, punctuated by the slamming of the door.

Aggie shifted back to Human before Grace could ask. She stepped up onto the deck, legs shaking, swallowing down the howl of fury and terror that made her nauseous with its force.

"Dan wouldn't be stupid enough to hurt Brody. Not in any way that could be traced to him. He probably just left Brody somewhere inconvenient."

"He'd better," Aggie growled.

"Who's ready to eat?" Jack called, stepping up to the sliding door. He grinned and hefted the bags full of Kentucky Fried Chicken and all the extras. Jack always bought enough to feed ten people. "How about we eat outside tonight?"

"That's a good idea," Grace said, forcing up a smile. She glanced at Aggie and shook her head.

Aggie understood. They wouldn't say anything about this to Jack—and she knew her mother would find an excuse for her to leave as soon as possible to start looking for Brody. She would start downtown at the boarding house and work her way outward, investigating all the places a wolf might go for some relief in the middle of the city.

# Chapter Nineteen

Brody crossed the street in Human shape and scuffled his feet in the gravel as he approached the Rapid station. Three hours of running as a wolf and then walking as a Human had helped him work out most of his physical reaction to that afternoon's surprises. He didn't even feel bruised from his fall. Mostly he felt tired and hungry. Maybe a little ashamed about acting like a snot-nose brat. It still hurt, thinking about Allison and the others knowing all about him and pretending they had just met him. His stomach tried to churn again as he thought about Aggie making friends with him, all the while knowing who he was and waiting to pounce. When were they going to hit him with their questions? Did they know he had come to Cleveland to find L. Monroe and get some answers? Were they laughing at him right now?

He snorted and paused at the foot of the steps to go into the train station. No, his mind wouldn't let him conjure an image of Aggie making fun of him. If anything, she was probably worried. He imagined Allison had called Aggie and told her everything that had gone wrong. Brody smiled a little, imagining them searching everywhere to find him. Maybe he would call them when he got back to his new hotel room.

He lifted his foot to climb the steps and felt the prickle down his back that meant someone watched him. Evil intent rode in that focused gaze. Brody felt his fur stand on end in his wolf body. He flexed his fingers, almost feeling his claws breaking through. It took an effort of will not to let the wolf come out. He heard voices coming down the stairs from the stationhouse. His enemies wouldn't attack with witnesses around. He climbed the stairs.

Brody stepped into a covered walkway. Open doors led him to the stairs and up to the station. The other way seemed to lead under the tracks, probably to the other parking lot. Brody grinned and headed for the parking lot. All his walking and wandering had given him a good internal sense of where he was in relation to the long stretch of park roads. He understood why it was called the Emerald Necklace. Each jewel in the necklace had been like an oasis. He plotted his path to take to get back to the closest jewel. Dusk fell, and it wouldn't do him any harm to spend the night in wolf shape, and frustrate his enemies into a headache. If he was lucky, he would lose the hunter immediately.

If he wasn't lucky...once in the Metroparks again, Brody knew the territory would be all to his advantage.

The tension hit him from a new angle the moment he stepped out of the doors and started across the other parking lot. Brody snorted at his own stupidity. Of course, if there were two entrances and his enemies expected him to take the Rapid to get back downtown, they would wait at both entrances. The trick would be to cross the road and pass the Ford plant before they could get through traffic and follow him.

The tension caught up and followed him all the long walk down the road past the Ford plant. The streetlights left only small gaps of darkness and no place where he could shift to wolf and vanish into the night. Not without giving his enemies ammunition to use against him. He didn't need another reporter hearing about wolf sightings and following the story here.

Brody walked slowly, hands flexing into fists and then claws as he jerked them out of his pockets again. His muscles screamed to break into a run. He could run like the wind even with boots on. He opened his senses to the sticky warm night, listening to the sounds bouncing off concrete, inhaling deeply the myriad aromas, the stink of machine exhaust

He traced the outline of his birthmark with the tip of his index finger. It tingled, like the vibrations that buzzed in his fingers and toes when he had visited the Metroparks.

Good sign, or bad sign? Blessing or warning?

"Doesn't matter anymore, does it?" he whispered, and smiled.

Nothing happened by the Ford plant or when he crossed the railroad tracks and walked past Brook Park City Hall and the National Guard building. Brody took a right at the next intersection, aiming for Eastland, which had brought him to the airport and Rapid station in the first place. His sense for open spaces and less traffic guided him now. With every step he took, he sensed he came a little closer to clean soil, open air and deep-rooted trees.

It wasn't that long a walk to the Metroparks entrance in Berea. He could run the entire distance without being winded. The tension coiling through his body gave him the energy. His shadow hadn't made a move to intercept him yet. Brody had seen the same truck pass him four times already, going up and down the road. Someone was keeping an eye on him, maybe reporting to others. He hadn't quite figured out what kind of game his shadow was playing and how many other players were involved. If he started running, they would panic and move in for the attack. He didn't want to signal the enemy that he knew they were there until he reached familiar territory.

Territory familiar to him, anyway.

It was going to turn serious soon, Brody sensed. He had to change it to his game, played by his rules, without the enemy knowing he had done it. Whether he managed that or not, the game wasn't over by a long shot.

He turned right when Eastland crossed Bagley and headed toward the center of town, the path Aggie had taken this afternoon. Brody played with the idea of going to the Harsey house. Maybe confronting Aggie with what he had heard from Allison. For all he knew, Dan Moon was there right now. Brody didn't doubt his shadow or shadows were Dan's goons. No, he wouldn't involve Aggie just yet. He had to take care of this problem, first.

It was good to be the hunter for a change, and turn his enemies into the hunted. Brody grinned into the darkness and picked up the pace.

He turned down Front Street, heading for the Metroparks entrance. He wondered if his shadow thought he headed toward the Harsey house. He hoped they panicked. He hoped they all had cell phones and were making frantic calls to everyone involved, trying to figure out what to do. They couldn't run him down or kidnap him in the center of Berea, with the police station just a few blocks away.

Brody breathed easier when he came to the Triangle and the Civil War monument and saw the big grindstone on the other side of Bridge Street, which marked the Metroparks entrance. Brody nodded, grinning as he noted the 'do not walk' sign had stopped flashing, meaning his green light was about to turn yellow and then red. He raced across the street. A stream of five cars, including that familiar truck, slid through the light. He started left up Bridge Street, aiming toward the Harseys' house.

The truck passed him. He turned around and ran for the Metroparks entrance. Car horns blared and brakes squealed. For all he knew, all five cars were involved in the hunt. Brody laughed.

Time to make the enemy sweat. Make them panic. No matter what they intended for him, they had to know their plan would die the moment he reached the park and vanished among the trees.

He wouldn't vanish immediately. He would lead them deep inside by staying along the road, within the lights, taunting them, making them think he was easy prey.

His fall at work today had not been an accident or a nasty prank; someone wanted him hurt, badly. Maybe even dead. What was to stop them from running him down with a car or using a gun? Nothing and no one—except him, his wits, his wolf self.

In the park, he would be king. The energy flowing through the ground there was like a second heartbeat that came up through his feet. It illuminated the shadows as bright as day to all his senses. He knew where every path led, where each animal denned, where the fish leapt and the birds nested on the water at night.

Did Aggie and her friends, with their mysteries and their ideas of doorways to other worlds, feel the energy throbbing through the park? Did they catch that glimmer of magic in the air? Did they see the sparks that he had seen come from Lara and Allison and Greg?

Brody doubted they did, or they would have done something about it long ago. Different was dangerous, as he had learned almost before he could speak English. They would protect themselves, not open themselves up to danger and torment by trying to find other freaks. Like him. There couldn't be others like him in the world. God wouldn't be so cruel.

Or maybe God wasn't so cruel. Brody had the sensitivity to find places where he could be safe and strong and could hide from his enemies. The park here felt more like 'home' to him than any place had ever been. No one would hurt him here.

Was that why Aggie had wanted him to come to the park? Was that why Allison had brought him there this afternoon? Brody nearly stumbled as he passed the man-high grindstone at the entrance to the Metroparks. Maybe if he hadn't been so angry, he would have sensed something else—maybe he might have stayed around long enough to listen and learn. Maybe they understood.

Maybe he had made a huge mistake.

He would have to take care of that in the morning. Right now, he had trouble to handle.

Brody stretched his legs out as far as they would go. He wished he could have taken off his boots, first.

Headlights speared him like a pin for a butterfly. Two pickup trucks and an Escort hit their brakes in succession. Brody only gave them a passing glance as he rounded the first bend of the road leading toward the stone arch of bridge over the river. He nearly hit a tree with his shoulder.

He thought he recognized all three vehicles from the construction site. Behind him, engines roared and men let out whoops and tires squealed. Headlights scraped the curving road down into the park.

No time.

Brody's boots pounded gravel and asphalt. He came up over the stone bridge and slowed as he skidded around the turn and started down Valley Parkway. He couldn't afford one unsure step, and skipped over the rocks marking the line between grass and jogging trail. Another sideways step and he hit the grass. The headlights caught up with him. He put on a burst of speed and crossed the road. He was inside the park and still not safe.

A quick glance in either direction showed no other car headlights to be seen anywhere. Brody couldn't even use traffic to buy himself some time. On one side was water and mud shallows; a waterfowl refuge. On the other was the open field, gravel parking lot and bath-house for Wallace Lake. Brody ran, pushing until the bushes and road signs blurred in the darkness. The thick stands of trees that meant safety, that would put his enemies on foot and force them to leave their cars to pursue him, were still hundreds of yards away, by the par course and the ford in the river that buzzed with energy.

Brody ran, reaching out his clenched fists and pumping arms for the safety and darkness only a minute or so ahead of him. He couldn't see the trees through the darkness, but he felt a sense of waiting, something holding its breath, as if the trees knew he was there and reached to give him shelter.

There! Moonlight on open water and an open meadow glimmered just ahead. Brody heard the engines roaring, gaining slowly on him. He imagined his pursuers, grumbling at how quickly he could run. None of them had the brains to wonder why or how he could move so quickly, or suspect they might just be in trouble.

Brody skidded on gravel as he leaped off the jogging path and crossed the parking lot for the par course and ran behind the far side of the bathroom shelter. The trucks and car slammed on their brakes. A muffled thump and the sound of metal and plastic colliding reached through the hammering of his heart in his ears. His lopsided grin faded when tires squealed and the vehicles behind him skidded over the berm, over the asphalt trail and across the grass.

*The rangers are going to be furious in the morning.*

Brightness touched his senses, a mix of sight and sound and scent beyond all previous experience, beckoning to him from the right. A sense of light unseen. He skidded on the night-damp grass and turned, listening to his instincts, scuttling his plan to run into the trees and hope his pursuers wrecked their cars. Brody followed the asphalt trail weaving in and out among the trees and the exercise stations. His tactic confused the trucks' drivers, judging by the squealing of tires and blaring of horns. Brody didn't hear that particular, welcome crunch of truck metal against any of the wooden and plastic posts of the par course.

The path curved up and to the right a little. He smelled water flowing green with weeds and rich with silt over stones still warm from the day's sunshine.

He remembered from this afternoon the road rose a little and turned and there was a swinging gate of metal bars to block the road when the water was too high—and the road dropped down abruptly to the ford, forcing drivers to slow down or bottom out and damage their cars. Brody ran faster, skimming over the ground until he felt his feet climbing the slight incline, then looked down and saw moonlight on sparkling dark water. Purple, blue and green sparks spun around his face for two seconds, then vanished.

The jogging path split, going right to cross the road and left into the darkness of the woods. For two seconds, Brody hesitated, longing to run into the shadows and the trees that ran along the river. If he could cross the river, they couldn't follow without leaving their vehicles. Or would they take a chance on losing him and drive the long way around, hoping to catch him coming out on the other side?

The river sparkled in the moonlight and darkness. Brody dropped and rolled through the grass and gravel toward the footbridge on the right and the water's edge, taking himself out of the flash of the headlights. His ribs banged against a rock but Brody could only gasp against laughter. The first truck flashed by, going too fast to stop as it crested the rise, slamming down hard heading into the ford. He heard the thump-bang-grinding shriek of transmission hitting rock and the splash of tires in water. The first truck died abruptly.

Two seconds later, the second truck slammed on its brakes, laying hot stinking rubber in the roadway, tires screaming protest. This truck too crested the rise and dropped into the ford at a lower speed, but still too fast to avoid slamming into the dead truck. A second engine shriek-crashed into silence. The men in both trucks were stunned frozen for five long seconds.

Brody got up onto his knees as he heard the Escort squeal around the curve in the road, a good hundred yards behind its fellows.

One car, he could handle.

He stood and ran, not caring if the men in the trucks saw him. He darted out into the roadway with his arms spread, eager for the Escort's headlights to hit him. Despite the glare in his eyes, Brody made out Doyne and a welder named Pinkley in the front seat, staring open-mouthed at him. As the car brushed past him, he spun and kicked, putting a dent in the car's side panel. Then he ran.

The Escort turned, tires protesting with dull squeals. Its engine roared and coughed as Pinkley forced the car to perform maneuvers it was too old to attempt. Brody ran at half speed, letting headlights nip his heels. The car never caught up with him, though he jogged for more than half a mile back along the trail. When he reached the par course parking lot, he darted around the bathroom shelter, forcing Pinkley to follow him up across grass and asphalt toward the trail that led into the woods. An extension of the lake and some swampy area lay there among the darkness of the trees.

Brody considered tricking Pinkley into driving his car into the water. The trees that formed a tunnel over and around the trail weren't far enough apart to allow even the rusty old Escort to pass. He cared more about damaging trees than about hurting Doyne and Pinkley.

The path curved right, past the leg stretch station. Brody stayed on the asphalt trail, heading for the gaping black mouth into the safety of the trees. They stretched their limbs toward him, promising safety.

At the last moment, he darted to the right, heading for the open meadow ringed by pines and maples.

The Escort screamed. Its engine roared—too fast and too clear. Brody looked back and in the moonlight, he saw the car pivoting on two tires. Somehow it had hit the leg stretch station and became partially airborne. Gasping on breathless laughter, Brody watched the car wobble along five more yards, heading right toward him.

The engine coughed and died. The car held still for two breathless seconds. Creaking, it wobbled and fell over onto its roof. The men inside yelped as they were thrown from their seats—no seat belts.

Then silence.

Brody crouched in the damp grass, breath quick and shallow, straining all his senses to read the situation.

Far behind at the ford, he heard the sounds of men's voices. Shouting. Angry. Frightened. Confused. He heard a truck engine cough and sputter and grind to a halt. Brody grinned and knew it would take a long time to get those two trucks out of the ford. Maybe it would take tow trucks. Maybe even the help of the park rangers.

Doyne and Pinkley remained silent and still. Brody crept forward on all fours and reached in through the open window to touch Doyne. The man still breathed. He moaned a little and wriggled in protest of his crumpled ball state, wedged between the top of the seat and the ceiling of the car. Pinkley seemed all right, exhaling a cloud of alcohol fumes, curled up along the window with one arm sticking out. After a few seconds of thought, Brody dragged both men free of the car and checked them more thoroughly for injuries. He jabbed them with a forefinger in arms and legs, testing their reflexes.

No broken bones. Breathing fine. In the moonlight, they looked a little pale but he didn't think they would stay unconscious.

He contemplated the overturned car and unconscious men and listened to the growing sounds of argument coming from the ford. He had to teach them a lesson. He had to figure out how to keep them from coming after him again. He didn't want to be the coward and not show up for work tomorrow. Simply walking away from this apprenticeship job felt like a coward's way out, though it would save him trouble in the long run.

He would gnaw on those questions tomorrow. Tonight, he was going to have some fun, if he could. He had an idea. It was nasty and it was infantile. Mom Cooper would shake her head and sigh in disappointment, but Dad Cooper would laugh. It might get him into trouble, but it would also open up a lot of questions that couldn't be answered without getting his enemies in trouble, too.

Brody bent down and braced his shoulder against the open window frame. He wedged both hands under the roof of the car, took a deep breath, and heaved. The Escort made a resounding, satisfying, hollow bang as it flipped over onto its wheels again. He got in and tried the engine. It started without a hitch. He grinned as he imagined Pinkley and Doyne tied up in the back seat, waking up and realizing *he* drove them.

Where should he take them? Brody got out, walked to the men and knelt to untie their bootlaces and unfasten their belts as he considered.

It had to be some place public. Some place where they would be seen by their friends. He had to teach all Moon's men a lesson about leaving him alone. Brody tied the men's hands and feet together with their own laces and belts and he laughed, soft and low. The moonlight rippling down over the meadow and trees seemed to laugh silently with him.

# Chapter Twenty

*Aggie?* Lara's voice in her head startled her and cut through the renewed panic racing through her thoughts. *Are you looking for Brody?*

*And trying to figure out how to kill Dan Moon and half my Dad's crew without going to jail. I know they're up to something and they did something to Brody—but I can't prove any of it!* Aggie sat down, wolf-shape, in the shadows of the lagoon in front of the Cleveland Museum of Art. *Why? What's up?*

*Allison told him we were looking for him.*

*When?*

*This afternoon. Dan dropped Brody off at her place. Brody got mad and took off. She's over here with Greg, crying her eyes out. Greg took her over to the boarding house and found out Brody moved out. She's worried sick.*

*She's not the only one.* Aggie leaped to her feet and started running. She had a long way to go to get back to the construction site, where she had left her car.

*I wouldn't be. I think Brody just got back at all those jerks.* Lara laughed. *There was a big mess in the park, out by the par course. You could hear tires squealing and guys swearing and there's about a dozen rangers and police. I hopped on down—you can't miss it, with all the mental static going on.*

*You didn't!* Aggie laughed silently, teeth bared, and ran a little faster. For Lara to teleport anywhere usually happened by accident, without meaning to do it. When she did it on purpose, she needed the utmost concentration so she didn't land off target or inside something.

*I recognized a couple of the creeps from your Dad's company. They were swearing and yelling about 'that weird kid.' From what I could pick up, they were chasing Brody through the park and he tricked them into trashing their trucks.*

*Where is he now?*

*Nobody knows. But I think he's going to be okay.*

*No, he isn't. I'm going to kill him, when I find him.*

*No, you won't. He's your brother.*

*All the more reason.* Aggie laughed, and the sound came out as a howl that got more than a few slammed brakes in response. Nobody saw the black streak of wolf racing down the dark streets, even when she passed only a few feet away from them.

There was no sign of Brody when she reached the ford in the park, and all the rangers and tow trucks were long gone. Aggie laughed, imagining what kind of revenge her brother had exacted on Dan Moon's goons, and made herself go home and go to bed. She would find out in the morning, which would come soon enough.

⁂

Aggie woke to the sound of the phone ringing at six in the morning. Today was supposed to be her day off and she needed to sleep in, to make up for yesterday. She rolled over, burying her head under her pillow, until she heard Jack swearing. He stomped around in his bedroom and she heard the slamming of the closet door and the banging of drawers. She sat up, still half-caught in her dream, where she found Brody and the air split open the moment she touched his hand, so they fell into another world.

The sound of Jack's car starting finally cleared her mind. She crawled out of bed and scrambled down the stairs. Grace sat at the kitchen table, rubbing sleep from her eyes.

"What's up, Mom?"

"The police called. Something happened at the site. Smithers is in a panic. All his dogs ran away."

"I'll believe those dogs can run when I see it," Aggie said with a snort. She dropped down into the chair opposite her mother and propped her head up in her hands.

"What could make the dogs afraid enough to run?"

"Nobody but me." She sat up straight. "Or someone like me."

"I think you found your brother." Grace made shooing motions and laughed.

⁂

When Brody reached the construction site, only a few cars had arrived. He looked for Aggie's car as he walked to the office trailer to put his carton of milk away for lunch. She hadn't arrived yet. Jack's car was there, parked crooked. Dan Moon's truck was conspicuously missing, and he was always there before everyone else. Brody wondered if he was somewhere having a meeting with his gang about all the mishaps from the night before. Grinning, he stepped up into the office.

"I wondered when you would show up," Dorayn greeted him. The white-haired man lounged in Dan's desk chair. He leaned back just enough to see out the side window and looked up, toward the top of the building.

Brody stiffened, wondering if the man knew what he had done. He liked Dorayn, and it suddenly occurred to him that he might be disappointed in him for the nasty tricks he had pulled last night.

"I'm early," Brody said instead, and opened the refrigerator to put away his milk. "It's still quiet, hardly anybody here."

"It's quiet because the emergency trucks haven't gotten here yet." Dorayn just grinned wider.

"Emergency trucks?" His heart picked up the pace, though he managed to sound calm and innocent.

"Everybody is up topside, trying to figure out how to get those two idiots down. Good job."

"They said I put them up there?" Brody groaned, realizing too late he should have said, 'what idiots?'

"Not yet. They're still too incoherent to say much of anything. When you get a chance, I want to hear all the gory details." He stood and sauntered toward the door. "Since Dan's not here yet, it's up to me to help Jack figure out what to do. Probably nobody had the brains to call for the emergency crews." He paused at the door and looked back over his shoulder at Brody. "You and Aggie really should sit down and talk."

"Aggie?" His heart sped up, and sweat gathered on his back and under his arms. "Why Aggie? Talk about what?"

Dorayn only shook his head and stepped out of the trailer. Brody followed him. A few more cars had pulled into the parking lot since he arrived. The new arrivals ran for the elevators and ladders, attracted by the shouts from up on the highest beam of the newly stabilized framework. Someone perched on a narrow platform of two girders. It wasn't a very wide platform, even at the best of times, even if the people standing on it didn't shake and weave and let out pitiful shrieks to the men racing onto the construction site.

No boards reached across the gap from the girders and I-beams on either side. From where he stood, Brody couldn't see a single board long enough and thick enough to bridge the gap and let the stranded men cross on solid footing. He grinned, not caring who saw him, and felt immensely pleased and proud of himself. The topper on last night's success had been terrorizing those smelly, drooling Dobermans into running away, yipping like puppies.

Dorayn and the others climbed up. Brody heard the squeak and groan of the elevator coming down, and voices raised in shouts and curses and even some laughter. He stayed where he was, head tilted back a little and a hand raised to shade his eyes. How long he could stand there and enjoy his handiwork, he didn't know. Right now, he didn't care. Shaking his head, he settled down on the office steps and made himself comfortable. In a few seconds, the yard was empty as everyone headed for the top of the building to help.

Before he got comfortable, Aggie's Cavalier growled into the lot and parked next to Jack's car. She got out and strolled barefoot across the gravel. The commotion moving up the building caught her attention. She stopped at the foot of the steps and pointed.

"What's up?"

"Somebody's stuck up there."

"Who?"

"Somebody who probably deserves it." He grinned.

"I think you know who's up there."

"Doyne and Pinkley."

She grinned. "Wouldn't happen to nicer guys." She wore denim shorts and a T-shirt and her hair was tangled from sleep—definitely not dressed for a day at work. "Can't say they don't deserve it. Lara caught a little of last night's action. I'm glad you weren't hurt." Aggie looked around the parking lot, and smiled even wider when she noted the empty spot where Dan's truck should have been. "Brody, we have to talk."

"Naaah, not now." He hooked a thumb toward the figures at the top of the building. "I want to hear what they say when they finally get down." He grinned, all mischief.

"Brody, we have to talk. Now." She tugged on the collar of his shirt, loosening another button so his birthmark was revealed. "I wish I had seen this before I started washing your clothes yesterday. It could have saved us a lot of trouble."

"Huh?" Now he paid more attention to her.

"Get in my car."

"Aggie, what's going on?"

Instead of answering, she grabbed hold of his left ear with forefinger and thumb and twisted, effectively bringing him to his feet. She was half a head shorter than him, and it would have been funny if it hadn't hurt.

"Stop that! You're always yanking on my ear. You're always bossing me around and—"

Brody stopped short, mouth hanging open, eyes staring, the breath frozen in his lungs. An avalanche of shattered memories flooded through his mind, scorching and shearing away a black wall that divided his life into 'before the storm' and 'after the storm.'

"Remember me now, Kaenarr?" she said, grinning despite the trembling of her mouth.

"Aguirra?" His voice cracked.

Aggie nodded and let go of his ear and tugged down the neck of her T-shirt to show her own birthmark.

"Why didn't you say anything before?" Brody sank back down on the office steps.

"I tried. I've been screaming since yesterday afternoon, but your mind is blocked and you couldn't hear me. Try listening to the dreamrealm for a change, would you?"

"Dreamrealm," he said slowly, tasting the word that was strange and yet a moment later as familiar as his own face. "We've forgotten so much."

"I think maybe we've been forced to forget." She nudged his foot with her bare foot. "From some things you told Allison, maybe you wanted to forget, too."

"You know how you want something so bad, and it never comes and then when it finally does come, you don't recognize it?" he managed to say. It was hard to talk, hard even to breathe.

He reached out a hand and she took it and a buzzing sense washed over them, a tickling sense of well-being that made them both want to laugh. Aggie tugged her hand free, but he wouldn't let her go. She finally nodded.

"You know, that's a crazy idea, but I must be crazy because it makes sense."

"How did we get here? How did we get separated? What happened?" he blurted.

"Lara and I have been looking for answers. We only remember bits and pieces, nothing that's worth anything. Maybe with three of us, we'll remember more."

"Lara—Alaria?" He winced and dug his knuckles into his temples, to fight the sudden ache that came from memory. "I remember her. As a little girl. Somebody tried to kill her and we were caught in it."

"That's because we're sworn to protect her."

He shook his head, overwhelmed by the tiny prickles of memory trying to push to the surface of his mind. He remembered himself and Lara and Aggie running across a meadow, little children, laughing and chasing sparks that turned into multi-colored creatures with wings, impossible creatures, that splashed against their faces and tickled and made them laugh.

Aggie's face twitched, as if she fought tears, but she smiled too.

"Aguirra," he whispered, his voice catching on her name. How could he have ever forgotten his own sister, his twin?

Brody leaped to his feet, arms open—and paused, wanting to grab hold of her and make sure she was real, half-afraid he would find out she was just another dream. Aggie let out a choked laugh and stepped closer and they hugged, hard, digging lean fingers into each other to hold on forever. Brody laughed and spun her around, making her feet fly off the ground. Aggie held on tighter and laughed.

Dan's truck spit up gravel as it skidded into the lot. Brody put Aggie down but he didn't let go of her as they turned to face Dan.

He looked like a storm was about to burst from his face. Brody wanted to shift to wolf right there and leap on the man and tear his throat open for the trouble he had been causing Aggie. His sister. Brody felt everything inside him rise up in loathing for the man. His blood and bones demanded that he avenge his sister's honor and drive away

WOLVES ON THE WEST SIDE

this unwanted suitor.

"You've got a lot of explaining to do, Cooper," Dan growled.

*He's good at looking dangerous, but he's got a lot to learn about the scents to go with it,* Brody thought to Aggie.

*Toothless old hound,* she retorted.

Brody snorted, trying not to laugh.

"No, you've got a lot of explaining to do, Dan," Aggie shot back, and tightened her arm around Brody. "Your goons tried to kill my brother last night."

"Brother?" Dan took a half step back and his mouth dropped open.

"Dan! Get up topside," Jack yelled, barreling across the construction yard. "We've got a major problem." Then he saw Brody and Aggie standing there with their arms around each other. "What's going on down here?"

"Dad, Brody is my twin brother," Aggie said, as calmly as if she ordered eggs in a restaurant.

Jack opened his mouth to deny her words—Brody could see it, and smelled the panic that washed over the man. He stopped short, mouth open, stunned speechless. It was Dan who started swearing. He reached for Aggie, to tear her from Brody's hold. Brody growled and braced to lunge. Aggie swung, clocking Dan across the side of his face and knocking him back two steps. The blow knocked Dan into silence and unplugged Jack's voice.

"Aggie—honey—it's got to be a trick."

*Show him,* Aggie thought, and pulled down the neck of her T-shirt. Brody tugged open his collar at the same time. Jack stumbled to a halt again, blinked, shook his head, and stared at their matching birthmarks.

"It's a tattoo," Dan sneered. His words came out muffled, because he had his hand against his mouth. The smell of blood slowly seeped through the air.

"Mine or his?" Aggie challenged. "We can call up the police reports from when we were found. They probably have all sorts of photos to show all our injuries, and these birthmarks will be in those photos. Brody is my twin brother. Take it or leave it."

"But, honey, even if you do have a brother, where has he been all these years? Does he know where your parents are?" Jack said, half-whining.

"No. Sir," Brody added quickly. "The people who kidnapped us were trying to kill Al—Lara. Aggie and I were just in the wrong place. That's about all I remember, after the way they beat us up."

"I don't buy it," Dan said. He glared at Brody, as if he blamed him for all this.

"You don't have to buy it." Sudden glee washed over him as he realized he didn't have to live in fear of Dan Moon. "It's the truth. And here's some more truth you never paid attention to before. My sister doesn't want anything to do with you."

"Oh, you know this after only being together a few hours?" the man sneered.

"Anybody with brains can see it," Brody snapped. "Half the crew says you're marrying Aggie to take over the company. The other half is laughing behind your back because they know Aggie'll never let you touch her."

"Take over the company?" Jack echoed. He lost his confused look and frowned at Dan.

*Good one,* Aggie thought, accompanied by a few snorts of laughter. *Why didn't I ever try that tactic?*

*That's what brothers are for.*

"Dad, I'm taking Brody home." Aggie slid out of the curve of his arm and headed for her car.

"Home? Honey, I know you believe he's your brother, but there are still tests and—well, think about the shock to your mother."

"Mom knows Brody is my brother. I told her yesterday, when I saw his birthmark." She pointed up to the top of the building. "Don't you have a couple idiots to rescue?"

Brody knew better than to hang around while Dan heard what he had done last night. He hurried after Aggie, to climb into her car. He couldn't resist one last smirk at Dan, who still stood there and glared at him.

"You have to come up here to live," Aggie said, once they had put two intersections between them and the construction site.

"I don't know—"

"The answers are here. When Allison took you to the park yesterday, did you see—"

"Sparks? Blue and green and purple?" He felt like he had been punched in the diaphragm and couldn't get enough air.

"Things happen when we're in the park. The more of us there are, the weirder the things we see and hear. With five of us, who knows?"

"You, me and Alaria—and Greg and Allison?" he guessed. Brody slouched in his seat, feeling like he hadn't had a wink of sleep for four nights straight. "We have a lot of catching up to do."

"Tell me about it. Start with last night!"

"After what happened last night, I don't know if your father will want me around."

"Mom and I got the general idea from Lara, and Mom wants you here. She was getting the spare room ready for you to move into, when I left." She grinned at him and Brody grinned back. "So, what *did* happen last night?"

It was as natural as breathing to pinch all his memories together into a tight little packet and pass them mentally to her. Aggie's eyes widened and then she burst out laughing.

"Oh, they deserved it!" she sputtered as she drove up the ramp to merge onto the highway.

"Aggie? Now we can go home?"

"In theory." Aggie nodded and wiped her eyes.

"Where is home, Aggie?"

"That's what makes it only a theory. We're a long, long way from home."

"Too bad we just can't find someone to throw us back to Oz."

"Is that where you think we came from?" She snorted, grinning.

"Face it. We're freaks." He frowned as a new thought came to him. "Or is it just me?"

"We have parents and cousins and we're all Werelings—is that what you meant?"

"How could I forget what we are?" he moaned. "Is Lara like us?"

"No. But she can do lots of things that she just hasn't figured out yet."

"She gives off blue sparks. So does Allison, and Greg gives off green. Were they dumped here, too?"

"They were born here, they're not like us, but for some reason they're like Lara." She shook her head. "There's so much we have to catch up on. And remember."

# Chapter Twenty-One

Aggie thought Brody would cry, when they arrived home and Grace hugged him. The smell of her mother's special apple and raisin spice pancakes drifted through the warm morning air. Grace snagged Brody's duffle bag from his hand and ordered them into the kitchen immediately.

"I know Aggie well enough to guess you're starving now that it's all over," she said. "We can settle you in your room once the two of you have eaten."

*This is too easy,* Brody commented, and followed Aggie and Grace into the house with his backpack in his hand. They had stopped at his hotel to pick up all his gear, after he told Aggie why he had moved out of the boarding house. *I'm waiting for something to go wrong.*

*Probably when we contact the social workers to get permission for you to stay here. Will your foster-parents be any trouble?*

*They'll miss me—I hope—but they'll be happy for me.*

"You two are awfully quiet," Grace said. She stepped over to the oven and pulled out the wide casserole full of pancakes.

"That's because we can talk in our heads, Mom."

Brody choked on the glass of orange juice he had just started drinking. Grace put down the casserole and snatched up a couple paper napkins to blot the table.

"Aggie didn't bother telling you that I know, did she?"

"Know what?" Brody's face was red. For a moment, Aggie expected him to bolt.

"About Werelings, and your name is Kaenarr." She stepped back to the stove and picked up the saucepan full of apple and raisin spice sauce.

Brody glared at Aggie for three long heartbeats. Then a wide grin cracked his face and he slouched back in his chair and laughed.

⚜

"My foster-parents would have freaked if I ever told them, much less showed them," Brody said late that night.

The day had passed quickly, relating stories of how they had survived and adapted after the storm that separated and nearly killed them. Brody's new room was next to Aggie's, and she had showed him immediately how to remove the screen to make it easier to take night runs without Jack finding out. He was sympathetic when she told him about the one time Jack saw her shift from wolf to Human, and his reaction.

They met Lara, Greg and Allison for a picnic dinner, to give Jack some breathing room and time to adjust to the idea of Brody living in their house. Before Aggie brought Brody home, Grace had made calls to the social workers and the Coopers. She explained the situation and began the long process to allow Brody to move to Berea to be with his sister. Neither twin wanted to think about all the tests and questions and doubters they would have to deal with in the next few days and weeks.

Now, they had come to the park, to run in the moonlight and shadows of the forest. They had run for nearly an hour, as Aggie showed Brody all her favorite places. They went to Bonnie Park and she showed him her memories of that stormy July day. The sparks didn't appear and they were both disappointed. The sparks had been out thicker than the mosquitoes when they had eaten with Lara, Greg and Allison.

They stopped at the ford on their way back to Berea, and relived Brody's chase with the trucks and car the night before. They laughed silently, wolf-fashion, and ducked into the shadows when a ranger approached and crossed the ford. When the car had vanished from sight and sound, they shifted to Human, climbed up onto the bridge, sat with their legs hanging over the edge and talked.

"Some can take it. Some can't. I think Allison and Greg wouldn't even blink, if we showed them," Aggie said after a moment.

"Hope so." Brody gave her a sideways look and a grin. She knew, without any images from his mind, what he was thinking.

"You and Allison really hit it off. I'm glad."

"Does she go to Berea High with you?"

"Would that get in the way if she didn't?"

"Nope."

Aggie tried not to sigh too loudly. Lara had Greg. Now it looked like Brody had Allison. That would serve Mike Henderson right. His idiot cousin Allen had showed up for the summer—Allen always came for the summer, to 'relieve the pressure on his parents.' Aggie tried to feel sorry for Allen, whose parents had been separating and reconciling for years, but Allen made the sludge at the bottom of the barrel look good. The only good thing he had ever done was to express enough interest in Allison that Mike always paid more attention to her while his cousin was in town. Allen had changed from a skinny, snot-nosed, pimply, undersized jerk into a hulking football player with clear skin over the last school year. Suddenly, he was a rival, and Mike had paid more attention to Allison in the last three weeks, but not enough.

*Too little, too late,* Aggie decided, and kept her thoughts very private. They were too smug and nastily delighted to even share with Lara.

Mike had finally realized Allison was a girl worth going after, if only to protect her from Allen—who wouldn't take no for an answer, even when accompanied by a big brother's fist. As far as Aggie was concerned, it served Mike right to lose Allison to someone else. Aggie was happy for her brother, even though she felt jealous. Not because Brody had a girlfriend, but because she still hadn't found anyone. The only men who ever showed interest in her were wimps who needed babysitters, or arrogant jerks like Dan Moon.

Why couldn't there be more men in the world like Dorayn, but younger?

That thought startled her, so she didn't hear Brody's question.

Dorayn? Why hadn't she ever considered him before?

Besides the fact he had to be at least thirty years older than her, maybe forty?

He was just the kind of man she wouldn't mind hooking up with for the rest of her life. Strong and smart, dependable, with a good sense of humor, steady despite the circumstances. He met all her wolf criteria, too: clean scent, strong body, graceful, alert and quiet when there was no need to speak. Despite his white hair, she realized he had never seemed 'old' to her.

And best of all, just like Allison and Greg, she didn't think he would go over the edge if she showed him her wolf side.

"Hey, Aggie." Brody nudged her. "Where did you go?"

"Go?" She blinked at him and shook her head.

"Your body's here, but your brain is in another world."

"It's been a really long, weird day."

Brody just laughed.

They were back in wolf shape, on their way up the park road, almost to the spot where Grace had been shot, when Aggie smelled trouble. The wind blew from her back, but it shifted as she sidetracked to get a drink at the edge of the fishing lake. She caught a faint whiff of sweet, burned rope smoke as she lifted her head. Brody growled when he caught the scent. Through a screen of branches hanging out over the water, she saw the faint glow of the tips of cigarettes. She made out the dull silver outline of a rowboat. Aggie dismissed them as fisherman out late, hiding from the rangers and stupid enough to do drugs while out on the water. She was about to turn and go on her way when another smell filtered through the marijuana sweetness.

It was a mixture of spicy, dirty sweat, laden with beer and dirty denim, mud and rancid aftershave. She almost didn't recognize it, being inextricably linked in her mind and memory with melting snow and blood and fear-loosened bladders.

A growl rumbled in her throat and Aggie silenced it only with great effort. She slipped around the edge of the old quarry-turned-fishing-hole and came around behind the boat where it bumped up against the shoreline.

*What's wrong?* Brody asked. He followed her.

Aggie couldn't answer. She fought too hard not to let the residue of her fury and tears from that winter night overwhelm her. If memories took over, she would lose control, leap into the boat and bite out a few throats.

They weren't fishing. They lay across the seats and in the floor of the rowboat, drinking and smoking and staring up at the stars with blank eyes. If she ripped their throats open for what they did to her mother, would they even notice?

*Revenge is better if it takes a long time, and they're conscious enough to know it,* Brody said when she finally showed him her memories.

The faces of the young men in the boat matched the faces that had leered at her mother. Their scent matched. Brody's mental voice calmed her, even as his vicious glee and mental images of tormenting the foursome made her want to howl. Her teeth bared in a lupine grin as a plan came to her.

When the foursome stumbled back to their car two hours later, they found the camouflaging blankets pulled away from the car and ripped to shreds. Dozens of deep claw marks gouged the car's paint, on the sides and hood and roof. The hood ornament was gone, replaced by a neat little pile, courtesy of Brody. All four tires had deep gouges. Aggie had given up on biting holes in the tires after the first foul-tasting bite. Two were too badly damaged to be safe on the road. It didn't matter even if the four had tried to drive away, because the other two tires were flat, the valves ripped out completely.

As a crowning touch, Aggie had shifted to Human long enough to open both doors and roll down the windows, while Brody used his talent for influencing animals to persuade two skunks to come take a nap on the front and back seats.

The twins hid upwind from the car in wolf shape and watched the discovery of their work. They laughed silent wolf laughter until their ribs ached and they fell off their feet to roll in the dirt. The four made enough ruckus to wake the people living on the edge of the park. Those people called the park service and rangers came to investigate. They helped remove the skunks with only slight spraying and fined the four for being in the park after hours. The skunk stench covered the smell of marijuana.

"It's not enough," Aggie whispered, when she and Brody returned home, shifted to Human in the backyard and settled down on the deck to grin and unwind. "It's not nearly enough, but it's a start."

"So, we just harass them until they stop going to the park?" The vicious light in Brody's eyes told her he didn't believe that. He wanted revenge for Grace's sake, and that warmed and comforted her.

"No. I want them to pay."

"You're not going to kill them, are you?"

"No. That would make me like them."

"It'll give them power over you," Brody said, and caught hold of her hands for emphasis. "Dad Cooper told me a long time ago, when those stupid reporters were really bad, there's what people do to you and what you do to yourself. You can't control what people do to you, but you can control how you change, how you feel, the things you do. Don't let them change you."

"I won't."

"Don't get caught in the trap you lay for them."

"I won't." She squeezed his hands. "You'll help me, won't you?"

"Try and stop me."

⟡

"You patrolled the park for months after your Mom got shot," Lara said, coming back into the tiny living room of her apartment. She set three mugs of chai on the trunk she used as a table, and settled down on the floor. Aggie and Brody had come straight to her house after she got off work Saturday afternoon. "This isn't going to be easy, catching them and getting enough evidence."

"I have to trap them and find a way to let the police know it's them without having to answer a lot of really tough questions." Aggie clenched her fists until the image of all four murderers with their throats bitten out faded from her imagination.

"We thought maybe you could do some of your Internet magic," Brody said. He pulled a piece of paper out of his pocket and handed it over to Lara before picking up his mug.

"Dummies left their wallets and other stuff in the car when they went out in the boat," Aggie explained. "License numbers, social security, insurance. Brody and I tried to remember everything we could."

"You didn't take any of it to keep?" Lara asked.

"Too much risk," Brody said, shaking his head. "We're pretty good at memorizing, even if we're not geniuses like you."

"Are you sure you don't remember anything from before?" She grinned at him.

Aggie sighed, thoroughly happy with the feelings in the room despite the topic of conversation. This was how it should have been all these years, the three of them working together, teasing and comfortable.

"We tore up everything and dumped it in the mud," Brody said, shaking his head. "Including all their money. Wads of it. We may be vindictive Werelings, but we're not thieves."

"Smart. Be triply careful, even if there are two of you playing the Wolf of Wallace Lake," Lara said, nodding. "They shot your Mom. They might have guns, and you just didn't see them this time."

"I'm scared," Aggie admitted. "A little. What if someone catches us? Dad was bad enough after he saw me once as a wolf. To find out about two of us..."

"What I'm worried about is Dan Moon taking over the business if your Dad goes into the loony bin," Brody said.

"Then don't take the risks," Lara said.

"We have to," he said, before Aggie could open her mouth. "What about all the people they've hurt in the past and will hurt in the future? If we can do something that no one else can, and we can use it to help people, shouldn't we?"

"Yes. In theory."

"What about real life?"

"You're seventeen years old." Lara wrapped her fingers around her mug until her knuckles turned white. "Don't you think maybe we should find out what real life is, and what we are, before we try to save the world?"

"Yeah, I know but..." Aggie looked away, sighing. Then a grin touched her face as a new thought came to her. Brody laughed when she shared it with him. "Those creeps won't come back to the park for a few days, but when they do, we'll be waiting. The Wolf of Wallace Lake strikes again!"

"And they'll be seeing double," Brody added.

"Just be careful. Make them mad enough, they'll start hunting you."

"We know. The only way to trap them is to get them mad enough they get stupid. But we need you to use that info to find out everything you can about them, first."

"You know I'll do whatever I can to help you, Aggie." Lara held out both hands, palms up, facing the twins.

Without thinking, Brody and Aggie linked hands with her and each other, palm to palm, fingers interlaced. It was a gesture as natural as if they had done it a thousand times. A spark of blue light danced on each of their knuckles, stinging their skin before leaping into the air and forming one ball of light that flared and vanished, all within the space of two heartbeats.

"What was that all about?" Aggie said.

"I think we're getting closer to answers," Lara whispered.

⁂

Monday morning came too quickly, despite the strained feeling in the house all weekend. Jack tried to be nice, but his doubt of Aggie and Brody's claims was evident in his face and voice. He started to suggest several times that Brody not come to work at the site, always stopping halfway through. When Monday morning came, Aggie welcomed it despite knowing how strange everything would be at work.

She and Brody said nothing on the drive downtown. They didn't need to, with images flashing between their minds faster and clearer than words could ever be.

"Think Dan'll leave me alone, now that he knows I'm not a threat?" Brody muttered as they circled down the ramp to get off the highway.

"Like you said, he wants the business. He'll either see you as the heir apparent, if Dad adopts you—"

"I don't think so," he said with a snort.

"Or he'll suddenly become your best buddy, to get you to influence me."

"If I ever say anything nice about Dan Moon as your mate..." Brody frowned. "Okay, that was weird."

"What? Mate?"

"Yeah. Have you ever thought about things that way?"

"Lara and I always remember more bits and pieces when we're together. She thinks now that you're with us, more pieces will come together. Maybe something usable for a change." Aggie shrugged. "So, we're half wolf. We think of our husbands and wives as mates, that's all."

"That's all?" He shrugged. "Anyway, if I ever say anything nice about him marrying you, shoot me. Somebody else has taken over my body."

"Only if you promise to do the same if I start looking at him like he's a movie star."

"Swear." He held up his hand. They touched palms, fingers interlaced, sealing the promise in the new-old way.

Dorayn waited for Brody when they pulled in. He just grinned and shook his head, and gestured for Brody to get his tools and follow. The twins laughed. Aggie took their lunches into the trailer and Brody got to work.

✍ ✍

Bo Timmons had remained Grace's friend, and had climbed the ladder in his field, putting him in a position of authority. When he snapped his fingers, he got the information on Brody and Aggie without any delays or questions. By Friday, all their case records had been compared and the results of the blood tests had come back. More exhaustive studies were needed to prove conclusively that Aggie and Brody were brother and sister, but the odds were overwhelmingly in their favor that they were close blood relatives.

Just as Aggie had said, the earliest photos proved both she and Brody had their triangular black birthmarks when they were found. That refuted Dan's theory. And as Bo said during their final meeting, if the marks were tattoos, it would have been even better proof they belonged together, because it had been done deliberately.

"If my theory was right, it could just be proof that the same weird child sacrifice cult had stolen both of us," Brody said, when they were safely in the car on the way home from their last meeting.

Aggie reached over the seat to where he sat in the back and slapped him on the leg. Grace, who was driving, sighed and shook her head. She met Brody's gaze in the rearview mirror and smiled.

Grace called Jack when they got home and gave him the news. Then Brody called the Coopers, to give them the final verdict. Aggie watched her twin and ached for him. She knew how she would feel if the circumstances had been different and it was necessary for her to leave the Harseys to go live with Brody and his foster family.

The answers were linked with the Metroparks, especially Bonnie Park, where she and Lara had been found after that freak storm. Brody had gone back to the area where he had landed after the storm, and had never seen sparks of magic or heard things that didn't belong there. That was proof enough that the Metroparks in general, Bonnie Park in particular, was the jumping-off place. Maybe even the key to the answers they wanted.

They still couldn't figure out *how*.

It would take weeks for the paperwork to go through, but they already had planned their lives from now on. Brody would live with the Harseys. He would go to Berea High School with Aggie for their senior year. They would keep looking for others like them, to find more answers.

"What do we do when we graduate?" Brody asked, as he and Aggie and Lara waited in front of Lara's apartment for Allison and Greg to come get them for a celebration picnic.

Mike was to meet them at the park, since he had been part of the research effort. He said he would come if he could get Allen to go somewhere else. Aggie found the conflict between the cousins amusing. She wondered if Allison even realized that Mike had been her champion. From the way Allison looked at Brody, it was a good bet she had forgotten Mike even existed.

"I don't want to think about graduation," Aggie quickly responded.

"Whatever you do..." Lara shrugged. "I don't think you should go very far away from Berea."

"So we don't go too far from the doorway?" he asked with a grin.

Aggie didn't like that shiver that ran over her whole body, like the wind blew the wrong away against her fur. "What doorway?"

"Allison's theory, that there's a doorway to another world hidden in the Metroparks." He shrugged. "Makes sense to me."

"Allison could tell you the moon was made of white chocolate, and you'd believe her."

"It isn't?" He gave her a wide-eyed look of false innocence. She growled and bumped him hard with her hip, knocking him off the bench where the three of them slouched.

Greg and Allison showed up just in time to stop Brody from reprisals.

Mike waited for them—with Allen sulking in the car. Brody led Allison away to walk along the riverbank and keep Allen from realizing she was there, while Mike filled Aggie, Lara and Greg in on what had happened.

"We're stuck with him until he gets out of high school, at the very least," Mike said with a hint of snarl in his voice. "His folks are breaking up and neither one wants him. Surprise, surprise. Mom's talking with the lawyers and whoever, to make sure everything's legal and we keep him. She thinks the yo-yo effect is what makes Allen such a jerk."

"She might be right," Lara offered.

Aggie started to bristle, then remembered several facts. First, Mrs. Henderson had a degree in child psychology and volunteered at the Berea Children's Home, working with emotionally damaged children. And second, she had been Lara's foster-mother and there was a lot of love between them.

The picnic ended up at the stables off of Albion Road where Mike kept his big rawboned stallion, Omega and helped take care of the horses of a few friends. To Aggie's surprise, Allen wasn't a quarter as slimy as usual.

Maybe knowing he wouldn't have to go back to his parents at the end of the summer made a difference. Which meant Lara and Mrs. Henderson were right. That disturbed her. Still, Allen was better company than usual, though he did show off, trying to do trick riding on his black gelding, Trotter.

*That's because he thinks he has an 'in' with Allison, thanks to his horse,* Lara commented, when dusk finally arrived and the five climbed back into Greg's car to go home. *He was so busy showing off, he didn't realize she only paid attention to Brody.*

*Allen who?* Brody said, his mental voice thickly smug. Aggie was hard pressed not to burst out laughing, because then she would have to explain their whole mental conversation to Greg and Allison, and that wouldn't be good for any of them.

# Chapter Twenty-Two

Greg drove past the lane leading to Bonnie Park, on their way home. That thrumming sense of power the five always felt in the park washed over them, but twice as strong.

"We've never been here all together like this," Lara said, when the ripple of awareness shivered through the car and Greg slowed down in reaction.

"The five of us, sure," Allison said.

"Mike and Allen are right behind us," Aggie said, hooking her thumb back over her shoulder. *Do you see what I see?*

*Purple sparks*, Brody said. *Just for a few seconds. Attacking Mike...or coming from him?*

"This is getting really irritating," Greg said. He stomped on the gas and went ten miles over the speed limit, getting beyond that section of winding park road.

Nothing more happened to them by the time they crossed Pearl Road, other than that awareness, that sense of energy, like high tension wires humming in the marrow of their bones. Aggie liked the feeling. There was so much potential and promise in the feeling.

They drove down Valley Parkway, following the winding two-lane road all the way to Wallace Lake. Aggie thought she heard something as they turned back onto Old Quarry Road by the Music Mound parking area—a voice raised in fear, a sharp sound like a hand hitting flesh—but she couldn't be sure. She knew better than to ignore nudges and hunches when they were in the park.

"Greg, pull in?" She gestured at the gravel parking lot across the street from the Music Mound.

"What's up?" he asked as he complied.

"Oh...I've never really explored through here," she said, with a smile and a shrug. "All these years, and I've never looked at that little amphitheater thingy over there." She hooked a thumb over her shoulder, across the road to where stone seats in a depression in the ground created an outdoor stage. "Want to go take a look?"

The smell of sweet smoke met them before they quite reached the thick bushes separating the lawn of the Music Mound from the road.

Aggie stopped short, nose wrinkling. Brody snorted in disgust. The others continued another step or two before they saw her reaction. Greg opened his mouth, about to speak when he stopped short and wrinkled up his nose.

"Drug-heads," he grumbled. "Everywhere you go nowadays, there's some idiot messing up his brain cells. Maybe this isn't such a good idea."

"Yeah. Some other time." She turned and headed back across the road to the parking lot.

"It's funny," Allison said with a wistful little smile. "Do you guys feel like our private playground just got taken away from us?"

Later, Aggie thought that over and knew Allison was right. Something special happened when they gathered in the Metroparks, anywhere in the Emerald Necklace. It gave them all a proprietary feeling, as if they had a responsibility to the park system, and special interest in it.

She didn't think about that until much later, when she and Brody said good-bye to the others and started walking home from Lara's apartment.

"You can smell it from here," Brody said, and turned to face into the warm summer breeze coming up through the park directly behind them.

Aggie caught whiffs of something through the sweet smell of burned rope. A familiar odor, though it was hard to detect and identify. It made her shiver a little, the way a hunting dog shivered, waiting for his master to pull the trigger. Aggie knew better than to ignore that sensation of anticipation; a warning to be prepared, to investigate.

"Kaenarr ..." Aggie knew she had to get back to the Music Mound now. The haunting bits of odor and unintelligible whispers of memory pulled at her, turning into a shriek of insistence she couldn't quite make out—but she knew she had to follow.

"Let's go." Brody took a running step, arms stretching out, and shifted to wolf. She was only two steps behind him.

Their claws clattered as they crossed the asphalt and slid back into the trees and darkness. The smells coming from the music mound were stronger in wolf shape. Aggie's stomach didn't rebel now at the reek of alcohol, smoke and dirty, rancid sweat. Her wolf-mind catalogued the odors and what they meant and waited quietly for directions.

Aggie and Brody loped side-by-side through the woods and immediately came upon a car, parked in the shadows, hidden. How had the dope-smokers managed to drive it around the stone wall and through the trees? The sweet-sour green smell of torn bark and broken branches answered that question almost before it was fully framed in her mind.

She knew that car. It took a moment to realize blue paint had been swapped for green. She knew the stink of burned oil from the leaky block and the shape of the car.

*Still smells like skunk,* Brody said, jaw dropping open and tongue hanging out in silent wolf laughter.

Aggie sniffed and snorted agreement. The faint reek of skunk still emanated from the cushions despite the overpowering cloud of artificial cherry deodorizer. They had done very good work that night they discovered the fishing boat, and it was only the beginning.

Raised voices made the twins duck into cover of the trees. Peering out, Aggie saw two of the foursome stagger toward the car, each with his arm draped around a scantily clad girl. She recognized one girl, with a bruised face and torn top; a sophomore at Berea High. As they passed her, the reek of drugs and alcohol rolled off them all in a wave.

What would they do if the four saw her and Brody? Aggie was willing to bet they wouldn't be too stoned to remember. She decided to let them know who had damaged their car last time.

Aggie waited until all four were in the car. She took two running steps and leaped up onto the trunk. Startled yelps pleased her. Digging in her claws, she climbed to the roof, leaving long gouges in the fresh paint job. Aggie leaped down to the hood, purposely heavy-footed so the car bounced, and turned to face the passengers. Brody howled and leaped up onto the trunk and repeated the procedure.

*Remind me to stay on your good side,* he said.

It was hard to snarl with four white faces staring wide-eyed at her while she choked on laughter. Aggie managed, digging in her claws again with a sound close to nails on a chalkboard.

"That's the—" A muffled stream of profanity streamed out of the driver's mouth. He was the pimply one Aggie remembered from that icy night of snow and blood.

Aggie lifted her leg on the windshield for good measure and leaped down with a farewell scrape of her claws. Shouts answered her, but no one got out of the car. Brody leaped up onto the roof, added his own signature, and slid down the front and bounced off the hood with a flourish of his tail.

*Trying to impress the ladies?*

*You're the only lady I see,* he retorted as they fled into the darkness.

Mission accomplished. For tonight, at least.

Lara was suitably impressed, but cautionary, when Aggie stopped by her apartment after work the next day to report on what she had done. "They're going to come looking for you now, you know. You've given them a challenge and a target."

"That's the idea." Aggie swirled her tea around in her mug, watching the loose herbs form spinning patterns. "I figure, the harder I make the hunt, the more they'll try. Especially if I keep scratching at them.

Sooner or later, they'll mess up and get careless and I'll lead them straight to the police."

"What if they decide to shoot?"

"They couldn't hit me before, when I came right at them. They could only hit a sick, frightened woman when they had the gun pressed against her chest." She fought an urge to growl and swipe at something with claws that were invisible but tangible just under her skin.

"Aggie." Lara reached across the table and squeezed her hands. "Revenge isn't worth getting yourself hurt, or even killed. What'll Brody do without you? What will I do without you?"

She had no answer for that. She had considered the possibilities. Aggie knew she couldn't rest until she had brought her mother's attackers to justice. Much as she wanted to bite their throats out, she would have to settle for trapping them and letting the wheels of justice turn.

Meanwhile, their senior year was fast approaching. Brody had registration to take care of and a dozen other details if he hoped to attend Berea High School when the school year began. Aggie scolded herself to wait and be patient. The wolf half hated waiting, but the Human half had to be in control, or she would never get her revenge.

⚜

Sixth period, first day of school, end of the day for seniors, was mixed gym class. Aggie laughed silently as she changed for class and listened to a gaggle of girls on the other side of the row of lockers talking about 'that new guy.' Brody, of course.

*You've gained quite a fan club on your first day,* she called to her twin.

*Please tell me they aren't the ones who sat in the back of the class and giggled and whispered and...* Their mental link broke for a moment.

*Kaenarr?*

*No problem. I thought for a minute I had some sissy boys looking me over. They're impressed with my scars, that's all. Should I tell them where I got them, or just play quiet and mysterious?*

*Oh, puh—lease.* Aggie yanked extra hard on her shoelace and snorted to muffle laughter. *I'm on my way out.*

*Finally! Protect me, big sister.*

She did laugh now, and didn't care what strange looks she got as she scurried out of the locker room, into the gym. Because of the mixed class, both basketball coaches were in charge of the class. Coach Michaels beckoned for Aggie and tossed her a basketball, which she immediately dribbled down to the backstop at the other end. Aggie felt Brody come into the gym and race up behind her.

*Time to show off!*

She spun and passed it to him without looking. Brody took it wide, wove around the gigglers and went for a shot from the far end of the key. The ball yanked hard on the net as it went through. Aggie raced in and caught the ball on the rebound and went under the basket, tossing up and over and in.

"Who's showing off?" Brody said with a grin and caught the ball on the rebound.

"You want them to beg you to be on the team, don't you?" she retorted.

By the time the remainder of the class had come into the gym, Aggie and Brody had made fifteen baskets each, zipping in and snatching the ball in a smooth, intricate dance, with overtones of their hunting partnership. The two coaches approached the far end of the gym, where a good dozen classmates stood on the sidelines making comments and feeble attempts to get hold of the ball.

"Game over," Aggie said, barely out of breath. She tossed the ball to Brody, who put it down and held it in place with his foot on top of it.

"Where did you come from and why haven't you signed up for tryouts?" Coach Martin, the Varsity coach said.

"Mercer," Brody said.

"What school is that?"

"It's in Pennsylvania."

"Oh. You're the transfer kid." Coach Martin looked over his shoulder at Aggie. "He's staying with your folks?"

"Yes, sir," she said, and fought not to burst out laughing when that innocent question raised a flurry of whispers.

"Who has—"

"My parents are Brody's legal guardians for the duration."

"Who is that guy?" Lisa McGuire whispered loudly over Aggie's left shoulder.

Her question fell in that unpredictable moment of quiet when even a whisper could sound like a shout in the echoing gymnasium.

"My twin brother," Aggie said with a shrug.

*Timing is everything.* Brody grinned and kicked the ball straight to her. She let it bounce off her toe and up into her hands.

❧

"I swear, I'm suddenly the most popular girl in school," Aggie announced, coming in the back door after the first home basketball game of the season. "And it's all Brody's fault."

"What?" Grace paused in taking a roast chicken out of the oven and laughed.

"You don't care about being popular," Jack said with a snort. "Did you win? That's the important thing."

"Sure." Brody finished hanging up his coat on a hook by the back door.

"Sure, he says." He rolled his eyes and shifted around in his chair, stretching out his left leg, encumbered by a cast from his thigh to his heel. "I wish I could have been there."

"Allison and Greg were there, and they got it on video," Aggie said. She sighed as her second boot came off and stood up straight. "Gee, Daddy, I ought to be jealous. You were never so anxious to see my games."

"I never had to miss any of your games, little girl, because of a stupid accident. This is important to your brother. New home, new family, new friends—"

"Center in the starting line-up," Grace said. "For goodness sakes, the two of you, stop grinning and sit down. I know you're starving. Jack, don't you dare make Brody tell you about the game until he's eaten at least half his dinner."

"I can eat pretty fast," Brody said.

"That's my boy." Jack exchanged a nod and grin with Brody that had both Grace and Aggie fighting not to cry and laugh at the same time.

Aggie was content to sit and eat slowly and bask in the warmth around the dinner table. She pretended to be jealous over Jack's enthusiasm for Brody's talent in all sports, but she was grateful. Her father finally had a son to boast about. It didn't seem to bother Jack that Brody had come to their family so late. They hadn't gotten to the point of Brody calling him anything but 'sir,' but Aggie knew that would come in its own time.

Life was nearly perfect now. Dan Moon had toned down his pursuit of her and had released some of his more troublesome followers from the construction crew. Of course, it helped that with the winter weather, there wasn't that much work for Harsey Construction. It also helped that Jack had stopped letting Dan do whatever he pleased. Hearing that Dan wanted to marry Aggie to get control of the company had been a shock for Jack. He asked questions and examined things he had been willing to let slide before. He had started making reforms in the way business was handled and had given Dorayn more power to monitor the 'pecking order' on site, so good workers weren't driven away.

Aggie wondered if the accident at the construction site had been another petty revenge scheme from someone who had been let go, or if some of Dan's loyal followers had done it to make Jack slow down his reforms. She couldn't say it aloud, but Brody knew how she had felt and he had mentioned it to Dorayn, who had promised to keep an eye out for more signs of trouble.

"Now," Grace said, after Jack and Brody had dissected the other team's past record through the meal. She set the apple pie and bowl of whipped cream on the table. "What's this about you being popular and it all being Brody's fault?"

Brody groaned and leaned back in his chair. Aggie turned a giggle into a snort.

"It's just a good thing he didn't go out for football, that's all I can say. The coaches are fighting over him being on track and baseball in the spring. And he has groupies waiting outside the locker room after every practice." Aggie batted her eyelashes at her brother. That earned a guffaw from Jack.

"Jealous?" he asked, and winked.

"Hardly. Guys don't like athletic girls—unless it's posing in swim-suits," she added. That earned a snort and a grin from Brody. "And if I did have a bunch of guys hanging around the locker room, you'd be standing guard with a rifle after every practice."

"Darn right, I would. Nobody treats my little girl like a prize or a toy." Jack's smile went crooked and he met her gaze for a moment before looking away.

Aggie sighed. Sometimes, winning battles wasn't as wonderful as she had dreamed. Jack had finally realized that Dan's persistent pursuit of her wasn't as wonderful as he had imagined. Now he was doubly protective of his daughter and his company, and his partner wasn't the dream come true he had seemed. Aggie wished Jack hadn't lost that confidence and pride.

Maybe Dan Moon was responsible for practically everything that made Jack unhappy or worried for the last few years. If only she could get the proof of that.

But for now, Aggie vowed, she would put such things out of her mind. She would even forget she was a Wereling, with gaping holes in her memory and past. She wanted to be nothing but an ordinary high school senior, reunited with her twin, enjoying life, looking forward to the best Thanksgiving and Christmas of her life. Even senior panic season didn't look so bad.

꧁꧂

"Allison's folks..." Brody leaned against a tree trunk, twitching his shoulders as if he could scratch his back through his winter jacket.

"Yeah, I know. They like us, but they're scared of us. You're pretty sure they don't want you dating Allison, but at the same time they're nice to you and they don't say anything." Aggie shrugged and kicked a gob of snow into the ice-bordered river. "Of course, it could be that they're not too happy about their little girl riding in cars with boys," she added a moment later with a grin.

Brody had used his summer construction money and what he had earned working for Mr. Cooper to buy a car. Aggie was sure the long hours he and Jack spent investigating used cars and debating the merits of different makes and models had helped bring the two closer together. Brody had spent Christmas break touching up the paint and tuning up the motor, and that evening had taken Allison out. Aggie had expected her twin to come home glowing from a date where he didn't have to depend on someone else to drive them around. Instead, he had been unusually quiet and thoughtful. When she mind-called him, he hadn't hesitated to shift to wolf, leap out the window, and race with her to the park to talk.

"I've got the feeling, whatever the problem is, it's enough to distract them from that," Brody finally said, after frowning and thinking over her suggestion for a few moments.

"Probably doesn't help, but Lara's been getting the same reaction ever since she moved in with the Hendersons. The Terrels are nice, but sometimes I catch them watching us like they expect..." She gasped and stiffened and felt the fur around her neck in her wolf body stand up straight. "Like they know what we are, what we can do, and they think we'll just...I don't know, break all the rules and starting running wild. But they don't dare say anything because they don't want us to know that they know...and do I sound crazy?"

"Not to me." He shrugged. "Allen's practically breathing down Allison's neck. I wish we didn't have rules, so I could scratch him, just once. Bite him where it'll leave a scar he'll never be able to ignore. Just make him leave her alone."

"When I get totally pissed at Dan, I rip up his yard."

"Hendersons are too nice to do that to them."

"Allen's going out for track, according to Mike."

"Why?"

"Because you're the sports hero and he wants to impress Allison."

"What does that have to do with wanting to bite his throat out?" Brody kicked at an ice-covered stump and barely flinched, though Aggie knew it had to hurt his toes.

"He goes jogging in the park every morning and every night." She fluttered her eyelashes at him.

"The Wolf of Wallace Lake rides again?" He laughed, and Aggie was relieved when the sour tension in his scent began to sweeten.

*Doesn't even have to be you,* she said after shifting back to wolf. They started down the animal trail through the snow, heading for home. *Ask your critter friends to make things rough on him.*

Brody laughed so hard, he nearly tripped, and nearly broke out in howls.

The laughter didn't last long. When they were home and safely in their rooms, Aggie curled up to watch the moon through the gaps in the curtains. The questions started pouring through her mind again.

*What's wrong?* Brody asked, when she was sure he had fallen asleep and she was the only one awake in the entire world.

*Do you ever think about home?*

*What little I remember.*

*There are a lot like us, aren't there?*

*I think so.*

*But none like us here.*

*If you're holding out for a Wereling boyfriend—*

*Maybe we don't have the right to think about falling in love and...all that stuff.* Aggie couldn't even make herself think the words: *get married. If we're so different, if there's nobody like us in this world, maybe it's wrong. To think about taking mates.*

*Did you ever wonder why we are the way we are?*

*Magic.* The word was too simple an answer, and yet it seemed to cover all the various angles.

*I figure, we're both owed something for all the hassle we've gone through. Lara, too. If we don't have any right to take mates from this world, that goes double for her and Greg, because she doesn't even know what she is yet. I figure, we have the right to be as happy as we can. You're gonna have to drag me into another world to keep me from getting together with Allison.*

*Maybe...where we come from, it's okay,* Aggie ventured. She closed her eyes. The moonlight streaming down on her, across her bed, had warmth and weight. *Allison and Greg have magic sparks, so maybe it's okay.*

*But what about you, right?*

*Hey, no fair reading my mind without permission.* She tried to smile, tried to put laughter into her voice.

*Somewhere out there in the world, your mate is looking for you, Aggie. We'll find him. We found each other, didn't we?*

*Yeah, we did. G'night, Twin.*

What she dreamed about, Aggie couldn't remember, except for fragments of silver sparks raining down through her dreams and the feel of an arm around her waist and a man laughing and standing so close she could feel his warmth. The feelings that lingered from that dream made her smile even through her dreaded history exam. She was sure that if she could have caught his scent, she would have known him anywhere, when she woke. But she didn't.

# Chapter Twenty-Three

Just after spring break, Aggie noticed conversations that ended abruptly or took a U-turn the moment she walked into the room. She asked Brody if he noticed Grace and Jack acting strangely, hiding things, but he was useless. Between track practice, dodging girls determined to trick him into taking them to the prom, finding time to be with Allison and harassing Allen, Brody had no time or energy for anything else.

Business increased at Harsey Construction. Jack's general mood improved, but Aggie still caught him studying the company records, struggling through the computerized accounting system, and smelling of worry, anger and sorrow even when he kept a smile on his face. She took to spending her Saturdays at the construction site, working on the constant pile of forms, applications, government reports and requisitions. She had a vague idea that if she spent enough time there, someone would say something, or she would catch a hint as to how the wind blew. But just like her tactic of haunting the Wallace Lake area until she had enough evidence against the men who shot her mother, she gleaned very little, and none of it was usable.

There were usually half-crews working every Saturday, men eager to earn time-and-a-half to put the latest project ahead of schedule. Dan was often there, supervising, but he left her alone even when Jack wasn't there.

Aggie was grateful, though sometimes when Jack looked more worried, she wondered. Maybe if Dan was busy chasing her tail, acting as if they had a relationship, he wouldn't be doing whatever he did to worry her father.

"Jack's been asking a lot of questions," Dorayn said, when Aggie came to him with her worries. "He's asking everybody but Dan, for a change, and he's not too happy with the answers."

"Is Dad in trouble?" Aggie remembered that problem during the summer, with a building inspector who found problems that he shouldn't have—because he shouldn't have even come out to the site. "Is he going to lose the business?"

"Not if he can prove he didn't know what was going on."

"How? What kind of businessman lets someone else handle everything?" She groaned, knowing part of the answer.

"A good man who trusts everyone because he's trustworthy. A good man who wants to believe everyone else is fair-minded and generous." Dorayn shrugged, offering a crooked smile. "A man who'd rather go to high school basketball games than take care of paperwork."

"What can he do?" she whispered.

"Exactly what he's doing. Asking questions and taking back the reins of the business. And dissolving the partnership."

Aggie caught her breath. So that's why Dan was leaving her alone so thoroughly. He was keeping his nose clean—or trying to wipe his fingerprints from a lot of shady dealings before her father found out. Either way, Dan was playing the saint to convince Jack, yet again, that he wasn't the bad guy.

From the weary look in Dorayn's eyes and the tone of his voice, Aggie guessed he had discussed these very things with her father. Jack Harsey knew there were problems, and he was doing his best to solve them. There was nothing she could do to help him. Not even tearing up Dan's yard or harassing Smithers and his dogs would help this time.

Sometimes, Aggie really hated being a Wereling with such unique talents, and all of them useless.

⁊ ⁊

Aggie was glad she had decided not to go out of state for college. She didn't want to get more than an hour away from Wallace Lake and Bonnie Park, in case something happened. Maybe Allison's theory was more right than any of them could guess, and a door would magically open between worlds and let her, Brody and Lara go home.

Sometimes, a nebulous idea floated through the back of her mind, partially hidden by the blank wall that had slammed down on her memories during the storm. Aggie sensed that something momentous would happen this summer, either on her birthday or around graduation. She didn't want to be too far away when it happened.

Then one Saturday evening, Dorayn came over for dinner and he asked her about her plans after graduation. Aggie liked the idea that Dorayn worried that much about all the little details of her life, to ask.

"I'm going to go to Tri-C and get all my requirements out of the way," she said. "I'm still not sure what I want to major in, and this way I can try a lot of things without wasting money."

"That's the smart move," Dorayn said, nodding approval.

Aggie felt something deep inside relax in pure relief and pleasure that Dorayn approved of her plan. Aggie didn't know why Dorayn's approval and support was so important to her, and she didn't care. In some ways, she felt he knew her better than her parents, almost as well as Lara and Brody.

"I mean," she continued, leaning against the deck railing, "think of all the money I'll save."

"Doing what?" Jack said, coming out onto the deck with a platter of steaks.

"Aggie's plan to work part-time for you, come fall, and go to college at Tri-C," Dorayn said.

"You don't know how much your old Dad appreciates that," Jack said. He set the platter down on the table next to the smoking gas grill and wrapped his arms tight around her. "We've been through some hard times the last couple years, haven't we? I don't know what your Mom or I would have done without you here." He kissed her forehead and stepped back over to the grill.

Dorayn grinned at her over Jack's head and Aggie bit her lip to keep from laughing. Emotions still made Jack shudder, but she couldn't doubt the genuineness of his love for her, even if it took second place to getting the traditional Saturday night steaks on the grill.

That was another change Aggie appreciated: Dorayn sharing Saturday night steaks instead of Dan. Since Brody showed up last summer, Dorayn seemed to find more excuses to come by the house. He had even accepted Grace's invitation to Christmas and Thanksgiving dinner, which he had never done.

Life was far more pleasant with Dorayn as Jack's right-hand man, and Saturday night steaks certainly tasted twenty times better with him sitting across the table, telling jokes and stories or just sitting in silence while they played card games.

Brody was out with Allison, ostensibly to pick out a new dress shirt and tie for graduation. That made it just Jack, Grace, Dorayn and Aggie for dinner that night. Full dark had fallen by the time Aggie got up to take the dirty dishes into the house. Grace and Jack wandered through the garden, lighting the citronella torches that Jack had put in just the week before. Aggie breathed deeply of the lemony scent as it wafted through the windows of the kitchen.

"Never smelled anything like it, until I came to this—to this town," Dorayn said. His smile looked normal but he didn't meet her gaze as he handed her a stack of dirty serving dishes.

The phone rang, cutting off Aggie's question. She saw Smithers' name on the caller ID and knew the pleasant evening had officially come to an end. Dorayn read the name on the display and stepped outside to call Jack to come inside to take the phone, even before Aggie answered it.

According to Smithers, a gang had cut through the fence around the site, torched three separate piles of supplies, and started a fire in the office trailer. Jack had to go down immediately to talk with the police and inspect the site. A storm was expected before morning, and it could wash away all the evidence. Dorayn volunteered to go with Jack to the construction site to inspect the damage, but Jack waved aside the offer.

"Smithers and the police will be there. Grace has to go check out the office anyway. I'd appreciate it if you'd stay with Aggie until her brother gets back, though."

"Dad," Aggie moaned, and rolled her eyes. That earned laughter from her parents.

"We shouldn't be too long. I wouldn't be surprised if they decide it's a graduation prank that got out of hand."

Brody came home before Aggie and Dorayn had finished washing up the last of the dishes that wouldn't go into the washer. He didn't buy into the idea of the fire and vandalism as a prank, any more than Aggie had. He waited until Dorayn had left before he said anything.

"Think maybe they need some help down at the site?"

"Yeah, Mom might want to bring home files and things from the office. Especially if the police want to close up everything until the investigation is over." She picked up her shoes. "Are you driving?"

"I'm thinking they could use some wolf-style investigation." He tossed his car keys up once in the air.

Neither one said much on the drive down the back roads, heading for the industrial park in Medina. Brody had maintained from the start of the convenient little accidents that Dan Moon was behind all the troubles plaguing Harsey Construction. Aggie was inclined to agree with him, except she knew how much those accidents would hurt the value of the company. Dan lived for the company. He had too much invested in it. Hurting the company would hurt him, too.

"That fire got the electrical lines," Brody said, as the car turned down the long asphalt road leading to the newest section of the industrial park.

Aggie nodded and shivered a little. She wasn't afraid of the dark, but there was something very wrong about the thick patch of blackness that was usually lit by floodlights on tall poles. She leaned forward, resting both hands on the dashboard, as if she could make the car go faster.

The headlights suddenly illuminated a dark shape lying in the middle of the road. Brody slowed down and veered to the right to go around it. He growled and slammed on the brakes and leaped from the car.

"Kaenarr?" Aggie left her shoes in the car and got out to accompany him.

"Stupid, toothless..." Brody lifted his head and in the headlights she saw angry tears gleam in his eyes.

One of Smithers' dogs lay sprawled on the dirt-strewn asphalt, still twitching, with a pungent trail of blood marking its path. Aggie bent down to touch the dog. It opened its eyes, convulsed once, then went limp. It was still alive, but not for long. In silent agreement, the twins shifted to wolf and followed the blood trail.

They found the other three dogs, all with multiple gunshot wounds. All dead or near it. The last dog, the first to die, lay in a heap where its shattered legs had given out. Smithers was a still, cooling pile of whiskey-scented meat and bloody, torn uniform.

*Whoever set the fire came back,* Brody finally said.

Aggie swallowed the need to howl. She ran, a dark streak of movement, heading for the office trailer. Jack's car sat in front of the trailer, the passenger door hanging open and light spilling out on the gravel-strewn work yard. Thunder rumbled in the distance, promising a storm.

*Smell that?* Brody stopped next to her. He snorted, as if he wanted to get the smell out of his nostrils. *Familiar?*

Aggie turned her head into the faint breeze and breathed deeply. The scent was fading, but the stink of dirty clothes and sweet marijuana smoke, alcohol and the faint reek of skunk all combined to paint a clear picture in her mind.

*What are they doing all the way out here?*

*Unless that attack last year wasn't an accident? Maybe they were after Mom all along?*

Aggie didn't try to deny Brody's theory. Terror propelled her into the office trailer.

Nothing had burned. She noticed that first; the lack of smoke scent, the lack of charring anywhere in the trailer.

The sweet smell of the rose hand cream she had bought Grace for Mother's Day fought against the stink of cooling blood and fear that created an almost visible cloud in the trailer. Jack and Grace lay curled up together on the floor by Grace's desk. Aggie envisioned Jack throwing himself in front of Grace to protect her, and both of them doing down under a hail of bullets.

*Aggie.* Brody nudged her with his head. *Come out.*

*No.* She stayed frozen on the doorstep, staring at the still bodies, willing them to move, willing the smell of pain to overwhelm all the others, some proof that they lived. She couldn't see Grace's face, hidden under Jack, who had his back to her. From the puddles of blood, Aggie knew they had to be dead. There was too much on the floor. There couldn't be anything left in their bodies.

How long of a delay had it been between her parents leaving and Brody coming home? Half an hour at the most?

*This was planned,* she said. *No accident. It was planned.*

*Come out,* her twin repeated. *What if they're still here?*

*Good!*

*They have guns, dummy. If you get yourself killed, how can you get revenge?*

That broke through the rising wall of fury and vengeance hunger. Aggie followed her twin out of the trailer, back through the field and the gap in the chain link fence, back to his car. They had to drive to the main road and down another half mile to find a gas station and a pay phone.

⊱≈⊰

According to the Medina police, no one had reported a fire and no officers had been called out to the construction site until Brody called. The only fire on the entire site was a small spot near the gates. Enough smoke to convince Jack and Grace that Smithers hadn't lied when he called.

No one could decide if Smithers had been forced to make the call, or if he had been gunned down by his partners.

The office had been ransacked, the petty cash taken. Jack's wallet and Grace's purse were gone, their watches and wedding rings. The robbery made no sense—why go to the effort of luring the Harseys out there to rob them? The police were just as stumped as Aggie.

Through the next few days, as she waited for the coroner to finish examining the bodies and as she planned the funeral, Aggie thought about Brody's theory. She knew he was right. By the scent, the same men who had attacked her mother the year before had been involved in this attack. Did that mean they had been after Grace back then? Why? What would anyone have to gain by killing Grace? Was it a side-lined attack on Jack, to begin with? Why go after Grace if Jack was the target? Why kill them both?

Dorayn showed up at the funeral home when Brody and Aggie went to make the arrangements. Aggie couldn't remember calling him. But then, she hadn't called Lara, either, and her friend had shown up, along with Allison and Greg. Dorayn put an arm around her and Aggie gladly leaned into his comfort and warmth. Dorayn had always been there when she needed him, and she was grateful.

He accompanied them back to the house and bullied them into eating some dinner. Dorayn stayed after Lara, Greg and Allison left. He badgered the twins until they admitted they had classes and homework and a major, four-school track meet that weekend, and basically forced Aggie and Brody to lift their heads out of their misery.

"If you stay here through the end of the school year, we might just make it," Aggie managed to say without losing her voice to the agony that tried to strangle her. She and Dorayn stopped on the front step, halfway to his car.

"Princess, I'll always be here when you need me." His crooked smile struck chords of memory.

"You've always been here. Right from the start," she whispered.

The dam broke. Aggie crumpled and the tears she had been holding back, the memories of terror and falling and darkness and being horribly alone washed through her with the force of a tsunami. She went to her knees on the steps. Dorayn wrapped his arms around her and held her, rubbing her back, letting her soak his shoulder and down the front of his shirt. Aggie clung to him, taking comfort in his familiar scent, in his warmth. It wasn't an illusion, a wish. Dorayn had always been there during the truly terrifying, harsh times in her life. Even when her twin had been torn away, and all her memories, Dorayn had been there.

Aggie clung to him even after she had cried herself dry and headachy. Dorayn's arms stayed wrapped tight around her and he rocked her a little. There was no need for words, she sensed. He knew she needed the contact more than any advice.

Dan found them that way when he drove up to the house just moments after Aggie's last tears dried. It was nearly ten o'clock.

*Jackal on the front lawn,* Brody warned.

Aggie snorted, muffling laughter, and raised her head. The breeze blew from behind Dan, bringing her the scent of the beer and the stink of cigarettes from whatever bar he had visited before coming here. The hot spice of anger mixed with musky lust. The sour stink of excitement that had turned cold and disappointed.

The rose scent of Grace's hand cream.

She pushed free of Dorayn's arms and stood. Dan stopped a few steps away, breathing heavily, fists jammed into his hips, and glared at them.

"What do you two think you're doing?" he growled.

"Not that it's any of your business," Aggie said, "but I was crying and Dorayn was holding me. I'm allowed to cry, since my parents were murdered." She took two steps closer to him. The scent of roses grew stronger, definitely coming from Dan.

Along with a faint reek of that dirty-sweet compound she identified with the four who had attacked Grace in the park.

Aggie shivered as pieces and clues snapped together inside her mind. A wordless exclamation came from Brody, inside the house. She heard his feet thumping on the hardwood floors as he hurried down the stairs to join her.

"You're supposed to cry on me," Dan said, and thumped his chest for emphasis. The definite, soft chiming of metal rang through the quiet night air. Aggie caught a soft flash of silver inside the open collar of his shirt, reflecting off the front step lights. He wore a chain around his neck, and something hung from the chain.

"Why would I ever let you touch me?" she said with icy calm that would have stopped a stoned football player in his tracks. Dan brushed it aside.

"After everything I've done—you're supposed to be mine." He spat and gestured at Dorayn. "Not spending your time with the old man."

"He's not old!" Aggie snarled.

"Get out of here." Brody barreled through the front door.

"What did you do, Dan, that you think you have a claim on Aggie?" Dorayn's calm, quiet question stopped all three in their tracks.

"Whatever it is," Brody said, "it's not good. Why does he smell like Mom's hand cream?"

"I thought I was imagining it," Aggie said, nodding.

"Hand?" Dan's hand started to rise to the little lump under his shirt, right where Aggie imagined something hung from the chain around his neck.

She gasped as her imagination painted a horrified picture.

"You took them as trophies."

"Took what?" Dan's eyes glittered with fear, then his anger returned. "You're upset, Aggie. It's understandable. I want to take care of you. You need me. I can help you. I can make you happy."

"The only thing that would make me happy is to rip your throat out with my teeth."

"Aggie?"

She shifted to wolf and leaped on him. Dan shrieked and staggered backwards and sat, hitting the ground hard. The sound shattered as she landed on his chest. One paw ripped open his shirt. She caught his chain in her teeth and yanked hard. The rings hanging from the chain chimed softly as Aggie leaped off him, with an extra hard shove that snapped two ribs. Dan stared, white-faced, too terrified to even react. Aggie shifted back to Human and took the chain from between her teeth.

"My parents' rings. Stolen by the men who killed them. You sent those four idiots to attack my Mom last March."

"I don't know what you're talking about," Dan whispered.

"Tell the truth!" Dorayn thundered. Silver sparks swirled around his head and out, hitting Dan with enough force to make him yelp.

Dan tried to sit up. The silver sparks spun around him, biting like bees until he whimpered and curled into a fetal ball in a futile attempt to protect himself.

"All right," he gasped, wincing every time a spark hit him. "I had to get Grace out of the way. When Jack started breaking up the partnership, I had to kill him. I can't lose the company. It's my last chance!"

"What good is a confession here and now?" Brody said. "He has to tell the police."

"Go tell the police everything," Dorayn said. More silver sparks swirled out from around him and hit Dan, making him whimper and writhe, as if they were bb pellets hitting him. "All the details. Tell the whole truth of what you did and why. Now!"

The twins stayed where they were, watching as Dan climbed awkwardly to his feet and stumbled down the sidewalk, toward the center of town and the police station only a few blocks away. Aggie's mind spun with the implications of what Dan's stumbling confession meant. Grace had to be taken out of the way because she had disapproved of Dan's interest in Aggie. How or why owning Harsey Construction was Dan's last chance didn't matter.

Dorayn crumpled slowly, first dropping to his knees, then sprawling facedown in the lawn. Brody leaped forward, just a second too late to catch him. The twins rolled the man over. Aggie gasped and jerked away. Just in those few seconds, Dorayn had visibly aged, maybe another ten years.

"And that, children," he whispered, "is why I don't do magic anymore. Not unless it's absolutely necessary." Dorayn tried to smile. The effort drained the color from his face.

# Chapter Twenty-Four

"Silver sparks," Brody whispered. "You kept me from breaking my neck when I fell, didn't you?"

"You saved your own neck. I just healed your cuts and bruises. Werelings are like cats. They always land on their feet."

"You know what we are." Aggie felt like an idiot. Of course—Dorayn had been there from the beginning. No wonder she had always felt he was familiar. Then she really looked at him and pushed those questions aside for later. She had lost her parents. She and Brody couldn't afford to lose Dorayn. Not after what he had just done. "What can we do to help you?"

"The park. It's...it's like the Greening Lands. You don't remember what those are, but the Greening Lands are...they're magic." He managed to sit up. The twins wrapped his arms around their shoulders and stood, dragging him upright with them. "The first rule of magic, children, is that your power has to come from somewhere. If you have a source, an anchor, that person pulls the magic up for you and amplifies it a hundredfold as they pass it to you. In the untamed lands, magic wielders are bound to specific areas." He grunted as they slid him into the front seat of Brody's car. "In settled, tamed land, magic wielders are called enchanters. They're specialists, limited in what sort of magic they do. They draw their power from the air and the ground...and they aren't nearly one tenth as powerful as the uncivilized ones."

"What kind are you?" Brody asked as Aggie climbed into the back seat. He started the engine and pulled the car out into the street without looking for oncoming traffic.

"I'm a healer. Minds and bodies. Specialist, I suppose." He sighed. The sound was ragged, like he couldn't decide whether to laugh or cry.

"Why can't you draw power from the air and land?" Aggie asked. She was grateful for the distraction. Anything to take her mind off the revelation that still reverberated through her.

"This world doesn't have any magic. Not the kind that we're used to. The park...it mirrors the Greening Lands. There's leakage between worlds. I can't get much power, but there's enough to restore me."

Dorayn put up a hand, stopping Brody as he opened his mouth to ask more questions. "Please, let me rest. Just a little while."

They took Dorayn to the Music Mound. By some miracle, no one had come there, despite the beautiful, warm weather. Aggie imagined that people with ordinary lives were too busy preparing for graduation or had other chores that kept them busy on a weeknight. She was grateful. She didn't feel like playing at being the Wolf of Wallace Lake tonight.

Brody helped Dorayn sit on the ground, leaning against the stone wall. He kept guard, while Aggie walked off a distance and called with her mind for Lara. She showed her friend everything that had happened.

Blue sparks blazed in the gap between the trees. A moment later Lara limped out into the moonlight to join them. She glanced back over her shoulder at the place where she had emerged from thin air. A few sparks still hovered.

"I'm going to need a ride home. Only one miracle a month, I think." Lara tried to smile, but it faded as she turned to look at Dorayn.

He had regained his color, and some of the ravages of his magic had smoothed away. Not enough, though. The furrows along his nose and around his mouth were deeper, the creases around his eyes longer. His hair seemed thinner, and not the healthy, thick crown of white but almost transparent in spots. Aggie shivered, realizing he had sacrificed his strength for the sake of truth—for her.

"Well, we're back to the way we were," Dorayn whispered as the three settled down facing him. He smiled and closed his eyes, as if he could go to sleep right there.

"Why don't you give off silver sparks the rest of the time?" Lara asked. "Aggie and Brody can see my sparks, and Greg and Allison's. Why can't we see your magic?"

"My magic is different. Not as strong. I'm...my ancestor committed great crimes, so my magic is bound. Just as the Werelings are bound by vows to serve and protect you, I'm bound to serve them. That's the only way I managed to come through with you. Thank the Bendici I could." His eyes fluttered open. "I have more control than you do, so I don't leak, to put it crudely. You live here at the edge of the park, so you have a constant flow of magic to feed you. You'll be strong, when you return home."

"How do we get home?" Brody said.

"I don't know. You three will have to find the doorway yourselves. All I've been able to do is keep track of you, try to help, influence people so you'd be safe."

"It's drained you," Aggie said slowly. She understood instinctively, but the details hadn't reached the point where she could put them into words. "You've hurt yourself, for us."

"Worth it." A ragged chuckle escaped him, ending on a sigh. "Princess, would you believe I'm only ten years older than you?"

Aggie choked on a whimper and tears filled her eyes.

"Why are we here?" Lara reached to put an arm around Aggie's shoulders to hug her. "Someone tried to kill us, didn't they?"

"Your mother is—your mother was a powerful magic wielder. Her domain was the Greening Lands, which reached through all the untamed lands for thousands upon thousands of miles. She made it possible for lesser magic wielders to find the lands that called to them. But in time, those lesser enchanters decided that as long as she had power, she could take their domains away from them."

"They gathered together and attacked my mother. Both my parents," she whispered, nodding. Tears made her green eyes gleam like emeralds in the moonlight.

"Her very last magic was to send you away, to a mirror world, where you would be safe. The vows of blood and kinship sworn by your parents, the day you two were born, brought you along." Dorayn nodded to the twins. "I tried to stay to help in the battle, but I suppose the curse on my ancestors brought me along to help watch over you. I'm glad."

"No matter what it did to you?" Aggie whispered.

"It's good he was here," Brody said, shaking his head. "You put magic on us, to take away our memories, didn't you?"

"Safer if you didn't remember." Dorayn nodded. "You remember now? When I tried to help you escape the hospital?"

"How could it be safer if we didn't know anything?" Aggie blurted.

"No, he's right." Brody caught hold of Aggie's hands and squeezed hard, as if to force her to understand what obviously seemed clear to him. "Without memories, we fit in better. The more we remember, the more uncomfortable we are here. The more we fight. The more trouble we get into. All that trouble with the gossip rags, I brought on myself."

"So, now do we get our memories back?" Lara asked.

"When you need to remember, when you need to know, the memories will return." Dorayn braced himself with his hands and struggled to get to his feet.

"Shouldn't you sit for a while longer?" Aggie said. She leaped to her feet and reached for him.

"It's not safe for me, Princess. You've been here when purple sparks have shown up? That's your enemy, searching for you. Alaria's mother—" He smiled ruefully when all three flinched at the use of Lara's full name. "Her mother put shielding spells on you. But not me. With my magic so weak, the enemy can try to reach through the torn fabric of reality to find me, and through me, find you."

"That's why we've never seen you in the park with us," she whispered, nodding, as more understand spilled through her. "That's why you don't live near here, even though it would have kept you strong."

"Worth it, Princess. You three are more than worth it." Dorayn gently cupped her cheek for a few seconds.

Aggie shivered deep inside, very certain he meant *her* more than the other two. She wondered why.

Hadn't Dorayn said he was only ten years older than her?

He was only twenty-seven or twenty-eight, though he looked like he was in his fifties or sixties.

Knowing that made her ache, even as her mind tried to leap free of the shock that still stunned her.

"So what do we do now?" Lara said.

"How do we find the door and get it open?" Brody added.

"One thing at a time, children." Dorayn supported himself against the raw stone wall as he took a few testing steps. He inhaled deeply, nodded, and turned back to face them. "Bury your parents, graduate high school. Heal as much as you can. Worry about the battles waiting on the other side of the doorway when the doorway opens."

*The End*

# About the Author

Michelle Levigne has lived most of her life in Ohio, on the North Coast. She started writing her own stories in junior high, when she couldn't find the books she wanted to read in the library and didn't have enough money to buy out the bookstore. Her first professional sale was in conjunction with the Writers of the Future contest.

Her first place winning story, "Relay," appears in Writers of the Future Volume VII. Between that publication and the release of her first novel, Heir of Faxinor, she wrote and published more than forty short stories and poems in fan fiction, ranging between "Star Trek," "Beauty and the Beast," "The Phoenix," "Highlander," "Starman," "V" and "Stingray." This included a brief foray into fan publishing with the 4-issue fanzine "Starwheel."

She has a BA in theater/English from Northwestern College and an MA in communications/film from Regent University. Published titles explore mythology, epic fantasy, and futuristic adventures.

Please visit her Web Site:
www.MLevigne.com

Printed in the United States
77293LV00005B/199-216